Stories from the Psalms, Volume 1

*A Devotional of
Short Fiction Inspired by
Psalms 1- 15*

Daniel G. Keohane

Other Road Press
otherroadpress.com

Other Novels by Daniel G. Keohane

Plague of Locusts
Margaret's Ark
Solomon's Grave
Plague of Darkness

The Photograph
(with David Hilman)

Writing as G. Daniel Gunn

Christmas Trees & Monkeys
Destroyer of Worlds
Nightmare in Greasepaint
(with L. L. Soares)

For anyone who has ever wondered if their
art could be used for worship.
The answer is, always, yes.

Volume 1

Psalms 1 - 15

Table of Contents

An Explanation of What You're About to Read

First off, thanks so much for picking up this book. You might be asking what this little experiment is all about. A collection of short stories? A devotional? An instruction manual on how to read the Book of Psalms? Yes, Yes and No. Let's go backwards.

Please, please, do not look to this book in your hands (in whatever form that takes) as anything but an imaginative, artistic leap of faith one writer has taken to show how the Word of God can come alive if we allow it to. It is *not* a literal interpretation of anything written in the Psalms. It isn't saying, "This Means This." It *is* saying, "This is the image that was given me, as a writer and follower of Jesus, when I prayerfully read the Psalm in question and asked the Spirit to help me craft a work of fiction inspired by the verses."

That's a mouthful, but it's the best way to describe the process of writing this book. I've been writing stories, from horror to science fiction to contemporary fiction for years, including a number of devotionals. One day, the idea came to write a devotional, but in fiction form.

Is it something the masses might be interested in? No idea, and it doesn't matter. Like past devotionals, I took my first tentative step into Stories from the Psalms as a tithing of my writing time. I would pray for an image or character to come to me then read the Psalm. The next step is important: whatever image came to mind, I began writing around that. No worrying about the plot or setting, I simply wrote what I saw and let the characters drive the story. Sometimes it came fully formed after the first few sentences, other times I did not know what would happen, literally, until I wrote it. When finished, without looking back, I would pray over the next Psalm, read it and write whatever came to me.

Again and again.

Over time an odd thing began happening. With a couple of exceptions, characters from one story returned for the next. Or stories began to connect through location or an overarching plotline. I've read the book of Psalms a dozen-plus times in my life, and one aspect I hadn't noticed until now (I can be a little dense) is that they are often clustered with common themes. These patterns drove me, unconsciously perhaps, to writing interconnected stories. And yes, there were other times it was more of an artistic choice.

I'll give an example. When reading Psalm 7, an image of a dead man lying in a hole came to mind. I wrote the story first from the perspective of a boy spying from his apartment window, then from the man whose body we'd seen. When done, I read Psalm 8, and saw another young boy standing on his roof at night speaking to God. I realized this was the same boy from the previous story. When finished, I wanted to follow this character into adulthood and so, biased in this way I found a method of bringing him back as an old man when an image of a wooden sign on the wall of a church was inspired by Psalm 9. And so on.

Here's the question you might be asking yourself, standing there with the book in your hand: what is the point? Will I learn anything from reading these stories?

I'm glad you asked, and (aside from the sheer joy creating these worlds has been for me) the answer is also what kept me writing. I want people to see God's Word in a new way. When you read a Psalm, do you picture people in robes and sandals, King David hiding in a cave, or old dusty scrolls piled in a catacomb? How does this relate to our world today? I hope these stories paint new images in your mind around how God's Word timelessly applies the everyday world around us. Is "sin" a hole we dig for ourselves? What does that look like in twenty-first century Brooklyn? How does the act of keeping one's promises affect a high school student running for class president? How would God make Himself known on a future world with no knowledge of Him whatsoever?

How we apply the Psalms of David and others are as varied as the number of people born on this planet. What you're about to read are only fifteen possibilities, parables written by someone who never ceases to be amazed how alive and interactive these ancient words can be.

Part One: Tian Tang

Stories from the Psalms, Volume 1

An Introduction to "The Path"

Please understand one thing right away: none of us know what heaven is like. Jesus deliberately (I assume) refrained from describing it except through metaphors and parables. Yes, there are descriptors such as *no more tears*, and some more striking images in *The Revelation of John* of a massive city with streets of gold and light.

Don't think ill of me, please. I am madly in love with Jesus, but from a purely human, personal perspective when I step into the eternal kingdom, if it's only a massive city paved in gold I'm going to be disappointed. Now and then I enjoy a visit to Boston or New York, but I find more joy in the beauty of my hometown, or an occasional jaunt to the mountains. There, among the natural world, I feel closest to God.

What *place* do you see in your mind's eye when you think of true Joy? (That's Joy with an uppercase J.) I see myself sitting on a hillside looking over unending miles of nature spread before me (hence the story you're about to read). For my wife, it would be a blanket on the beach facing the ocean. For my mother, a quiet mountain lake with the haunting song of loons drifting overhead ("Norman, the loons!"). That last one is a close second for me, minus the ghostly loon cry. What do *you* see?

Many people can relate to the reference in Psalm 1 of the tree at the river banks, drinking the life-giving water and yes, this immediately struck me as well. One other balancing image also struck me: two paths, one of which is where leaves *do* still wither and die. This other path, just outside heaven's border, intrigued me (being the broken human I am).

Do we come to heaven perfect, without the scars of this temporary life? The question I ended up asking was this: what if we don't? What if some pain might linger even in the One Place we have longed to be? Picture the following answer, which I call "The Path," as simply *one answer to this question.* For the purists out there, remember that what you are about to read is not scripture, merely one person's *response* to it.

Prayerful Art.

Sometimes it's all we have left with which to worship.

Psalm 1 - The Path

Oh, the joys of those who do not
follow the advice of the wicked,
or stand around with sinners,
or join in with mockers.
But they delight in the law of the Lord,
meditating on it day and night.
They are like trees planted along the riverbank,
bearing fruit each season.
Their leaves never wither,
And they prosper in all they do.

For the Lord watches over the path of the godly,
but the path of the wicked leads to destruction.

Psalm 1:1-3,6 (NLT)

The Soul wondered, in that other forgotten life was this her idea of Heaven? Sitting on a hillside overlooking distant mountains, green everywhere. All of it surrounded by, and filled to the brim with, the Loving Water. From this place the Joy of a billion souls was felt exploding outward towards the sun who was God Himself shining over everything. It *was* sunny and warm here most of the time, though a breeze drifted through and between everything, cool enough for a nice balance to the overall environment. She closed her eyes and breathed in smells of grass and leaves and just a little decay in the background, an Autumnal, nostalgic presence. How long had she been here, not specifically *here* on this hillside but under this sun, smelling so much Life and Joy on the breeze, living in Heaven? A blink, or a thousand-thousand years? Time meant nothing. It belonged to that world beyond the veil she'd left behind.

The Soul's eyes stayed closed, faced turned up towards the Light hovering above and everywhere.

It wasn't always sunny, however. No, God's light did not dim nor turn away from the Joy rising from the multitudes around Him. Nothing like that. The world around her simply dimmed to allow the overwhelming stars to break through above. Day. Then Night.

Too much of a good thing is a bad thing, someone said in her past life. The Soul did not know who that was, or who *she* had been in that time and place, if she'd even *been* a she.

Too much of one thing, perhaps, caused eyes to wander, look for new things hidden in corners. Sometimes it rained, and these moments were celebrated. People emerged from whatever home or shade or personal corner had been their respite before then lifted their faces to the drops pouring over them like tiny baptisms. It never got too cold, merely wet. Wet *did* give a chill at times, with that slight breeze all around.

A thrill of a chill. Life.

The Soul wrapped her arms around her bent knees and sighed. She was in Heaven, for heaven's sake. Why was she being like this? She hadn't been this melancholy before, not when she'd first crossed over. Then, she'd stood in the very presence of God and all His forms, including Jesus, the Man born into the world beyond and Who set things moving in a better direction before letting His death be the bridge between there, and here.

Jesus, who shone like the sun above her and settled in her presence like dew amid her cries of joy. He emanated peace whenever He sat beside her, embracing her like a best friend. He knew her intimately, even the *who* she'd been before (those having crossed that metaphorical bridge never remembered, nor wanted to).

And of course, there was the Spirit of the Father filling everything, riding every raindrop in those moments of communal joy, drying every strand of hair with every ray of sunlight. The One who whispered love to her as she praised with the multitude or, like now, sat or walked in solitude and meditation.

Always, the Father, the light over everything; filling the universe with His presence even in those moments when He deigned to allow what she once called *night* to wash over this World Beyond Worlds.

Darkness was important. Without it how could one appreciate light? The Soul didn't think that was an actual quote she carried with her. It was simple common sense.

She adored the days or months or years when the sky darkened and filled with a billion million stars. In the before-life, these had represented balls of fiery gas warming a million billion planets and moons and gave life to other multitudes, somewhere, somehow. Is that what they were, up there, in this place?

She wanted to ask these and so many other questions but in moments when she was in Jesus' presence, the urge to ask anything so mundane left her. Sometimes, especially when alone like this, she wondered *why* she thought that those questions were mundane.

Maybe she wasn't ready to know. That thought came often, and she quickly buried it, as well as the consideration that she should not be able to bury *anything* here.

Gazing down the rolling, unending expanse of green before her, the Soul wondered all these things, including why she wondered them but never asked, how she could keep secrets in her heart, or at least fool herself into thinking they were secrets.

"Because it was not time to ask," He said, taking a slow seat beside her. Jesus was tall, dark-skinned with a face smoothed with the bottomless peace He carried with him always. His skin was marked with scars, some frightening to consider and others barely visible unless she stared long enough. His appearance was almost rugged, in jeans and a loose flannel shirt. Not necessarily handsome, at least she did not find herself attracted to him in that sense. *Drawn*, yes, a pull so fierce she yearned for it like a yawn or a stretch that never quite satisfied.

Except for those moments when she got caught up in herself, like now, and wondered about things.

He was looking at her, elbow resting on one bent knee and pressing a closed hand against His cheek. Waiting for her to come back to the present, perhaps.

He probably put that thought into her head.

"Sorry," she said to the man who was also God sitting beside her. "I'm preoccupied."

He lowered his arm and gently wrapped the other around her. She scooted closer and let herself be pulled into the embrace.

"With what?"

"Why do you ask me when you know the answer?"

"We'd have nothing to talk about otherwise. Eternity would be a lonely place if everyone decided I already knew what they were going to say. I don't, you know."

She blinked, looking lazily down the hill. Clearing after clearing, edges of woods and copses of trees like darker flows of color, a drawing on a canvas of grass and flowers washed in ever-darker green under an exploding blue sky. All of this intersected by a soft shadowed river snaking its way in and out of sight. She said, "You don't… know what I'm going to say?"

She felt him shrug in her embrace. "I *could* know, if I looked ahead. Time doesn't have a hold on anything, or anyone, but I choose not to look. Why would I? Life is so much more interesting hearing your words for the first time."

"You *do* look." An accusation, but without malice.

"All the time, just not at any conversation I might be having with my brothers and sisters."

"But you know what I'm thinking."

"I know what you're *feeling*. Not your thoughts. I could, and did often when you were there," he nodded in a random direction she knew indicated beyond the veil. "Here, we choose not to know because good conversation is such an important part of love."

"But you *could* look," she insisted again, beginning to worry she sounded like a petulant child trying to get the last word, "if you want to."

"We can do anything we *want* to. We're God."

She leaned harder into Him. This time, after so many times, she remembered.

"What are stars? If the Father is the sun shining on us, aren't the stars just a reflection of Him? A bunch of little Hims?"

"There is only one God - in three persons, but we're still One - and all creation is a reflection of Him. But poetic imagery aside, those are actually stars. Other suns, other systems."

She sat up, looked back at him. He wasn't smirking, like he did when teasing.

"There are other planets up here in Heaven?"

Jesus did not smile. "No, and, well, yes," he said, shrugging. "What you see when the night comes are the same stars you once saw as a mortal across the way, though in that place you saw with far less clarity. When you look up now..." as he spoke, twilight came on, progressing quickly. The Soul sensed the others sharing paradise with her suddenly shout with joy, verbally or silently, as night draped over everything.

The night was full of stars, a few at first, then so many their clusters were thick as clouds. Jesus continued, "...now, you are looking beyond the veil, into the world from where you came, when you were broken yet so perfect."

"I can see back there, right now?" She stood and turned slowly, then glanced lower, across the tops of trees. "Can I see more than just stars?" He was beside her. She hadn't remembered Him standing but of course He moved like that all the time.

"Not at the moment, you haven't learned how, yet. Honestly, you could have seen any time you wanted, merely didn't think to ask." He gestured casually skyward. "You can visit those planets and see other worlds, other perfect beings like yourself that look like nothing you've ever imagined."

She stared and walked, trying to find wonder in that but could not, not in this moment. His earlier words kept pressing into her, like a pebble in a shoe. The Soul finally looked down at him - He was her height but she stood a few steps uphill. "That's the second time you said something like that. I could have *seen*; I could have *asked*. But it wasn't time."

He shook his head. "No."

"Why is now the time?"

Another of those non-committal shrugs. Then he was gone. She was alone, as alone as one could ever be in this place. The Soul felt the presence of every other in this existence, though right now she could not *see* any of them. People sometimes chose to be alone for long stretches, to consider the universe, talk with God, be at peace. Now and again, being with others was *necessary*, and they would appear, around a tree, or sitting in a shop having coffee. The coffee shop would not be visible until those moments when her need for people blossomed into *necessity*. She never dared question if what she saw as a coffee shop was something else entirely for others. A park or intimate kitchen. She thought of the coffee shops as way-stations, a communal church to gather her extended family of God together. *Coffee in the Stars*, she called these places.

Sometimes the Soul hated them.

Recently - how long *recently* meant could be anything from a day to a century in this time-loosed universe – the Soul was suffocated by their confines. Quick as that, she'd be back on this hill to find her connection to God again and worship in her own way, her own voice. Until she yearned for reconnection, be a part of the chorus again.

This time, something felt different. First, the morning returned so soon after night had draped over heaven that the Soul expected to hear disappointed sighs from the others. Of course, *their* nights may have lasted longer. For her, morning had broken because it needed to. Dew glistened on every leaf of every tree; the grass underfoot was cool and damp. She walked forward. The hillside was again the explosion of green life rolling away, but dimmed somehow, less distinct, the color falling into a background hue.

Except one spot, down the hill to her right. A few paces from where the eternal river curved away from the edge of a long and wide forest. Its presence, and color, was like an arm bumping against a friend, saying *come this way, follow me*. She walked down the slope towards it, the grass under her bare feet dryer here. As she drew nearer, the forest changed. The colors were so fierce and sudden the Soul worried it had been set alight. Green fell into yellow. Then, oranges, reds both deep and bright. From this point onward as far as she could see, the woods were blinking into a picture of New England foliage. A beauty that burned like flame deep in her chest.

She walked towards and into it. By the time she'd reached the true edge of the woods, the colors were not as vibrant, even with the Light above. The change continued as she walked. Fall had come. Something came after all of this color, but she struggled to remember.

A path opened before her that not existed a moment ago. It led deep into the color-scape of trees. She hesitated, unconsciously rubbing her upper arms with her hands. She realized suddenly that she was naked, and understood what the word meant. She looked down at herself, wondering if she'd always been like this, even in the coffee shops with others. She didn't think so, seemed to remember Jesus Himself dressed like some hipster lumberjack earlier, then wondered again why any of that mattered.

It once did. Long ago, beyond the veil.

A cold wind gusted from down the path, far down and away. She shivered, gooseflesh running across her body. The Soul tightened her arms about herself and began to walk, quickly, deeper into the woods not because she wanted to but from an understanding that the sooner she did this, the sooner she could return.

She wasn't in Heaven anymore. Or, if she was, it was a corner where no one wanted to be. This was the veil.

Still surrounded by the brilliance of Autumn, she walked the edge of some unseen cliff leaning over the chasm between her heavenly Father and the world of broken humanity. She saw none of this, assumed the Spirit was with her, as always, whispering truths. Beside and above them towered trees with yellow and orange and red curling into brown and black before the leaves fell dead around her. They were a shower of crisp sighs landing with a hiss on the ground and on top of each other. Beautiful in their finality and choreography. The Soul was not sad, not exactly, merely more introspective than she'd already been, stepping over these discarded husks of former lives. Stretching her arms to the sides, the touch of a leaf now and again alighting, then bouncing off her skin. Below her feet the ground was a thick bed of it. The only indicator where the path led was merely the lack of trees. At some point, the Soul was certain she'd left the path altogether. She was safe, however, would always be safe.

Then why was the cold growing more painful, pushed by a wind which hissed angrily through bare branches? Fallen leaves covered everything, lifeless. Even the sky had frozen to a harsh gray, the cold a coarse blanket. Rubbing her arms did nothing. She was too cold, *beyond* cold. Stumbling into a clearing, surrounded by bare trees, she knelt. Walking any farther would only lengthen the return journey. She could not go back. That certainty was a harshness wedged into her brain.

The Soul's shivering became violent. Too cold.

Why was it like this, in the place between, in the veil? Was it winter where she'd come from?

Things fell from the steel sky. Tiny flakes. Beautiful and lonely. Each snowflake could be seen and felt, even heard infinitesimally as it landed on the ground, on the dead leaves and her flesh. Her shivering worsened. She wanted to lie down, curl away from the snow but there was no place for protection. The metal cold of the air and the wind danced among the branches above like spirits searching her out... and others? Were there others with her? She was too cold to know, but felt something, a kinship with the invisible crowds. This place pressed her kneeling body lower and lower. Why wouldn't Jesus come with a blanket, with the clothing she thought she'd never need again? Why was He absent now, of all *nows*? The snow was a blanket over everything, taunting and teasing, slowing her shivers until every pixel of skin felt suddenly warmer. A distant, screaming part of her mind knew this was a bad development. The sky, the trees, the frozen ground under the fallen leaves under the falling snow under her legs which curled tighter in agony. She was paper in a frozen blue fire. Pressing in on her, crushing any existence she'd ever....

Then the Soul saw -

- the face before her, eyes rolled and lost and guilty, but still determined. This memory and the sudden harsh sensation of human touch was not welcome. She knew this image, this moment, one repeated again and again and the feel of hands on her flesh, hands not invited but touching nonetheless, hands that once meant safety but were not safe and she rolled away but could not escape then was suddenly alone again on the frozen ground, half covered in the falling snow.

She screamed, "Why?" into the collapsing sky. Her voice was lost. "Let me back in, please. That isn't me anymore it's not - "

The snow melted on her lips. Everything had become damp and cold and unloving. No love. Nothing gave love and nothing could ever be real again - these were words rolling around her mind long unacknowledged then more images came of new faces looking down, never at her, not completely. Instead, their gazes were of a glutton falling back onto a bone, picking it clean of meat. That was her, that picked-apart bone, in this moment that had been, those few moments in that life when she became unreal but could still feel something, even if it was pain. The Soul was dying, thrown back into the coldness of the world beyond the veil. There had been a rule somewhere, a disclaimer she hadn't noticed in that wash of Joy on entering Paradise, falling into Jesus' arms and into Their love and warmth so deep everything behind her washed away. She'd failed, as she had failed when she was mortal, failed from birth, thrown away, grabbed for only passing amusement like a page of a newspaper with an interesting headline, caught out of the wind before being set loose again, flying away to drift and stumble until it no longer existed, not even as a memory.

That is not how your life ended.

The words were a thought, a consideration, and how the Spirit spoke to those on the other side before they could truly Hear.

No, this was not how her life ended. She had fallen eventually into arms that truly loved (a word she would not understand for another half lifetime), under gazes that truly saw. Such life-giving affection remained only a weak light compared to the radiance of her Savior when she was eventually carried through the veil, but they were glorious in that moment, for they were a reflection of Him. A love and acceptance she rejected at first, not trusting. They were patient, those arms from that broken life. They spoke with peace and let her exist in solitary freedom for as long as she needed to. The wounds had healed into scars, her hand eventually reached out for those reaching for her, and life became better. Not perfect. But better. It was there that she met Jesus. The others introduced Him, but her relationship with Him would take many years to build.

He was patient. And kept her safe as she emerged into the world anew.

Was this where the Soul was being sent back to?

She opened her eyes. Grass beneath her. Green, and soft. No snow. No cold.

Sitting up, raising both arms in front of her she inspected her skin. Smooth, unbroken. The Soul should have been excited, joyful, but this spot, this warm green spot was an island in a sea of white all around; an eternity above the beautiful death that was winter.

No, she was simply not comprehending. In truth, outside the circle where her kneeling body stared in silence, there was, truly, *nothing.*

Eternity was waiting. For something. For her?

"I-" she said, but her voice was swallowed up beyond the small circle of grass. She touched her ears. Still there. There was simply nothing to carry the sound.

"I-" she began again, then finally stood, brushing imaginary strands of grass from her skin. "Thank you."

For what?

For everything.

For the experience of suffering, for being lifted from pain and into arms which proved that love was not a vague concept but a solid, real thing that came with a cost worth paying.

For souls that existed to serve other souls.

For a God who was invisible to so many but there for everyone who reached out. Even for her when she had become *nothing* to everyone, everywhere. No, *not everyone*. For those who had become the *not everyones* for her.

For the moment when she'd accepted His gift, then later stepped confidently through into Heaven. For being reminded what Paradise was, by being shown, in this moment, what hell could be. What it was.

Even in the presence of the God who created everything, in His Light, the Soul had forgotten what Darkness truly could be. And how it could follow even into eternity if one wasn't careful.

Around her suddenly was *not* nothing, but pure eternal light. She stepped forward and wished for nothing but to thank Him again and again. The voices of the chorus rolled toward her like a wave, joyful, crying, laughing and singing and singing and singing and she was suddenly with millions of others, and millions more. Her voice became one of many yet distinct to the One hearing. Some day she would again step away, into the relative quiet of the *Coffee Shop in the Stars*, maybe spend more time alone on a hillside, only to eventually yearn again for quiet conversation after the silence of solitude, then crave the storm of worship that surrounded her now.

Paradise was only paradise when it balanced against corruption. Joy only joyful when it was freed from despair.

Green forest only beautiful if the beholder has also seen the decay of seasons. One could not be without the other, and she would scream and sing her thankfulness for this Truth forever.

An Introduction to "The Date"

Here, the first few lines of the Psalm struck me, especially in this modern day when people try to demonize Christians as hateful and unloving (thanks, in no small part, to a good number of Christians; let's be honest). How could someone like Behram stand firm in his faith and still find true love? Well, if we remember that having a relationship with God first means he has (and we have) already found true love, then everything else is gravy.

Or coffee.

Let's see if I'm right.

Psalm 2 - The Date

Why do the nations conspire
    and the peoples plot in vain?
The kings of the earth rise up
    and the rulers band together
    against the Lord and against his anointed, saying,
"Let us break their chains
    and throw off their shackles."

The One enthroned in heaven laughs;
    the Lord scoffs at them.
He rebukes them in his anger
    and terrifies them in his wrath…

Therefore, you kings, be wise;
    be warned, you rulers of the earth.
Serve the Lord with fear
    and celebrate his rule with trembling.
                    Psalm 2:1-5,10-11 (NIV)

"So, I was reading last night because I couldn't sleep? About that kid who got to see the Pope?"

Behram had eventually figured out how to listen to Rayyan, but not before a few false steps in the conversation. Whenever his date relayed a bit of information she'd heard or read, the statement sounded like a question. Mostly (but not always) they were *not*. Running as an undercurrent to everything said was

23

the consternation that *he* hadn't read or heard the same amazing facts.

Rayyan was not currently talking. So . . . waiting for a reply. Did Behram know the child she was talking about?

He raised the small cup of espresso halfway to his lips in order to look casual and said, "I don't recall a story about a kid visiting the Pope," before finishing the cup's journey. He wanted to add that he wasn't very interested in stories about the Pope since he was Methodist and before that, being a first generation American raised in a Pakistani home, Hindu. Though for his family that designation had mostly been in name only.

His parents left their country to protect his sister (Behram, too, though at the time he was merely a growing bump in his *Maan*'s belly) from the Muslim majority. Since then, the pull of any specific religion had no power in his home. Most in their circle assumed the Nawaz family were devout Hindus. He and Souma were taught their parents' language (and subsequently forgot it by the time they'd graduated high school). That language was Hindi, never the national language of Urdu. Any bit of culture specific to Pakistan, where their leaders stood by and let thousands of its daughters be stolen from their beds, was dead to them.

According to his mother, at least. For her, all of everything prior to coming here was dead to them. She liked that expression.

Perhaps because of this, they hadn't complained as vociferously as Barhram had expected when he became a Christian. The act did spark in his *Maan*, however, a sudden need to set him up with as many Hindu women as possible among her friends and relatives. Behram didn't mind. He'd never thought his ancestral people were all that interesting, but they *were* quite beautiful. Unfortunately, finding many who shared his faith was proving to be problematic. Pastor Lucas would likely have something to say about risking "uneven yokes" with these occasional blind dates.

His pastor might worry less if he could hear Rayyan talk, beautiful as she might be.

"Really?" she said in reply to his admission of ignorance. Sort of a question, rhetorical as it likely was. With growing fervor, she added, "He was called up, or his parents had an audience, or he won a lottery, something along those lines. Regardless," a slight toss of her manicured fingers in dismissal, "the Pope with all his robes opened his arms to hug the little boy? Can you believe this?" Undertone of question, not a question.

The coffee was good here.

She didn't finish the story, only looked at him with those eyes. Behram wanted to melt into them. Instead, he'd managed to work out what had happened even though the story she'd read was probably fake.

He said, "The boy turned away at the last minute and shouted Jesus is a lie?" He might as well use a question mark. Speak the language.

She giggled and nodded, delicately covering her mouth. "I mean, it was in Italian, but even so."

"His parents must have been so proud."

"Oh, I think they were."

Poor kid, he thought. Not that Behram believed in many Catholic tenets, but their current leader was an alright guy doing his best to bring the church out of the cathedrals and back onto the streets. Of course, doing the right thing often invited rejection. Safer to hide inside, away from the storms.

Especially if you're a church.

Rayyan's face fell a little, realizing her date didn't share an appreciation for the child's slam against Christianity. She lowered her hand, took a sip from her own small cup and smiled. She was trying, he gave her that, but already Behram wondered why he was doing this to himself, or to her.

She shrugged lightly and broached the subject he was certain *Maan* had skirted when arranging the date. "It's not as if we should feel bad for the old man. All of them are so... off."

"Catholics?"

She waved her hand again, shoulder height, taking in the general vicinity. "Well, yes, them and the others. There are what, a thousand sects of Christianity?"

Not a question, not a fact. At least, he didn't think so. "At least."

"And they're so intolerant."

It was his turn to shrug. "Some are, but every religion has their share of intolerance. Most of the Christians I know are pretty accepting."

She pointed in warning. "Be careful! They'll try and recruit you. It's all they care about."

"Well, yes, we like to invite people to church but there's also the serving-others part that I like best. Feeding hungry people, helping the homeless, all those widows to take care of and stuff."

She laughed, trying to work out the joke. He spared her any more embarrassment. "I'm a Christian. Methodist. One of the larger 'sects,' at least in the Midwest. We're a bit smaller in New England."

Her hand dropped. As did any pretension. Her stare was disconcerting in its directness. "Really." Not a question. More like a polite expletive. "I don't imagine your mother would arrange this date if she knew that."

"She does, actually. Does it matter?" He wondered, not for the first time, why so many people *didn't* think it did. What would Pastor Lucas say?

Her perfect eyebrows raised in surprise. "Does it matter?" She glanced, briefly, beyond his shoulder, eyes losing their focus. What had been uttered as rhetorical turned suddenly into an actual question she now pondered. Did it matter? *Maan* hadn't thought it would, or perhaps his mother was getting desperate. "Of course, it matters," Rayyan finally said.

Yes, it did. In the end one intangible word, "matter," meant something entirely different for her who, to this point, had shown him that her faith lay in makeup and status, the opinions of the faceless 'they' and being comfortable. Nothing was impossible with God, but to step any further in this person's direction would be to test that truth to its limits.

They fumbled for a few minutes more, Behram curiously probing her on how much she understood her own faith, what she'd read of the 'Gita. His questions were enough to, if not physically, then mentally push her out of the chair with a sudden, convenient text arriving on her phone. She excused herself, ordered a car before lowering the phone back into her bag, then stepped outside. He'd stood when she stood, waited until she was outside before sitting back down and finishing his coffee.

When he turned around, considering whether to monopolize the table a little longer with another cup, he caught the eye of a barista sloshing together an *Americano* for an impatient tapping-foot at the counter. She glanced in his direction and smiled, her blush obvious across smooth, Euro-pale skin, before turning away.

He didn't know her name. Had seen her a few times.

Behram groaned audibly, knowing he was hopeless and had to get out of here before he stumbled into another situation where she ended up being an atheist or a Wiccan. She didn't seem Wiccany, whatever that might mean. Later, maybe, some other day, some other century. He needed to spend some time doing anything other than talking to women. Best head home, see if Chen or Bennie were around, maybe get a game going. He looked forward to Sunday, maybe corner Xing-chi for a few minutes to get her silent take on today's car-wreck of a date.

* * *

Behram was tired. Up too late last night with his roommates and a world full of gamers spending too many hours in a fabricated, online world. He'd been thinking of the game's universe that way more often. False. A distraction. Their most recent campaign was called, appropriately enough, *Fallen World*. Behram's avatar was a winged chipmunk partially plated with cellindriate (not a real metal) and armed to the small, cute teeth with weapons that included the smallest but deadliest shooter ever invented: the Stryper Mallet Thing. He'd created it and was especially proud of the weapon's name and destructive power, as long as his winged chipmunk was able to find fifteen dropped acorns on the battle field in time (the game's most interesting feature, aside from escaping responsibility and one's real-world demons for a few hours, was its openness to player-generated weapons - provided they included some unique, and usually frustrating, requirement for use).

He spied Xing-chi in the corner of the church hall, half out of her seat as if preparing to rise but suddenly reconsidering. One thin, spotted hand gripped the top of her cane, adding to the illusion she was in motion. Behram knew better. The stance did not invite many to sit beside her and talk. She was a beautiful and very old woman who didn't do small talk well, and who found a polite way of avoiding it whenever possible.

Her eyes were cast down this morning, not noticing the occasional parishioner unnecessarily shouting their greetings as they passed. She glanced with a wry smile at little Ranita Cruz as the four-year-old offered a piece of her donut. Little Ranita didn't say much. The two were kindred spirits separated by eighty years, maybe more.

Xing-chi waved her hand lightly, said, "No thank you, lovely Ranita. If I eat that I won't poop for days." She winked. The girl covered her mouth in surprise, then skipped away.

Xing-chi (never just Xing or Chi - and Behram was reasonably sure the name was hyphenated) was now exclusively his for the next few minutes. He sat in the empty chair beside her. A slight tap of the woman's fingertips on his leg in greeting. "How was the date, Ram?" She'd been trying to make that nickname stick for two years, since he'd arrived at Hope Methodist in his senior year. It hadn't, and he made sure no one else used it. Still, it was lovely coming from her. More than once he wondered what she'd looked like when she was younger. *Who* she'd been. Very few knew, and those he suspected *did* weren't talking.

No matter. For the past two years, their relationship consisted of these brief few moments on Sunday after service. He sometimes felt closer to this Chinese woman than his own *Maan*, not that he didn't adore his mother. What did that say to his feeling for *this* one? He leaned gently, and briefly, against her and answered, "We were both swept off our feet in a wave of love; lifted higher than any two mortals ever deserved to be carried."

She continued looking down, the slight smirk from the encounter with little Ranita never quite fallen away, then nodded. "Sounds pretty terrible," she whispered.

"The worst. Actually, she walked out after learning I was Christian."

"Another Hindu girl from your Mama?"

"*Maan.*" She gave him an indifferent shrug in reply, so he added, "I guess so, culturally at least, but mostly just another God-hater."

"Lots of those around; a bit louder these days."

He thought about it a moment, said, "It's in fashion to dis the King."

"Dis the King," she laughed and nodded again. "Hmmm."

They said no more for a few minutes. Xing-chi's granddaughter Rebecca (introduced as such long ago: a stately, definitely-*not*-Chinese woman hovering somewhere in her mid-thirties) approached them. She bent over in preparation for helping her grandmother rise up for real this time. Xing-chi leaned into him and said, "You will know her when it's time."

Not Rayyan, he told himself. *Someone else.* "How?"

She still leaned weightlessly into him, while Rebecca whispered if she was alright, tried to help her straighten. Xing-chi obliged but looked into Behram's eyes as she did. "She will be there, present before you, when it's time. You'll know. Like a glimpse of *Tian Tang* for just a moment." She was on her feet, still looking at him. He had no idea what *Tian Tang* was.

She added, "Don't screw it up when it happens."

He thought of the barista he'd glimpsed on Friday after his date left. In his memory, she was in focus, everything else around her a blur. He hadn't gone back, tried not to think of her now. Instead, Behran offered the old woman a little wave. Normally with someone so close he would have given a hug, but that wasn't to Xing-chi's taste. Only those small touches, leaning in. It was how she embraced.

*   *   *

Staring at the screen, clicking through one link, reading the over-hyped news article littered with ads and not remembering any of it. The coffee was good, though, another *Americano*. Made by "Patis". The in-focus, present barista who smiled knowingly at him and towards whom he still felt a draw like no other in recent memory. This week, at least.

Honestly, all he wanted was *one* date that worked out. Even a little. And *no more blind dates*, especially those setup by *Maan*. When he'd sternly informed her of this last week, her self-pity choked him through the phone (he certainly wasn't going to confront his mother in person).

Behram focused his mind on the single task of not looking up towards the serving station. Hopefully, sitting here for the last twenty-five minutes on his laptop looked normal, even if he was working on the same...

Someone placed covered cup beside his empty one.

"If you're going to pretend to be busy at least buy another coffee." He was suddenly grateful for his Pakistani heritage which masked, at least a little, his blush from the presence of this blond, piercing-eyed woman.

"You're blushing," she said, smiling. "That's encouraging." She sat in the chair to his right (not the one opposite), extended a hand covered in either flour or sugar. He took it. Flour, not grainy enough for sugar. Something warm and comfy ran along his arm with the connection.

Stop it, stop it now.

"Behram," he said.

"Pistis," the perfect woman said. It sounded like *Peace Teace* but he probably wasn't listening well. Still, didn't match what was on her name tag. He gave it a shot. "PissTiss?"

She shrugged and shook her head, her upper lipped pulled tighter as if suppressing a smile, or a sneer. "I put Patis on my name tag because I got tired of people trying to pronounce my real name. But it's Pistis."

He pretended to follow what she'd just said. "I like it," he lied.

"No, you don't. You like *me*."

"Yea, I do, but that doesn't make much sense since this is the first actual conversation we've had."

"Ever."

That was *sort* of like finishing his sentence. Good sign. He finally released her hand and took a sip of his new coffee. As good as the first. Better, because she'd made it for him. He

31

looked at her eyes. Patient, maybe a bit demanding. He was in love and didn't understand how that could be possible. *The hell with it*, he thought, without a trace of irony. "I've been thinking about you a lot this weekend."

"Stalk much?" Spoken kindly.

"Not too often. Just when it counts." He smiled, too proud of himself for that stupid remark to worry about looking cool. She laughed, put her hand out again, laid it on his. She was probably in love with him as well, and could explain it no better than he.

Stop it right now.

"I write poetry," she said, "about things in my house and try to make them sound deep; meaning-of-life deep I mean. I'm not too bad."

Behram blinked. She added, "Just giving you a random fact about myself."

Those eyes. Blue like the picture of that lagoon in the old drug store calendar he used to hang on his wall years ago, a way to physically mark off days until the end of school. Why was he thinking about that?

"Why do you write poetry about things in your house?"

She leaned forward, tightened her grip on the top of his hand. He suddenly wanted to sing, but suppressed the urge. He'd probably regret being cautious later. She would have appreciated it. Or gotten fired.

"You forget the second part. Meaning of life. It's what poets do."

"So, you explain the pathways of the world, those down which we all must navigate, but which are sometimes impossible to find without the lyrical directions from poets like you?"

She leaned back, slowly, her smile never leaving her face, which now softened. In amazement, he hoped. She seemed to be breathing deeper.

Uh, Oh.

Finally, Pistis cleared her throat, never once pulling her hand away, but seeming to regain her carefully crafted, carefree composure (he was impressing himself even with the stuff he *wasn't* saying aloud). She said, "You next."

Here it was. The first of what would be two major tests he seemed to find himself struggling with on dates. What she'd told him in a casual way was, he guessed, something very personal. A thing she hid from public in some way. He needed to be honest.

There would always be hesitations when faced with choices. But hesitations were not denials. Pastor Lucas would explain this to him later, when minute details of this encounter were relayed to him.

Behram stepped forward, verbally.

"Well," he said, forcing eye contact and sounding as confident in his next words as he felt he was. "I'm a Christian, attend Hope Methodist across town. Graduated from WPI a couple of years back, engineering." His major or his job didn't matter. He forced himself to change direction, needed something artsy. All he had was truth. "And I spend so much time gaming online that I consume far more than I create, but have always wanted, in some way, to reverse that, if I only had a better imagination."

The hand had started to pull away during the Methodist portion of his rant hesitated, then suddenly gripped his hand harder. If humans could make wild, passionate love simply by holding hands, this was it. Something was different, or changing, in her expression.

She said, "The fact that you want to reverse the tide of your gluttonous consumption of the universe is a fine thing, young Behram. As long as you follow through with it."

"Start planting more metaphorical trees to replace the chasm of… something something."

"Ooh, the wordsmith stumbles."

"Happens to the best of us."

Her smile slowly dropped and her hand pulled away, not (he didn't think) from his reply but rather a change in mental channels. She looked away a moment, thinking. "Christian." Not a question. "Go to church because your mother asks you to every week, or you're one of those arms in the air shouting Halleluiah kind?"

He couldn't hesitate with this one and still look confident, so, "Arms in the air kind. Not a big shouter, unless the music's loud enough to mask my voice."

He knew what was coming next, had seen it before. This time, he didn't want to. Behram was grateful he hadn't had time to envision any other reaction, like Pistis telling him she loved Jesus, too, that she was active in her youth group and patiently waiting for the right man chosen by God blah blah blah blah. Instead, she said:

"I hate Christians." Spoken as casually and affectionately as everything else she'd said since sitting beside him. "They're intolerant, and live in the past."

He laughed. "Some might be, I'll give you that, but most of the folks I know are far more tolerant than the non-believers I know." *Most.* Not her, but to say that would sound like he was sucking up. He knew without much thought that she was doing what so many people his age, living outside the church, did. Following the popular swing of their moral influencers and the media. Usually not from any personal experience.

She considered his reply. "No, can't say that's true. What's your view on gays? On women's rights to do what - "

He reached forward and gently, so gently, took her hand which had been hovering at the edge of the table. He raised it to his lips and kissed the fingertips as lightly as possible. She looked as shocked as he felt doing it. There was such a calm inside him. She was the one. Tang-tang or whatever Xing-chi's word was. There could be no fear in love, didn't Jesus say that?

"I love the gays," he said. It sounded so bizarre they both laughed.

She squirmed a little in her seat, but didn't pull her hand away. "Don't know if I can hang with someone who believes that stuff."

The second crossroads was now upon them. Again, Behram didn't worry. The only way to respond was to stay true to his heart and beliefs. It helped mightily that he knew, without question, that this woman was going to date him, maybe more someday. Maybe Xing-chi could explain *how* he knew (she wouldn't, but she probably *could*). One step at a time, for now. Pistis was very significant, glowing before him, but she was *not* his highest priority and never could be.

Where any of this was coming from, he didn't know, but he trusted it.

He gave her hand a quick squeeze then released it, saying, "I believe it, however, and it's the most important thing in my life. But I'm also quickly beginning to believe you and I are supposed to be together." He got up, casually wiping the end of his lips with a stray, crumpled napkin for no other reason than to look casual. "But it's up to you." He wanted to grab her hand again, even bend down and kiss her on the cheek, but that would be so far down a creepy road he would never win her heart. "You know where Hope Methodist is? It's technically Hope United Methodist but that's too many syllables for most people."

Her brows turned inward, confusion bordering on consternation. "I could find it," she said, slowly, carefully.

He hesitated. "I am so totally into you." Not a lie, no matter how lame it sounded when he said it. "I really would love to hang out with you again. Maybe even go do some datey things." *Datey things? Keep going, keep going!* "But we need to work out this big line-in-the-sand for ourselves. Come to church, meet me there. Sunday, ten o'clock."

Pistis leaned back, laughed, everywhere but her eyes. "No."

She would be there. She of the unpronounceable first name would step beyond everything thrown in front of her to see him again. As he would, to see her.

He would pray until his eyelids bled that this was true.

"No selling flowers at the airport," he said. "Just hang out with me, ignore everything anyone else says, even the pastor. Just be with me."

He let his gaze linger a second longer. Then a quick, "Bye, for now I hope." He left, not looking back, because he didn't want to know if she and the rest of the gang at the shop were laughing at the weird Christian dude who just left.

She would come.

Or she wouldn't.

Didn't matter. He wanted to dance all the way home, then maybe later when he'd come down from this moment he could hide in a closet and cry.

An Introduction to "The Snow"

Lying down and sleeping without fear. Brings to mind those moments, as a child, when the world was simple and safe. Not everyone lives in safety, but even in those worlds there are still moments of peace. For me, a memory and image that comes to mind reading this Psalm is a tradition at Christmas in my childhood family home. Electric candles (the kind with red, green and yellow Christmas bulbs over false melting wax, cast in plastic) perched on the window sill on cold December nights (I grew up in New England, your mileage may vary). The window shade was drawn so the glow emanated in magical color around its edges.

When I stared at the colors waiting for the over-abundance of sugar in my system to thin enough to sleep, all felt right with the world.

I admit the next story ends rather abruptly. Sorry. I hate it when authors do that. But really, this story, about clinging to a sense of protection, even from fears that may not real, is ongoing even as grown-ups. Occasionally, all of us end up hunkered under our blankets and wait out the night, trusting – or trying to trust – that all will be well.

That struggle for faith never really ends, does it?

Psalm 3 - The Snow

But you, Lord, are a shield around me,
 my glory, the One who lifts my head high.
I call out to the Lord,
 and he answers me from his holy mountain.

I lie down and sleep;
 I wake again, because the Lord sustains me.
I will not fear though tens of thousands
 assail me on every side.
 Psalm 3:3-6 (NIV)

Nayla opened her eyes and pulled the heavy quilt against her cheeks. The window shade which Mother pulled down last night did not quite reach the sill. Through the gap peeked the darkness beyond, held in check by the glow of the candles. Earlier in the year the girl would know when it was morning because the window shades would glow grayish around the edges. Not now. Everything, outside, was cold and dark and stayed that way into the morning. Cold inside, too, because Mother and Father liked to keep everything set low. That was how they put it. *Set low*. Cold. Save heat, save oil, save electricity. As a concession, they gave her this quilt when the family moved here from Tennessee. It lay heavily atop everything, hugged her and her "stuffies" like Mother did once upon a time, like she sometimes still did, even though Nayla was almost eight years old.

Outside winter was dark and snowy, silent as a held breath. Waiting for the coming of Christmas. This waiting in the extended dark was hard, but the *Day* was coming, and that name did not mean Christmas. True, time moved slowly once the calendar changed to December, crawling along the frozen ground towards the holiday.

Day to day, though, the sun rose later and later, but it *did* rise, burning away any fear that something outside might claw its way inside her room. The light was her rescuer. Nayla had drawn a picture in school last year of a wobbly yellow sun pouring its heat onto a rendition of their new house. She was not a great artist, not like her friend Ranita, but her paintings had "passion" according to Mrs. Sampson. *The Day*, she'd written in large red letters in the sky above the house. Since then, now that winter was here, "morning" was too weak a label. It was The Day; a Knight slaying the Night.

Until it fully arrived, however, the candles were in their place. Yellow and orange in her room, blue and red in her brother's, small white cords dripping behind the shades while colors illuminated their bedrooms. These were another parental concession for the season. Her room was at least warm with color, even if in reality when she got up her toes would curl away from the cold floor.

With the candles, everything *looked* warm. *Felt* warm in her heart.

She hunkered under the quilt, sleepily watching the two windows, one after another. Orange glow, yellow glow, back again. Occasionally, something tapped and slapped against the glass, beyond the glare of the candles. Snowflakes blown towards the house or perhaps drawn to the electric candle color, like moths.

Snowing outside still, as it had been doing when she'd gone to bed.

All was calm, all was bright. She was safe.

The house creaked as it always did whenever she woke in the middle of the night. There was nothing to worry about, not in this colorful place. The candles were a sign that God would keep her safe. Mother and Father said so. Everyone at church, too, said God watched over the little children, so He would, right?

Nayla slid further under the blanket with only her forehead exposed, not really afraid but not wanting to see anything in her peripheral vision except the edge of the quilt warming her face, the barest glimmer of yellow and orange candles behind the shades.

She eventually fell back asleep, safe in God's arms, the colors, and the quilt.

*　　*　　*

In the risen light of morning, of Day, Nayla emerged from her cocoon. Her brother Kevin was being his usual self, talking louder than was needed. Why yell when it was just her, and him, and Mother and Father? Well, not Father. Apparently, he did not come home last night from work. He was a policeman in Worcester. Maybe something happened.

The snow happened. *All hands on deck,* he'd said when he left last night after dinner. Keeping people safe. *Other* people. No sign of his boots or coat by the door.

Reading her mind, between hurried flurries around the kitchen looking so much like Nayla's brother with her impatient motions, Mother said, "Your father had to stay at Uncle Armand's last night because of the storm. He's on duty again this morning."

Her brother waved one hand in the air and said with an annoying imitation of their father, "All hands on deck!" He didn't sound anything like the man.

Mother ignored the dramatics. "You'll see him tonight." Then, to herself or God, likely not realizing she was speaking aloud, "Oh, God, I hope he gets back here tonight."

That meant more snow was coming, not unthinkable in December, or maybe she was just worried. Nayla had asked once if working as a policeman was dangerous, but Mother had only laughed and said the worst that might happen to her father was a cut doing paperwork. She'd looked down when she said it, like she always did when she told a lie. Kevin taught her to look for that. Nayla wished he hadn't.

This morning, when she wandered past the breakfast nook, the tall windows revealed a snow-covered paradise. Nayla stepped to the front of the house, pushed aside the window curtain.

The driveway wound downhill towards a road that was out of sight beyond the trees. Their town wasn't very far from the city but sometimes it felt like another world. Like Narnia on the other side of Mother's wardrobe. Everything was buried in a foot of snow. More, actually, judging by how much of it had risen towards the bird feeder. She and her brother recently freshened the markers along the house-facing side of its post; every black tic meant four inches. She couldn't see the foot mark anymore.

Before bed she'd watched as the flakes begin to fall, a million white angels landing silently on their property like invading paratroopers. It wasn't the first snowfall this season. Father said Hillcrest was higher up than Worcester because of the mountain and so usually got snow when other towns got rain. Outside would be cold, the air becoming an angry neighbor who watched and waited for her to slip up and forget her hat or mittens.

With last night's fall, they would only be a spot in a vast sea of pine and white when viewed from the road. She usually liked being set back like this; it let her pretend to be anywhere her imagination could conjure. Until Mister Laub finally plowed the road at the bottom of their hill, then swing his truck up their driveway, Father would have to trudge through it all to reach them.

Mother did not like being so hidden up here. She would stare out the front window and wait for Father to come home. The man had been raised here, like Grampy before him, all the way back to when their big yard was even bigger and had cows and chickens and corn. He brought them to live here two years ago when Grampy died.

Mother didn't like being closed off from everything. She said so every time it snowed or rained or the power went out, usually under her breath when she thought no one could hear.

Her mother's fear crept like a snake into Nayla's heart. She closed her eyes and thought about the colored candles in her room, still glowing, always ready.

She pressed her face against the curtain. Cold seeped through glass that never quite kept the chill at bay. She thought of Father, his tall thin frame, curly hair struggling to stay in place when he wasn't in uniform. According to Mother he was too lazy to comb it when off-duty.

He was far away, now. Helping people. The snow would keep him there. Keep him away from Nayla.

For the first time, the girl worried about the things in the forest behind the house that wanted them all to die.

*   *   *

Scarf, once around. Never twice, Mother's rule. Twice around and you would not have enough freedom to turn your head, and thus be at the mercy of whatever was stalking from behind. Not that she ever gave *that* as the reason. That was her brother's explanation. Older by four years, Kevin enjoyed pointing out the things that existed beyond sight of their home, things which waited for her to foolishly wander far enough from safety to snatch her away. Usually, he gave these warnings when Mother or Father weren't around. Nayla didn't believe him; *couldn't* believe the stupid things he told her.

Her boots were thick, lined with actual fur. Father insisted. No artificial substitutes would cause her to lose a toe. She doubted anyone in Massachusetts ever lost a toe from wearing the Walmart boots everyone else got. Mother bought day-old bread and big bags of store-brand Fruit Loops knock-offs to save money, but they would spend hundreds of dollars on boots that made her feet sweat.

Father worried about losing toes; Kevin worried about things in the woods, or at least tried to make Nayla think he did; Mother worried about everything, mostly when Father was away. Too many worries. Nayla had trouble holding everything in. The weight of their words and fears pressed her deeper under the quilt at night. It only got worse when winter grew heavy, when the days got cold and too short.

It was Day now, though the light always had that gray, temporary feel to it. Not like summertime. The sun will be gone again before supper. What light there was, was pulled into the carpet of snow around them and reflected back up like confetti. Everything in winter made her squint: the light, the wind, the cold.

"Don't get eaten," Kevin muttered as he opened the front door, shovel retrieved from the closet just to the right. Shovels were kept inside because often this specific chore which began just beyond the threshold. She carefully whispered a couple of the finer curse words she'd learned from him. The boy chuckled, then began shoveling the small front porch. Mother shouted for him to move faster so he could close the door behind him.

Boots finally laced, gloves on, Nayla moved towards the back door, feeling overheated and craving the cold air. She did not *want* to go outside, especially when Father was not home. His presence had a way of neutralizing her brother's lies. When he was not around, Kevin's nightmares ran wild throughout their home. She opened the back door and cold slapped into the kitchen. From somewhere behind Mother yelled, "Door! Clear it quickly and get that closed!"

The second shovel was in her hand. The drifts against the door were not too bad, just a few inches. The snow was light, not sticky. Nayla pushed it away with the back of the shovel, enough to step outside and close the door.

Look around first, to make sure there were no wolves or otherworldly creatures creeping into the yard from the white-blanketed forest beyond the shed. She wished they had a dog like normal families. A dog would bound outside the moment she opened the door, chase away her fears. Like Father did.

Shoveling the porch was easy and mindless, then the steps. In her wake, a path formed away from the house, twenty feet distant to the shed where the lawn mowers and various tools hibernated through the season. The rarely-used snowblower was in there, too. Otherwise there would be no point in clearing this particular path, at least in Nayla's mind. She worked her way towards it and regularly scanned her surroundings, berating the fear.

They are there, always have *been there. They feed on small animals, birds... don't you wonder why we don't have a dog?* Her brother's nervous excitement when he'd said these words had been worse than any beating he might have given her. Not that he ever hit her, no more than an occasional shove out of the way. But these stories, told at night before the lights were extinguished and Mother and Father disappeared into their own shadows, were far crueler. Bruises and scrapes would heal. *These* scars, these *Scary Facts About What's Outside* blotted whatever daylight was left inside her as she later would spend too much time looking for so many *They*s skulking around, mentally scolding herself for being a baby because none of it was true.

None of it was true!

Mother and Father swore to each other they would never tell you the truth, he'd said.

The shovel hit the shed door. A sudden fall of snow from the slanted roof above made her *yip* in surprise then step back. *Stupid little baby!* she thought.

It came one time, when Max was tied out. Max was his name, you know. Our dog that was killed.

We never had a dog! You're lying.

Don't bother asking them*, they swore to each other never, ever to tell you the truth.*

Clearing around the front of the shed, she didn't look inside. Nothing to see there. She straightened. The snow was smooth beyond the corner, spreading ahead and beyond until swallowed by shadows and half-grown mountain laurel marking the start of the wood line. Above it all stood the pines, silent watchers casting everything beyond in shadow, more so every minute as morning waned and clouds thickened …

Something stared back at her from between two trunks. Nayla froze, waiting for the shape to move and reveal itself as a mirage or something normal like a branch. With the same thought she willed it to do nothing but remain the make-believe illusion her brain just invented. Father said nightmares were merely the brain making pictures, painting things that did not exist.

There was definitely something there, standing tall like a man, like Father who was miles away and would not be able to help. Wait, no, it had to be her brother trying to scare her. A spark of anger, then.

They're a race of creatures older than humans, old and surviving by sheer strength and aggression. And cleverness. They're very *clever. We pushed them here with our roads and cities, and they kept out of sight. But they are really mad about it.*

The anger she felt was not her own, however. *It* hated her, whatever that shape was between those two trees. She had been warned. Her brother wasn't trying to scare her, he was trying to protect her.

Even monsters as dangerous and savage as them have to be careful. We have guns and bombs. They hide until one of us gets careless, or they get too hungry to hide any longer.

Help me, please, she prayed, terrified suddenly that God might not be real. Mother took them to church, including Father when he wasn't working or sleeping in which was most of the time on Sundays. To Nayla, the tiny white building in Worcester with the cross on top was another home where she saw Ranita and other friends like Scarlett who went to a different school; where they watched videos and did crafts about Jesus or Daniel and the lions. Once, Mrs. Zari taught them how to pray. Maybe she'd been doing it wrong. Instead, just in case, she prayed to Father. That felt safer, more certain. Wherever he was, he would hear and come, lights blazing from the top of his car.

Nothing changed between those trees, not at first, then everything did. White eyes and teeth, but those could have been snow on a branch.

They wait, then they take. Drag their food into the woods and eat them so fast you hardly have time to scream before you're dead!

As she turned and ran along the freshly-shoveled path Nayla prayed to her brother, too, because she needed all the help she could get. The house was *right there* but seemed to pull away as she drew close. She slipped on a swath of snow and landed hard in the drifts beside the porch. Reaching out with one mitten, she managed to touch the first step but otherwise didn't move. She couldn't breathe. Lungs not working. What was happening, was she dying?

It was coming. Nayla heard its slow, heavy feet, claws crunching into the permafrost beneath. It thought it could sneak up on her but she'd heard it, she'd heard it, she'd heard -

Nayla curled in on herself then pushed upright with both feet, throwing herself onto the porch. She waited for two clawed hands to dig into her. It would be over then; she'd be dragged away and torn apart before she could scream.

Father, please come and help me!

The door handle resisted, locked? No, no it could not be! She tried again, mittens slipping. The knob turned, opened. She was in the kitchen without remembering moving. Kevin was there, standing just inside.

"What are you - "

She shoved past him. "Me, help!" She couldn't think rationally enough for better sentences. "Close the door, help me, chasing me!"

He looked as though he was about to say something mean, then a knowing expression illuminated his face. "Hold on. I'll check!"

With his coat unbuttoned, her brother ran with only his fists as weapons into the cold yard. She couldn't watch, but shouted in time with her brother's screams. He begged for help, choked on something. The shoveled path was probably covered in blood but she kept her back to it and would - not - look. The door was open. These things wouldn't step inside, would they?

Nayla closed her eyes and cried, "Stop! Stop!"

"Kevin Roy, knock it off and get back inside. Look what you've done to your sister!"

It was the creature, dripping with her brother's blood, using Mother's voice to trick her.

She wouldn't look. The fear simmering in her stomach was spreading through her, paralyzing her. No, it was the thing behind her, holding her in place. She was choking on a scream that could not come out of her throat. Until something grabbed the back of her coat. She screamed then, and thrashed her way out of it and ran, boots and all across the living room, into her bedroom, screaming and shouting words that made no sense even to herself. Her mother might already be gone and all Nayla could do was cry like a helpless baby. Maybe Father was dead, too. All hope was lost then. The thought was a wave rearing up behind her but she kept running on heavy feet. The bedroom, *her* room, illuminated partly with the candles behind the drawn shades and partly with dull light from outside. No time to wrap herself in whatever calm or peace these might offer. She climbed into bed, boots and all, then pulled the quilt over her head. She would not come out, ever, not until she was sure Father was home and could protect her.

Sounds were nothing but a thick buzzing of frozen bees inside the walls. Her universe collapsed into this single place of darkness beneath the quilt. Nothing else. The hot air soon made it hard to breath.

When the creature pressed both hands against the quilt, she sank deeper and deeper into the sanctuary of the bed, feeling like she was falling into another world, a secret entrance to Narnia beyond the wardrobe. She screamed and would continue screaming until everything was safe again. Everything would be yellow and orange lights peeking behind the blinds, the hint of snowflakes on the other side of the glass. Nothing else was real. That was OK because the thing beyond the blanket could not touch her. All she had to do was stay where she was and wait for Father to come home.

An Introduction to "The Shed"

This one is uncomfortably auto-biographical. Not of my childhood. Dad was pretty calm. But I got my random spurts of anger from somewhere, and I've stood before my own shed and fought the urge to trash everything in front of me. Anger is a coil always wound within us to some degree. Problem is, too many people refuse to acknowledge it's there. We relegate it to a far corner of the yard to deal with (or not) some *other* day. Everything that might control us needs to be brought into the light. Otherwise, it'll emerge some other way.

Psalm 4 - The Shed

Answer me when I call to you,
O God who declares me innocent.
Free me from my troubles.
Have mercy on me and hear my prayer.

Don't sin by letting anger control you.
Think about it overnight and remain silent.
Offer sacrifices in the right spirit,
and trust the Lord.

Many people say, "Who will show us better times?"
Let your face smile on us, Lord.
You have given me greater joy
than those who have abundant harvests of grain and new
wine.

Psalm 4:1,4-7 (NLT)

Corn fields... no not corn. Corn stalks were thicker, like those he would cheat and sneak past in the corn maze up in Hillcrest. These, here, were thin like overgrown grass in the field behind his home as a kid, with long heads on top he would break off and hold in his mouth in order to look like the farmer in every child's storybook. Wrong color, though. Wheat, then. Tall blades of wheat. Millions waving in unison one way, then another, dancers to a silent, unheard rhythm. Lucas Roberts knew it was wind making them dance like this, but the stalks towered so much higher than him he felt no breeze. Only enough for the wheat to share among its own kind.

His eyes opened and reality returned. Muffled shouting next door. The Henmans again, pushing each other emotionally, maybe also physically, to whatever edges led to the most pain. Was this real or another dream? Lucas didn't want to think about it. If it was a dream, he wanted it to change back to wheat. He closed his eyes and let go of the sounds, the thumping, and for the briefest moment was standing before the stalks again. This time, somehow, he was tall enough to see over them, hovering in that half-flying way that only existed in dreams. Their husks danced and swayed in a time-release choreography, spreading before him into eternity. Midwest wheat fields were so big, so unending. Lucas still did not feel any breeze, even now above it all. He was dizzy, riding atop a vertiginous frenzy spawned by the unending sway. Losing his sense of up and down, he moved with the wheat, flying too fast, bending forward at the waist and arching his back in an awkward attempt to remain airborne, all in time to a song he could not hear -

Lucas opened his eyes again, this time to faint daylight and his left hand gripping the edge of the mattress. He stared down to the floor, at his discarded socks, finally up at the clock on the bedside table. Five fifty-eight. The alarm was going off in two minutes. He usually woke before it, but never after such a vivid dream.

Renee shifted on the mattress behind him. In her own sleep she draped one loose arm over his shoulder. He smiled, stayed where he was. Carefully he reached up, shut off the alarm with a few seconds to spare before letting one leg slip out from the covers to touch the floor. A trick he'd developed years ago to keep from falling back to sleep. If he did, there was a good chance he'd fall out of bed.

Something else in the dream, or *between* the dreams. Voices, an argument. Mustn't have been a dream because he still remembered it, unlike the dream of wheat for which the details were already fading. He couldn't recall his neighbors ever arguing before, at least not like that, but seemed to remember thinking, when he'd woken earlier, *The Henmans again*, something like that. Why would he think that?

Lucas sighed, knowing he wasn't getting back to sleep, and shouldn't. Perhaps he'd swing by the neighbors at some point and see how they were doing this fine autumn day.

* * *

"Baby, you need to put the yard stuff and mower into the shed today."

"Daddy, can you play cars with me, like yesterday, before Mommy brings me to school?"

"It's supposed to snow, believe it or not. Don't forget."

"I need this form signed!" This last from twelve-year-old Madeline who obviously just remembered the form herself, yet sounded as if her parents were the ones with memory issues.

"What is it?"

"One of you have to sign it so I can play basketball!" Every sentence the girl spoke ended with an exclamation point. She turned towards Renee as if sensing her father's reluctance. Lucas looked to his wife, raised one eyebrow and shrugged.

"Daddy can you play cars? Here, you be the red one."

"I don't think we're going to have time, buddy."

Renee paused in putting Benjamin's preschool lunch together and plucked the form from Madeline's hand. After a brief glance, "Since when do you want to play basketball?"

Lucas assumed most of his daughter's friends were doing it. A moment later her angst-ridden reply confirmed that *everyone* was signing up and she *had* to do it and he reminded her she *needed* to go to practice, and if she signed up she was *not quitting* and, "Yes, yes, I know that," and the bus was coming and she had a test. Renee asked if she'd studied (while signing the form) and Madeline groaned but kept herself from actually screaming (she'd done that once and he'd taken her cell phone away for a week). Benjamin slammed his blue car into the red car which somehow appeared in Lucas's hand. Lucas twitched a little too much in reaction.

"Sorry, Daddy."

"Here," Renee handed the form to Madeline who looked sidelong at her father. Lucas took advantage of the moment and glared, as if his reaction to having his finger smashed by the blue car had been meant for her. Maybe it was. It worked, a little. The girl said nothing else and Benjamin went "brrccchhhh" and hit his blue car, more gently, into his father's red.

Lucas closed his eyes, imagined a scene of waving wheat fields, this lone remnant of the dream still lingering. It didn't take long. When he opened them, Renee had zipped up Benjamin's lunch bag and dropped it into his backpack.

Lucas bent down and lightly tapped his red car into his son's blue, whispering, "brrrcchhhh."

Benjamin smiled.

"Time to go, little one."

Surprisingly, the boy didn't argue.

His wife's beautiful brown face drifted closer to him, smiling in that way which, to a stranger, always looked serious but to those who knew her, only amusement, even joy. "You good, caveman?"

He smiled, hanging on to the last shreds of annoyance because they were his and he could hang onto whatever he wanted, then shrugged. "I'm good, my angel." He kissed her, longer than necessary. She let him. This time. Usually, she didn't appreciate distractions during the morning routine.

When they parted, Benjamin was watching them, smiling a

little.

That was good.

*   *   *

The sky was heavy steel, weighed down by what forecasters insisted would be the first snowfall of the season. Still two weeks until Thanksgiving, but Massachusetts usually got one decent snowfall early.

Lucas breathed deeply and relished a moment of clean, snow-scrubbed air in his lungs. There were two moments when the world around him brought this kind of peace: the hours before a snowfall, and just before a summer thunderstorm crashed over everything and the air danced in electric anticipation.

He stared into the shed.

It was a mess.

The fingers of his right hand began their usual, instinctive dance. His fist opened and closed as if itching to get going. Lucas did this unconsciously, staring at the fallen rakes, an ax, two hoes (one of which was far too rusted to use without first getting a tetanus shot), and other implements of landscape destruction he'd accumulated over the years. Some he hadn't touched since buying and using once.

Beside him the old push mower waited on the grass for him to find room inside. A nervous passenger waiting its turn for a life boat on this sinking Titanic of a yard. His first instinct was to force it inside with a blind shove. Most of the tools would probably scatter to either side. But no, not a good choice.

Something about this shed, every time he looked in, made the muscles in his shoulder blades tightened and his jaw hurt. What he needed was to pick up every individual tool … no, better: *remove* every tool from this hundred square foot box in the far corner of his yard. Lay them down, put them back one at - no, clean them, *then* put them back, one by one. But not before sweeping out ... not before. So many *not before*'s. He did not understand why this box was so chaotic and ruined while almost everything else in his blessed life was well-ordered. *Fairly* well ordered. Not perfect, but mostly ordered.

His fingers rolled faster. He was getting tense.

Neighbors. The vague memory of something last night, between dreams, maybe a dream of its own. The Henmans. Maybe he should pop over, visit them.

Clean the shed.

Later.

*   *   *

"Beer?" Geer Henman hesitated. "You allowed?"

Lucas laughed obligingly (how many people asked him this question?). "Yes, they do allow me to imbibe the lesser spirits from time to time." At his neighbor's blank stare, he added, "Yes, thank you." It was a Budweiser, but Lucas wouldn't say anything, though his preference was usually for the microbrew variety. *Good* beer in other words. He'd force it down for the sake of being neighborly. "I'm not interrupting your work, am I?"

"Oh, no, no," the man said. Geer was a big man, somehow fitting into his name though "Geer" wasn't very common as far as he knew. He also pronounced it like 'bear' and *that* fit the man perfectly. Large shouldered, arms the size of Lucas's thigh, he sat gingerly in an overstuffed recliner which received the man with only minor protest. "Been online since five o'clock this morning. Big install last night; I've mostly been monitoring today, little else."

Not knowing what any of that meant but assuming he didn't need to, Lucas leaned forward from his place on the couch, sipping the beer and making faux-pleasurable lip-smacking noises. "You were awake all night?"

Slow shake, bottom lip protruding. "No, mostly just kept the computer turned on and expected a call any moment from production support." He glanced over at the laptop opened on the coffee table. "No one called. Looks like stuff went well."

"Good."

Furrowed brows. "Why? Were you?"

Lucas laughed, more genuinely this time before shrugging. This man could easily tear him apart but, somehow, he wasn't worried. Probably because there were plenty of neighbors in their cul de sac to hear if Geer decided to beat him to a red splotch.

"Just woke up for a few seconds," he finally said, "and thought I heard shouting. A bit of a fight, sounded like. After ruling out the kids or Renee this morning, I'm assuming it was just a dream. Some old memory resurfacing." He raised the can in a half salute. "Figured I wouldn't be a good neighbor without checking if everything was OK here."

Geer chuckled, his large frame shaking in its leather womb. "Well, we can probably rule out Ellen on the other side of you, unless she had a man over."

Lucas *had* ruled her out, since Ellen O'Neil was almost ninety. He smiled and nodded anyway. "I agree, she usually doesn't get into very many brawls on weeknights. Ellen's more of a Saturday night fighter."

Geer raised his own can in salute without laughing and took a sip. Then, "No, honestly, Father. Things couldn't be better."

"It's not Father. That's Catholic. Everyone just calls me Lucas."

"Wh…. Well, what's your title then?"

"Minister, I suppose. Or Pastor."

"Pastor Lucas?"

He nodded, "My congregation's pretty split between that

or Pastor Roberts. Friends quickly drop the title, though, and it's just Lucas."

"Well, Lucas - Luke?"

"I'd prefer Father over that."

Geer laughed and took a deeper swallow. "Lucas it is."

They talked for another half hour, using the man's job as impetus for Lucas excusing himself and telling him not be a stranger. If he needed anything, anytime, just ask. Geer had seemed nonplussed at the initial questioning but eventually pleased that someone was concerned. He said as much, too. Lucas strolled along the sidewalk to his own driveway, assuming the big man was watching from his window.

His neighbor had been lying about the shouting match. Lucas long ago learned to spot lies, a talent that helped with his line of work.

People fought sometimes. Hopefully the situation at the Henman's wouldn't degrade into what his own parents had put themselves through for years, before Mama grabbed Lucas and his two brothers and drove them far away from the drunk man who came home every weekend and... well, no matter.

Old news. Old world.

God had given him a family of his own, and things could not be more opposite. It would remain so, for them at least. It was still a sad, painful situation faced by people in so many ways. Mothers would always be sneaking their children away from someone else's rage in the middle of the night. His youngest brother Shane once asked him if that's why he went into the ministry. To help people like Mama who needed it.

Maybe.

That sort of... *thing* wasn't selective. It was rampant, and had been since humanity left the Garden.

*　　*　　*

The shed was still a mess.

He sighed and walked with resignation into the dim interior. Daylight was waning; winter was coming. He looked around, not wanting to start and not understanding why. It was so dangerous in here. In one glance he spied twenty different ways the kids could hurt themselves. He picked up a metal rake, smeared with grime along its reinforced yellow handle. Its rakey end was wedged under a tamper he'd purchased a few years ago for the brick walkway out front. Lucas was proud of that one, even if he had to re-level a few bricks every Spring. Benjamin once called it "Dad's Thumper". He tried turning the rake one-handed to free it from the tamper's heavy base. It nearly came free before wedging under a single tine of the bamboo rake which refused to stay hung on the double nails hammered into the support beam. He'd put the nails there specifically to hold these stupid things up high, out of the way.

The rake fell over. The tamper tipped and knocked over the hoe, dominoes shaped like rakes and sledgehammers and gas-powered weed whackers which shouldn't have been left with the heavier tank-end on top because the thing was too top heavy that way, but he'd been in a rush to get inside and out of the rain a few weeks ago. All of them falling over the forgotten form of the rusty shovel which he used for digging the occasional animal grave behind the house. He had a better shovel mounted perfectly on its own nail further inside but this one existed now only to get in the way of everything else.

In this corner of the shed near the door, things had been causally or hurriedly discarded as each project came to a close. It was *his* place, his tool shed, and if he didn't want to organize everything perfectly that was his decision but now the chaos of it all tipped and fought him for control and Lucas suddenly screamed and wrenched the rake free. The thumper's handle tore up and slammed into his leg just below the knee. Everything narrowed for a few seconds as he shouted again and brought the rake down onto the thumper's handle, once, twice, screaming inside his mind to *stop it stop it* before everything broke and he would need to explain why he was buying yet *another* but this just fueled his anger more.

Three times, four, the rake's metal head was now twisted so it didn't matter anymore if he destroyed it. Its usefulness had ended. He swung it wildly to the right, crashing the bent tines into the wall just below the window. *No No No don't break the glass.* It didn't.

Could have.

What would he have done then?

His heart raced, shoulders tense, hands and teeth clenched. It felt *so good.* He wanted to break something else. Anything.

Stop.

No.

Stop.

He waited. Slowly, gently, Lucas Roberts's rational side regained control. It always did after these moments.

The hole in the closet door in the basement where he stored the paint cans was a reminder of the last time. Months ago, that was. Sometime last winter, trying to replace a blade on a hacksaw, it broke after ten minutes of unsuccessful coaxing. He'd tossed it across the room and the corner had dug into the center of the hollow door.

The kids played down there. No one mentioned it. Everyone assumed an accident, a toy thrown, playing too rough. No one asked. This fact sometimes bothered him. Didn't anyone wonder why that stupid hole was there?

Not surprising, then, that no one noticed the small signs of damage in *here.* Anything broken, anything *new* for that matter, was eventually swallowed by the mold and shaded darkness lurking everywhere. As if this was some outward expression of his mind, carefully culled from his body and hidden away, far from prying eyes. A purgatory where he might occasionally free the blind rage for a few dangerous minutes. Maybe someday he would burn this sty to the ground, find some lame excuse for the "accident."

If he did, where would the rage go to hide?

He thought of the hole in the door in the basement, where his kids played.

Maybe it would go there, or find a way upstairs.

Lucas walked out of the shed, leaving its interior more chaotic than when he'd come. Time to wash up anyway. Play with Benjamin who'd be arriving home with his mother in a few minutes, or try unsuccessfully to talk to Madeline when her bus lumbered home, about the happenings in her life. Back to the calm, normal world he'd been blessed with. For a moment, Lucas had allowed the anger and violence of the past to be set loose, let it stretch its legs only to cage it again, lock it away. It was better there.

He knew, without needing any deep insight, that the creature he was protecting his family from in the shed had followed him from childhood, leapt from his father's shoulders to his own and was even now following Lucas into the house. Biding its time, waiting to catch him off-guard.

Is this what Isaac Roberts, his father, had done all those years ago, to knowingly put his family at risk every time he opened a beer? Was Lucas doing any less by hiding it away?

He would be fine. If he was careful.

He could control it.

An Introduction to "The Birthday"

I should make clear one rule I impose on myself when working on this project: aside from normal editing changes, whatever story comes to mind for each Psalm cannot be changed. Editing *could* mean changing character names. I did that a lot, in fact, but in this case, I did so for a significant reason. Xing-chi's name in "The Date" was not originally Xing-chi and she wasn't even Chinese. I forget what her name had been. I think my subconscious was already making plans around her.

As soon as "The Birthday" came into focus when I read Psalm Five, I understood something. The conflict in this character between past anguish and suffering, and her hope in God for eventual deliverance, tied back to an earlier story. In that moment, I also remembered a piece I'd written years before titled, "The Box." Realizing that the character I'd created, the pain she'd been through, was the same person of that long ago story, I went back to "The Date" and changed Xing-chi's name and ethnicity, knowing at some point I was going to end this common thread of stories with "The Box." I'd thought the entire book (or at least this volume) would end with that story. Until I read Psalm Six. To me, as the author, there was no question what the Spirit was telling me: *There*, He said. *This particular story thread ends with Psalm 6*.

Wait, Dan, what about Psalm 5?

Patience, Grasshopper.

Now all of this creative revelation came together quickly, over a couple of days. When the dust settled, I sat down and reread Psalm 5. The same image and conflict was there, only now I understood better who the person dealing with all of this was. I needed make this both a standalone story in its own right, but also a transition into the next. The slight twist at the end of "The Birthday" was a surprise to me, too. Didn't know it was going there until about halfway through that final scene. I've said enough. I particularly love the language in this piece. Sounds like bragging, but it's not. We writers have no clue where the words come from most of the time. Well, *I* think I do, but don't tell my atheist friends.

It'll only freak them out.

Psalm 5 - The Birthday

O Lord, hear me as I pray;
    pay attention to my groaning.
Listen to my cry for help, my King and my God,
    for I pray to no one but you.
Listen to my voice in the morning, Lord.
    Each morning I bring my requests to you and wait
expectantly.

Because of your unfailing love, I can enter your house;
    I will worship at your Temple with deepest awe.
Lead me in the right path, O Lord,
    or my enemies will conquer me.

 But let all who take refuge in you rejoice;
    let them sing joyful praises forever.
Spread your protection over them,
    that all who love your name may be filled with joy.
For you bless the godly, O Lord;
    you surround them with your shield of love.
               Psalm 5:1-3,7-8,11-12 (NLT)

His eyelids fluttered then settled, but the sun found its way through nonetheless. Just a thin line across his lids. Behram knew if he pretended to be asleep long enough the sun would eventually move off of his face. A long, sender arm draped over his shoulder, the limb's freckled paleness contrasting with his own dark skin. He smiled and curled back against his wife as she pulled him closer. Pistis tended to wake him up this way every weekend morning. On weekdays he was out of bed before her but on Saturday he could sleep for as long as *she* allowed. That was fine with him. She nestled against the back of his neck and rumbled like a contented cat, "Beeeee-rrrrrammmm." Dragging out the last letter, tickling his skin and driving him senseless. He wanted to respond, but also did not want to break this perfect moment.

Mornings with his wife were as close to paradise as he imagined they would ever be this side of eternity. Xing-chi's *Tian Tang*.

Pistis gave his ear a little chew. Then a whisper, "Happy anniversary, baby."

Keeping his eyes closed, he slowly rolled onto his back. Pistis semi-purred again and draped herself across his chest. "What's it now," he said, "ten years?"

Into his chest, "Very funny. Though we *have* been married twice as long as last year."

"Math, yuck." He fell silent, letting the moment be only theirs for a while longer. Finally, "You know what this means, then?"

She curled tighter against him, then beat him to the punchline. "It's your Beloved's birthday, of course."

"Yes, it is."

"Are we going to visit her? What's she, two hundred today?"

"Close. I think she's ninety-nine."

"*Almost* two hundred."

"More math." Behram pulled her slowly higher until their faces met. "We'll visit her later. Much, much later."

*   *   *

Xing-chi stared out the window to the church property beyond her small backyard. The morning sun blazed through the glass, warming her hands. One of those hands unconsciously worried over a thumb-sized sliver of wood. It was all that remained of the box. Someone had given the remnant to her as a child and she'd somehow managed never to lose it. Those who understood its implications wondered why she hadn't thrown it out, or burned it.

It reminded her of God's righteousness, His protection, how evil thrives in this world but eventually falls under the crash of her Maker's shield. Something like that. There was a poem someone once wrote for her, a man she thought she loved, but who did not, in the end, stay for the "whole show." She never thought of his name, didn't think of it now, either, only his faded after-image. He hadn't known her story, not at first, about where she'd emerged as a child into this world. She made the mistake of telling him after they'd been married for four wonderful, uncertain years. Shouldn't you trust someone with your past, when you've been intimate that long?

Not in this case. The truth, *her* truth, was too much for him to hold in whatever space he had in his heart that had not already been filled with himself. He'd broken down, wept and took the shock of her story far too personally. As if it had been he who'd lived through it. In the end, he could not handle the pain - his words, never once finding any irony in them - and left, never to return.

An after-image, he was now. A flicker in the corner of her vision when compared to the span she'd spent on this world, certainly compared to the eternity she'd eventually spend on the other side of the veil, her *Tian Tang*. A smile, faint and sad, twitched at the corner of her mouth. It was also love, for the man who could not handle another's past pain.

Why did she do this? Her birthday should be special. Yes, he left on this exact day seventy years ago and was very likely dead now. No more pain for him who must not be named.

Today was special for another reason. Her listless, angst-ridden grandson Behram and his adorable, grab-life-by-the-horns bride were married two years ago. She referred to the boy as her grandson mostly to see the confused expression of others while they surreptitiously glanced between the ancient Chinese woman and young Pakistani man. Both Americans, but far from blood-related. It was fun to mess with people. Actually, it was fun to mess with people and be ninety-something years old. You could get away with it easier.

She turned the piece of wood over and back for a while longer before finally reaching to the window sill and dropping it into its long thin box, the latter intended once upon a time to hold a fancy pen. Its layers of velvet had been long-worn in the depression where the piece went. She replaced the cover, stood on her tiptoes and managed to balance it back onto the top of the refrigerator. She was still tall enough to just reach without falling over (years ago she wouldn't have had to stand on her tiptoes at all). The grabby tool Rebecca had given her this past Christmas, with its squeeze handle controlling a claw at the end of its metal bar, was on the sink where she'd left it. She used it now to push the box farther onto the appliance while leaving *just enough* showing to let her to find it. Next year. God willing. Her granddaughter (and Rebecca was, truly, her granddaughter by Xing-chi's son, Nant) had already called this morning. That was how she remembered it was her birthday in the first place.

No knock on the door yet.

It was their anniversary. She'd told them last year not to waste their special day on her. They could visit anytime.

They agreed, but she knew they would come back, and was privately thrilled.

Xing-chi had lived ninety-nine years on this planet, at least she was pretty sure that was the age Rebecca told her on the call. Sounded right. If so, then she had been *truly* born eighty-seven years ago.

She worked her way to the small, cushioned chair in the living room to wait for the couple. A small, weak part of her was afraid they would take her at her word and not come, perhaps wait until tomorrow. They might reason, *What difference would one day make?*

She prayed not to be alone today, then dozed in her chair. She saw God's mighty shield, golden but stained with grime and blood as it slammed down on her worries, one, two, three, four in rapid succession.

She blinked, felt a pressure on her neck, stared at the carpet before coming fully awake. She looked up from her tremulous perch on the chair. She'd nearly fallen out of it. More knocks, just a couple before the front door opened.

"Auntie?" Behram's voice.

Xing-chi laughed softly. *Auntie.* What a moron. Ram varied the named he addressed her with each time he visited. She loved him for that.

Quick breaths to get more oxygen into her system, needing a burst of energy. "Right here," she said as Behram and his bride stepped into the living room, crossing through the rectangular wash of sunlight coming through the front window. She needn't have spoken; they would have seen her the moment they entered the small house, but it was best to let them know as soon as possible that she wasn't dead in her chair.

*   *   *

Clink of fork on the plate. "We don't give each other presents." he said. "I mean, it's a little silly if you think about it."

Pistis looked at her husband, pulled her cake fork slowly

from her mouth and casually said, "Men shouldn't use the word 'silly'."

"That's sexist."

"Doesn't make it less true."

"Actually, yea, it does." He looked at the old woman who was carefully cutting a sliver of cake with her own fork. Anyone who didn't know Xing-chi would think she hadn't heard him, or was drifting into some haze of dementia. Her eyes hung half-lidded and unfocused as her hand moved slowly towards her mouth with the cake. It was, however, these very attributes that showed Behram that she'd heard everything.

Finally, the old woman said, "Labels that decry one's personal stance or opinion are by their very nature incorrect in the general context of human meaning and dignity."

Behram snickered but Pistis straightened and blinked twice. "That was very insightful."

Xing-chi smiled and reached out, patted Pistis' hand. "Do you understand what it means?"

"Not a word, but it was wonderful to listen to."

The woman's usual expression, one locked in an eternally-amused smile, broke open for a moment and she laughed. "I do like you two children. Very much. Can't say the same for this cake."

"But I made it from scratch."

"No you didn't. You bought it at the Piggly Wiggly."

After cutting himself another forkful Behram said, "We don't have Piggly Wigglys in Massachusetts."

"I know, and it's a shame. Piggly Wiggly is fun to say."

And so went the sparring between three people who loved each other deeply and for varying reasons, sharing similar tastes in humor and faith. They found a unique attraction in each other's company. Behram considered this during one specific back and forth between Pistis and Xing-chi. His attraction to his wife was natural, immediate, even fated (though Pastor Lucas would frown at that term). Why he should be so immediately and constantly drawn to this ancient, smirking woman since the first day he'd entered their church, he might never know. His best theory was that she broke every stereotype he'd ever built around the elderly. She was old, and frail, but full of more life and fire than some friends his own age.

She'd once said a believer's immortality began in that moment of acceptance of what she (and of course many others) called the capital G Gift, but very few lived like it. She, and he, and every other Christian, was immortal. So few believers truly realized they could begin to live in *Tian Tang* this side of the veil, or at least some aspects of it.

She was soon to shatter his assumptions of reality again, but he did not yet know this. There was a quiet moment, as the two woman fell to their respective verbal corners.

No one spoke. The silence was not uncomfortable, but Behram sensed something pending in the room. He waited for one of them to speak. A flash of Pistis announcing her being pregnant flashed in his mind, causing a jolt equal parts joy and terror, but that did not happen. It was Xing-chi who spoke.

"I'll be dead soon."

He glanced at his wife calmly. Like himself, she offered no reaction to the statement. Their friend started most major announcements this way. She had been putting her affairs in order for as long as he'd known her.

"And there is something very few people know besides my *Aunt*s, my granddaughter, and Nant..." Eyes suddenly downcast, voice quiet, "...but he's gone now, him and his sister. Both gone."

She always paused any time she mentioned this one. Not Nant, but his sister. It was a story she'd relayed in snippets over the past few years. He wondered if they would get the full story now, but that particular time in her life would forever be a mystery.

"My Auntie Susan." Her smile returned. Xing-chi blinked herself back to the present and looked up at them. "Susan Wu, in case any of you are assuming I'm messing with you again."

"She was your actual Aunt, then, by blood?" Pistis sat back in her chair, one leg folded over the other with the knee leaning against the side of the table. Her settled-back-for-the-ride stance. She sat that way in the car, too. He wondered what she would be like as a mother. Wonderful, he guessed.

"Ram, are you going to stare at your wife all afternoon, or listen to my story?"

"Can't I do both?"

"No." That got his attention. Her face was suddenly serious. "Not this time." To Pistis, she added, "Blood relative only in regard to our common Savior, my dear. But it's time, I think, to tell you how she came into my life." The woman looked down a moment, considering. Without looking up, she whispered, "How *I* came into my life. This one, I mean."

No one replied. She could be cryptic sometimes. Oftentimes. But she'd earned it. Looking up, and as a beginning, Xing-chi said, "There is a sliver of wood in a gift box on top of my refrigerator. Don't look now. Later. This, is about that."

*   *   *

Pistis' cries on the way home were the heavy, wracking sobs Behram had heard only twice in their four-year relationship. For someone who laughed as much as she did, when something struck her as truly sorrowful, she was all-in. The first time was when he'd proposed - and it took him quite a while to believe those tears were actually of joy, so deep were the sobs. The second was after seeing the movie *The Notebook* for the first time.

But this … this was different. This was sadness at a new

level, for something that had happened almost a hundred years before.

Xing-chi had been very matter-of-fact in relaying the details of her story. She'd been twelve years old a long time ago. Before the Internet, computers or television. The evil that one human could do to another was sometimes beyond imagining. It was why some still tried to pretend the Holocaust never happened. Or that an entire second grade classroom could never be attacked and murdered by one lost soul. Not because the people who doubted the reality of these events were, themselves, bad. Some inhumanity was simply too inconceivable to anyone with a shred of a soul.

And didn't everyone have a soul? Wasn't everyone worth saving?

Behram wondered sometimes.

He reached out to his wife, who took his hand into her own but continued staring out the car window. The leaves were changing, winter coming. It should be beautiful, and it would be again, later, but much of what they saw outside had always been viewed (and might again, in time, God willing) through a veil of innocence. Now everything seemed a little bit faded. The telling of a moment eighty-seven years ago, of a world far beyond this, was a troubling reminder how there always would be something dark and frighting just outside the garden walls.

*　　*　　*

Sometimes Xing-chi thought she could see the veil thinning between this physical world and the next, to the point where flashes of heaven shone through. This hallucination was either her eyesight failing, or her mind, or the Spirit Himself preparing her for the trip home. She played with the spoon in her empty cup - craved another tea but doing that would guarantee she'd be up three times tonight to pee. She had glanced occasionally to the top of the refrigerator while she told the young couple her story - or was it her testimony? No, more like an origin story, for she knew very little from her life before that time. Trauma did that. Flashes of her *before* years returned on occasion, but she'd long ago learned to ignore them, never sure if they were memories or wishful thinking. Didn't matter, not now.

What *did* matter was that she'd told someone else after so long. Past confessions had been given to a few people who were like family to her, or bound to silence for other reasons. A logical part of her mind understood *he who would not be named* had been an aberration. Knowing this part of her history should have drawn him closer. Shouldn't it?

Of course. You're being silly.

They would call, Ram and Pistis. Later, or tomorrow. She was not worried.

Hopefully they didn't linger too long. The air between her and the living room seemed thinner than usual, as if she might step through any moment. "No, Lord, not yet, please." The last thing she wanted was to drop such a bombshell on these poor kids only to die the same night. She smirked. It *would* be dramatic, however. And she'd have the last word.

There *was* something there, between the kitchen and living room beyond. A hillside rolling away, forever and ever. She imagined herself sitting on that hill, being a new creation. Who would she become? Saul the Pharisee had shed his old skin and became Paul the evangelist; Jesus gave Simon the name Peter. Maybe He'd give her one, too. Or ask her to choose one for herself.

Maybe there were no names on the other side.

Her smile was tired. It remained, even as she slowly lowered her head to the table and nestled it in her arm. With her other hand she pushed the tea mug aside. It was blocking her view of the hillside. The air was no longer thin. It was open and clear and her smile, nestled in the crook of her arm in the silent kitchen, became wide while Xing-chi's eyes lost their focus and her shoulders relaxed. The woman who'd lived many lives in this world stepped slowly, but with shaking excitement onto the hillside, leaving her name and life and memories behind her. All of it now washed away in the light coming from the man who now embraced her with more love than she could ever have imagined possible, even in eternity. The Soul stayed wrapped in those arms a long, long time and knew everything, everything, everything was finally perfect.

The phone rang in the kitchen. When the answering machine kicked in, Behram's voice called her name. Xing-chi did not respond, still staring half-lidded towards the living room. She did not rise, because she was no longer there.

An Introduction to "The Box"

Please be aware that the subject matter of this next story might be very disturbing to some people. Nothing overtly graphic, but some horrors of our broken world don't need to be spelled out for their dark truth to be obvious.

Nor should they be ignored.

I was stunned by the words of this Psalm, in light of what was going through my mind at the time (see the introduction to the previous story). I won't say any more, except that if you wonder how Xing-chi the elder stateswoman could be so strong in her faith with such a painful beginning of life, you have a too-small image of the Creator. I know and love quite a few people whose testimonies would curl your toes, and yet today they are much stronger than me in their spiritual walk with God. Because they understand this world is broken, but also that they are fearfully and wonderfully loved.

They know that *Tian Tang* is always within our reach.

Psalm 6 - The Box

Lord, do not rebuke me in your anger
    or discipline me in your wrath.
Have mercy on me, Lord, for I am faint;
    heal me, Lord, for my bones are in agony.
My soul is in deep anguish.
    How long, Lord, how long?

Turn, Lord, and deliver me;
    save me because of your unfailing love.
Among the dead no one proclaims your name.
    Who praises you from the grave?

I am worn out from my groaning.

All night long I flood my bed with weeping
    and drench my couch with tears.
                        Psalm 6:1-6 (NIV)

She awoke in darkness. Whether it was morning or evening didn't matter. Such concepts were lost to Xing-chi. Even her name, which had meant something to her father and mother, no longer had significance. She was she, with occasional labels and epithets spat by the men who came to her in moments uncountable. No light meant only that no one was coming to pull her small, cramped body from its home. And this was her home, an acceptance which had long ago crossed the threshold of her mind. Any hope of the world turning back to its proper shape had long fallen away, crushed under her sparse weight inside the box.

Time passed. Light gradually blossomed, vague and gray. She moved slowly in the tight space, long-practiced at silence to avoid attention, rising until her right eye aligned with the imperfect circle in the second-highest slat. Once a rough knot, it had fallen loose many months ago when her crate was lowered unceremoniously onto a platform much like the one on which it now rested. She stared through the hole, a surrogate Eye through which Xing-chi could view the world. She raised her left knee, bit down on her bottom lip as a sharp pain cut upward along her side from the neglected muscles, and held herself aloft on tips of slender fingers. Eye to Eye, looking into the gray.

This world was larger than the previous, wide and spacious with air that was at least cleaner than the damp shipping hold which served as the first of many worlds she'd traveled to after the leaf and tree of her childhood had been ripped away forever. Other boxes like her own filled the cavern. Many would contain lifeless cargo, bodies or books or machine parts, jumbled straw entombing a single expensive vase. Sometimes, in other places, she would watch men opening the crates as they followed a list on clipboards, adding items or taking them away. Always, if their puffy, sweaty faces turned her way Xing-chi would fade from the Eye, drift into the shadows of her home and hope she had not been seen either by the men, or their thoughts.

There were moments, however, when the box felt too tight and angry around her, when she welcomed their attention, rough and violent as it usually was. It served as confirmation she was not dead, was not mere spirit once drifting in the wind, now caught in a net and caged, never to see or touch the trees of the Next Life.

Her mother talked of a place like that. A world of joy and music and warm breezes. Tian Tang was its name, the point all must travel toward but never reach, not until the time they were lifted by the Light and delivered to its bosom. Her mother would sing of this place and read from her book. In those long-ago moments Xing-chi understood little but savored the woman's tone, the sound of her hope. She had forgotten her mother's voice now. There had been a father, too, a stern rock of a man. His gaze rarely fell on Xing-chi. She remembered he had smiled once but the reason for it was as elusive as her memories.

Maybe what she was remembering *was* Tian Tang. Perhaps she'd already passed from her old life and reached its perfection, only to lose her footing and fall backwards, into this box.

She raised herself higher until her head touched the top. Her small nose poked through the Eye. Xing-chi breathed in, quietly pulling into herself what smells she could draw from the room. Wood of course, so many crates. Something else, wet and greasy. No food, not yet, but this consideration sent saliva to run like a fever over her tongue and teeth. She licked her lips, swallowed, turned her ear to the hole as a distraction. Silence, the sound of waiting. A sniffle, far off from one like her, never too close, never a word or gaze to share with another.

There, a soft whimper, perhaps a yawn. All like her were careful with silence. Perhaps this girl had been inside too long and wanted to draw the men to her, if only for that craved attention, that confirmation of her being. All of them, trapped spirits. Flies in amber.

CLANG!

The sound was so abrupt Xing-chi curled onto the bottom of the box, away from the sudden light washing through the Eye. Tight, low voices uttering unknowable words. Their tones told Xing-chi that no new books or lamps would be unpacked this day. They had come for her, or another. The voices grew no closer, moved at a distance towards some other part of the world. The voices rose sharper, accompanied by the sound of wood being pulled free of its nails, a crate being opened. A girl's voice, high and delicate like broken porcelain. Xing-chi once understood the words she spoke, or those like them. If there was understanding now it was trapped outside the box, never to be reclaimed. She did not want to know, because there was no room in her dark place for another's pain. The voices passed back the way they'd come. She uncurled slowly, keeping to the shadows far from the Eye, saw shapes flitting past in the distance. One man, apparent by the hair on his large face, moving too fast to discern detail. Tangled black hair followed, its owner lower than the hole. Xing-chi suppressed the urge to move forward, to see who it was. The broken porcelain sounded again, but was hushed into silence. Another clang echoed in the cavern a moment before the light died. Xing-chi did not move, non-existent once again in the sudden dark, and waited for the gray to return.

She eventually curled back onto the floor, the top of her head resting on the wood, bare feet pressed to the far wall, knees bent and stiff. She thought no more about what had happened, simply let the activity, which had come and gone like lightening, drift about as a new shape in her shapeless world. They would return. They always did after one was taken. They would open her box and lift her out, let her wander in some far corner to stretch and defecate. If she was fortunate they might spray her with a hose and for a joyous moment remind her she was alive. Because if she was still in this First Life, shattered as it might be, then Tian Tang may still be waiting, may still be a hope.

Xing-chi closed her eyes. She was hungry, but would eat when food was offered.

*　*　*

A ripping sound. The shaking of her world. All was falling and lost. These thoughts stampeded through her brain as Xing-chi awoke. She tried to curl tighter but her movements were too sudden, the pain too sharp. The top of the box cricked open, angles of light widening as the top was hefted against the many nails holding it fast. Large, gloved hands pushed up and up.

The men had returned but she'd been sleeping, hadn't heard, could not prepare.

A pockmarked face mostly hidden in a thick, wiry beard loomed over her - the man she'd glimpsed earlier. His smile was lost in hair and cratered flesh, eyes narrow and wet. He spoke words and Xing-chi waited, still curled tight in the small space. A second head peered over the top of the box, long and thin with wide eyes. He licked his lips twice and they glistened in the artificial light.

"*One of our finest,*" the bearded one said. Xing-chi understood nothing except the tone. The thin-headed man would be taking her for a time, touching and maybe hurting. That was all right. Her existence was now a truth revealed in the trembling, expectant gaze of both men. The thin man said something. The beard replied with, "*Twelve or thirteen. Can't tell with this kind. Look like babies no matter how old, right?*" He laughed. Thin-head did likewise, without humor, glancing across Xing-chi's bent and naked body.

She kept her eyes open, looking sideways at the men, listening to words familiar from past conversations like this one. Would the thin man choose another? Did they not see her? She wanted to move, do something to attract his attention so he would lift her from the box and see her.

He nodded. The beard did as well and his head rose higher

as he lifted the top free. His chest was wide and muscular, like her father's only much, much bigger. He was going to lift her out like the lamps and books. She was here. She existed. The other man would have her for a time in some cold and distant corner. Xing-chi was both excited and terrified. She wanted to smile, and wanted to die. Tian Tang was again a hope, but the road was so hard.

Rumbling thunder of a dozen shouting voices. The large man had been reaching down but now he stopped and straightened, turned in unison with his companion towards the noise. He barked short words then was gone, the platform rocking back and forth with his departure. The thin-headed man looked down at her, fear and need swirling about his nose and lips like Autumn leaves. His arm snaked into the box. Tears ran down his face as he gently touched her leg. More shouting, closer, one word repeated over and over, "*Now! Now!*" Then, "*On the floor now!*" He continued to touch her as Xing-chi stared into his lost and defeated eyes. She tried to speak, tried to thank him for the contact. She could not, no more than she could move more than a few inches in such a confined place. Even so, she savored the proof of her existence in his –

A black-gloved hand grabbed the man's collar and pulled him away from the box. The word, "*Now!*" was repeated with such venom Xing-chi curled against the pain of her muscles and closed her eyes. The box shook. What came next would not be good. Demons and anger. A new word was shouted at her from the top of the box, "*Miss?*" making no sense, the tone too tight and wild. Xing-chi bent her arms about her head, forced herself into the wood, became the grain. Like the world of her birth, this terrible place was crashing, turning over and if the one which replaced it was worse than this, she did not want to be anywhere. She understood with constricting clarity that she had, indeed, fallen from the Next Life. It would be best, then, if she was no longer here or anywhere. Only patterns and swirls in the wood, lost inside a box in a cavern of gray light.

When the man's voice returned, it was softer. As all around her, shouts and frantic words filled every corner, the soft tone of Black Glove's voice dominated her small world. *"Miss,"* it whispered, like a warm breeze, *"can you understand me?"*

She did not understand his words. Her spirit was pattern and swirl, no more substantial than a lost memory.

*   *   *

The room was warm, filled with light. Warmth was a concept long forgotten. How cold had it been inside the box? Without choice, things simply were. She curled on the bed in the same position as when the soldier had lifted her out, wrapped her in a rough blanket and carried her away. She understood those moments with clearer thoughts now. The soldiers had come for her and the others, brought them here. She dared not venture further in her mind with these considerations, nor their implications. For if the tiny world in which she'd lived for so long was the same as that of her lost home, her mother and father... the meaning was too much, too terrible. She pressed against the mattress, tried to disappear into the sheets like she had done when the thin-headed man had been pulled away. Too much. All, of everything, was wrong.

"How long?" A new voice in the room. Not the yellow-haired woman who often came and spoke to her, touched her, shined lights into her eyes. Her long face was like the man above the box but softer, prettier. This new voice was also gentle, another woman. Xing-chi could not see the face it belonged to, nor did she care to. She closed her eyes tighter and pressed her face hard against the bed.

"*Best we can tell,*" the yellow-haired woman said, "*two and a half, three years.*"

A sudden intake of breath. "*Oh, Dear Lord. How.... why did.....*" Staccato words, but Xing-chi found comfort in their rounded edges, and the hope that they were speaking about her.

"*She's been like this for hours. Won't acknowledge anyone, but she probably doesn't speak English.*"

"*Can't you put clothes on her?*"

"*She won't let us. Not yet. Try to talk to her, Sue. Please.*"

Xing-chi let their voices lull her. So much like her mother's, especially this new one. Light footsteps, leaves across stones. "*Miss?*" That word again. Would this be her name now? A cool touch on her shoulder. Xing-chi flinched, but the fingertips remained, hardly there at all.

"Ni ming bai wo shuo shen mo xiao gu nang Ma?"

Every muscle in her body froze – not tightened as they often did at the sound of men approaching. She merely became motionless, fearing any twitch or movement would make the light filling her chest fade away.

She'd understood the words the new voice had spoken. *Do you understand what I'm saying, young girl?*

The touch remained, patient. Xing-chi had to show she understood before they gave up and went away. She opened her eyes, did nothing else, not yet. The mattress stretched out before her in a soft, white landscape. A figure moved like a cloud in her peripheral vision.

The voice said, "Ni ming bai Ma?"

Emotion poured into her, drowning her. She turned her head and a woman like her mother but not her mother sat on the edge of the bed. Her face was round and flat and loving. It smiled and spoke and Xing-chi died in her gaze. The world filled with water. She could no longer see, felt an arm curl around and lift her up. Xing-chi's own arms and legs remained curled, but she allowed the contact and knew it would not hurt. She cried against the stranger's dress, understood her own nakedness for the first time. She was an infant reborn into this world of warmth and light and perhaps she had made it... no, she would not think this, would not hope, only let the angel hold her and hold her.

*   *   *

Xing-chi sat on the bed. The woman remained, one arm around her shoulder, always touching, always this contact. She'd tried to wrap her in a blanket but the moment she felt its confining embrace a black terror sent her curved, angled limbs flailing until the blanket fluttered to the floor. She was happy the way she was, body open to warm air and the woman's arm, always around her shoulders, connecting the two of them like a newborn to its mother.

"Ni zhi dao ni ming zi Ma?"

The woman wanted to know her name. Xing-chi wanted to tell her, knowing that it was not *Miss*. She wanted to say *I am Xing-chi*, not knowing why she was called this. When she tried to remember the fear crept back. She wanted to tell this woman, this angel, something, wanted to *speak*.

She tried to say her name, but her mouth was broken, tongue disobedient.

"*That's OK*," the woman said in that strange language. The yellow haired woman said something equally alien before she crossed the room to a wide glowing wall. A thin, bamboo-like shade covered the window. She pulled on a chord and the veil was lifted.

Sharp daylight, so bright it was almost painful. Xing-chi needed to squint, but she kept her eyes open, needed see what lay beyond the glass. When she saw, understanding and joy flooded into her again, like sunlight filling her body. She gasped and tried to straighten her arm and point.

The woman said, "Ni xiang qu chuang kou Ma?"

Do you want to go to the window? Xing-chi reluctantly looked away and stared at her face, so much like her mother's. She could not say the word, but thought, *Shi, shi, shi*!

The woman nodded, helped her off the bed. Xing-chi's legs would not straighten, would not hold her weight.

"*Let me help*." The angel lifted her with both arms. Xing-chi leaned against her chest and held tightly to the woman's neck. Always, though, facing the window. When they reached the glass, brilliant sun poured over her. She reached out her fingers and they curled against the glass. She continued, letting the back of her hand bend, then her whole arm. She could not reach what beckoned from outside. So close.

"*She's trying to reach the tree*," the other woman said behind them.

Xing-chi accepted the futility of what she was trying to do, and instead pressed her palm flat, fingers splayed. Wide green leaves filled the world beyond, edges red and yellow. They were perfection, like the story of the first woman and first man from her mother's book. The outline of her hand spread like fog across the glass.

Xing-chi tried to speak but her lips bent funny. She ran her tongue along them, soothing, calming. She swallowed and focused only on the single word she wanted to say.

"Tian Tang," she whispered. The joy hearing it spoken aloud, and its truth, gave her lips strength to say it again.

And again. And again.

"The Hole"

Part Two: Looking Up

An Introduction to "The Hole"

Before we talk about the next story, I should point out that Part Two contains an entirely new set of inter-related stories, *none of which* are connected in any way to the previous tales. As I believe I've mentioned, it was never my intention for any of these to be connected, but you know what they say about best laid plans.

End of public service announcement.

Digging yourself a hole is a strong image in this Psalm. From his apartment window Young Mateo sees a body and needs to get close enough to *claim* his great find before everyone else makes the same discovery. As artists and writers, it's funny how some people we weave together have bigger stories than what we originally give them. They demand more air time, as we'll learn in subsequent stories.

Halfway through "The Hole," I understood that the body itself was a soul that needed its story told. I had to go back and find out where he came from. I truly loved every character I got to meet in the subsequent coffee shop scene, and miss them. I keep hoping they'll come back some day, in another story. But they haven't. Not yet. When this first volume is released, I'll still have a hundred and thirty-five more chances (there are a lot of psalms!) to visit them again, or to hear what the Lord might say to us through them. For now, let's enjoy our too-brief visit to this Brooklyn neighborhood.

Psalm 7 - The Hole

The wicked conceive evil;
    they are pregnant with trouble
    and give birth to lies.
They dig a deep pit to trap others,
    then fall into it themselves.
The trouble they make for others backfires on them.
    The violence they plan falls on their own heads.

I will thank the Lord because he is just;
    I will sing praise to the name of the Lord Most High.
                      Psalm 7:14-17 (NLT)

Seven-year-old Mateo stared through the apartment window, trying to decide if the man lying in the middle of the hole outside was dead, sleeping or had simply fallen in. The people who'd dug the hole still hadn't put any fence around *the damned thing.* That was how his *Madre* referred to the massive dig site in the lot across the street. He repeated it aloud only once, and hurt for the rest of the day. His mother couldn't stop him from *thinking* whatever he wanted, however.

"Mateo," Madre said quietly, her belly so big it seemed to pull her down towards the floor. *"Termina tu desayuna antes de que pienses salir a fuera."* She said most of everything quietly these days. His brother Neftali would be arriving any day now. Mateo imagined her swollen belly stretching beyond its limits and a fifty-pound baby tumbling out.

His own stomach flopped with the image but he shuffled reluctantly back to the small table and finished his breakfast as commanded. The road, the hole and empty lot outside the building were now out of sight. He finished his waffles quickly, brought the dish to the counter, rinsed the plate and left it in the sink. As he ran to his room his mother spoke, in English this time. "I don't want you to wander out of sight of the windows, Mateo."

"I won't!"

And he wouldn't. The hole was only across the street. As he dressed, he hoped the man was still lying there. He imagined being the only one who'd seen the body - if it *was* a body (of course it was, regardless if it was alive or not). Mateo might be interviewed on TV as *The Boy Who Discovered The Murder Victim.*

He dressed in record time. As he reached the apartment door, Madre said, "*Ven dame un beso.*" He did, with no reluctance. His mother was like an angel, tired as she seemed these days. He kissed her on the soft, perfect skin of her cheek and whispered, "I love you, Mama." She smiled, hummed her pleasure and said she loved him too, reiterating that he was to stay in front of the building, not to talk to anyone he did not know and absolutely *not* go into the lot across the street. As he ran down the hallway towards the stairs, he rolled that final instruction over in his thoughts. He could go on the sidewalk, to the edge of the hole without actually stepping foot onto the property. He would be able to see the man, close-up, without breaking any of his mother's rules.

The summer heat was only implied within the chipped linoleum lobby of the ground floor, but was a molten wave crashing over him as he pushed through the doors. Mateo excused himself past Mrs. Bykov, who almost got the door in her face from his haste. Dry, hot and... something else. A smell; a new smell. Like the subway but sharper. In the thin breeze it dissipated, but as he waited beside a crooked man in a blue suit at the crosswalk the smell came again. He stepped away from the man but the smell did not change. Wasn't him, then. That was good. What would it have been like for the guy if he had... the WALK signal glowed. Mateo and the crooked man crossed the white hashes together to the other side, keeping pace, as if racing to be the first to see beyond the edge and later interviewed on the news.

In fact, the crooked man was doing just that. He reached the edge of the property and stepped a few more paces to the left, staring down. Mateo looked up, noted his face, its long, bristled mustache, the curious, neutral gaze into the hole. The hole! He'd been too distracted. Others were standing beside them now, anyway, muttering to each other and staring down. Nearly ten in all. Mateo could hardly see past them, definitely not enough to catch sight of the body. He needed to get closer, but how without his mother seeing? She *would* look, make sure he was visible from their third-floor window.

Word was spreading quickly, more people arriving, his chance to get a close-up glimpse worsening. Two large men stood a few yards down the sidewalk, tall enough to see from their vantage. Mateo ran to stand in front of the heaviest of them.

"Bruno Angelo, lift me onto your shoulders."

Bruno Angelo - these were his first and middle names and if you called him anything *but* Bruno Angelo, he would beat you to death. Ravi told Mateo this at school once, about how two boys decided "to be smart" and call him "big guy" and were *still* in the hospital. Mateo had his doubts about Ravi's story, but Bruno Angelo had been his friend's foster brother once upon a time so he should know.

"Go away, Mateo Antonio (oh, and Bruno Angelo called everyone *else* by their first and middle names, if he knew them) and just push yourself closer to the edge. You're small enough."

There was no more time; blue flashing lights stalked around the corner of Pleasant Street. The cops were going to make everyone leave. *Nothing to see here, folks.* Mateo risked the hospital and grabbed the fat man's shirt, gave it a tug. "I need to see, and you're the strongest in the neighborhood." A lie, but what did he know, it might be true. "Hurry the *policia* are here. Hurry!" He raised his arms up and probably looked like a baby but *he didn't care*!

Bruno Angelo called him a bad thing in Spanish to his equally-large buddy, but was also smiling. "Turn around, *mi hermano.*" He did, and found himself rising over the crowd. He was suddenly on the man's shoulders, careful not to mess the slick black hair. The world rocked side to side. "*Ay Dios, Nene,*" Bruno Angelo shouted, "*avanza tu pesa!*"

Mateo steeled himself and looked. "*Que es ese olor?*" he asked, for the smell up here was so much stronger.

The man in the hole was white, not just Caucasian but white-white like a ghost. Mateo's arms drained cold. He held tighter to Bruno's Angelo's head, no longer caring about messing his hair.

In English, the man under him wheezed, "What do you *think* that smell is, *Nene bruto*, it's the body. That's the smell of the guy rotting."

Everything spun about them. Mateo's stomach was cold. The street corner dimmed as if the sun had fallen behind a cloud.

"*Ah, no!*" the second man shouted, pointing. "*Bruno Angelo, suerta lo que va vomitar!*"

Mateo found himself dipping and tipping then an unforgiving grip lifted him off the large man's shoulders. He knelt and leaned across the edge of the abandoned property. Then he threw up, hoping it wouldn't drip down into the hole towards the body. He shouted in misery as the rest of his breakfast came up.

*   *   *

Richard W. Phelan was a heavy, sweating man with high blood pressure. Because of this condition, his face was a constant shade of red. He ate full cloves of garlic as if they were miniature white apples, giving his sweat a pungent, heavy odor. He was also extremely rich, so few people complained. He'd grown up in Troy, eating lunches paid for by the state of New York most of his life. *Never again*, he swore to whoever might listen (willingly or not). There would always be money now, and more coming. If either of those situations fell short, he would push harder, cheat more, hurt whomever he had to.

Especially cheat. He did that a lot. Life was a game of monopoly where every time the banker turned his head or went into the kitchen for a beer, was an opportunity to grab more twenties from the stash. Turning in David Kardoff to Customs three years ago was one such example - the guy deserved it, had been monkeying with his manifests for so long that he'd been destined for prison eventually, regardless of anything Richard might do. In this case, Richard needed cheap concrete, and Kardoff's assets being frozen by the Feds opened a route for Richard to make a false claim against one specific container from Hangzhou. He knew Kardoff wouldn't dispute it. He was too busy making sure no one looked in some of his other boxes.

Customs was easy to fool. The entire city was, in fact. Not that the fine purveyors of the New York City wheelhouse didn't know when someone was pushing them the wrong way, but Richard could be a friendly guy when he needed to be, knew when to pay a little extra and when *not* to. Most importantly: how to keep his name out of the news.

He wiped a white cocktail napkin across his forehead. It

came back yellowed. He stared at it. That wasn't normal. Looked like he just wiped makeup off his face. Richard W. Phelan did not wear makeup. Not even in private. Sometimes he wondered if maybe he should, clog the pores and keep sweat from bursting across his body whenever he walked more than a few steps.

The city was hot tonight. This yellow discoloration was probably just soot from outside. As much as the Apple had been polished over the past few decades, it was still a dirty city. He crumpled the napkin in his fist then let it drop to the table.

Richard looked up in time to find two teenage girls staring at him. When their gazes met, they turned away quickly, shoulders together to block their whispers and giggles. Let the tarts make fun. He could buy them any time he wanted, ten times over. He understood that he stank, but the website said garlic was the healthiest thing to eat, especially for someone his age. People turned away from him all the time, talked in whispers and giggles like these loose dregs of humanity across the room. People who didn't know him; people who didn't want something from him; who weren't afraid of him: they didn't matter.

"Tarts," he whispered, and laughed a little. It was a fun word. His father used it all the time. Come slamming into their apartment in Troy yakking on about the latest "tarts" who used his cab at three in the morning. Richard, even as a boy, woke every night at the sound of his father coming home like this. Not that the man ever knew it. Richard never made a sound, even when his father occasionally came to *check* on him. It wasn't joy when he heard his father come home, only fear.

He had a fondness for the man only *because* of this fear, for it molded the clay of his childhood into who he was today.

His coffee cup was empty.

Why was he here?

He wanted to see the hole, that was why.

He raised the cup and waited for the girl with the dreadlocks to look up and see him. She seemed reluctant to catch his eye. "Darling," he said aloud, finally, "think I could have another?" Stupid place didn't let you get your own refills. She would probably charge him for it, too. Would probably *have* to. Cheapskate owner likely had rules around that sort of thing.

She came to the end of the counter closest to his table. He got up and leaned over - poor girl actually flinched when he drew close. He could buy her, all of them. Richard rose up, keeping one foot in the vicinity of the table in case anyone thought he was leaving. There were a few standing at the counter eying his seat. He held the paper cup as she poured then sat back down, not waiting to see if she asked for payment. Refills should be free. In his peripheral vision her image lingered, then moved on.

Richard W. Phelan sipped his coffee, unaware that in less than thirty seconds he would experience God, yet even then be oblivious to it.

The outside light faded, late summer twilight in East Williamsburg. *Juan Coca Beans* (the grammar in either language was atrocious, but the coffee was decent) was a triangular hole-in-the-wall bordered by Union, Majuer and South 1st Streets. He liked this table. Its vantage looked out the glass door, across the street towards the hole he'd paid to have dug three months earlier, when Spring was new and the ground soft. Not that there was much actual *ground* here. Mostly rock, old concrete and yes, some dirt tainted with a chemical Richard told the foreman never to write down or speak aloud. If it was bad, he needed to claim ignorance.

All of it, dug up and shipped under an anonymous corporation hours before any hazmat or zoning folks could arrive to find out just what the heck they were up to.

Now it was summer, and people had lightened up a little

with their screaming and whining about the sudden appearance of a hole in the center of their neighborhood. Having no fence was too dangerous, they said. More dangerous than living here? Granted, this neighborhood wasn't so bad, not like that of his childhood, but nothing close to upscale as where he currently lived, less than a mile west.

Gentrification, ladies and gentlemen. Classy living was spreading slowly but inexorably East from the river and Richard W. Phelan would be ready with one key piece of property that will, without question, increase in value by the time the wave of progress reached this block. Property never went down, only up. That's what his old mentor MacKenzie told him, and *that* tart was usually correct in her view of things. All he had to do was wait and dig an ugly, monstrous hole on the property to prevent anyone from squatting on it.

Through the windows, the hole was just a vague shape in the falling gloom. Now and then, a passer-by would stop, look into it, maybe toss a piece of something in. Like a penny in a well, or an offering.

He should probably get a fence.

Ten seconds.

He sipped the coffee. Hot, and good like the last one.

Maybe he should give up the table, even pay for this second cup. Leave her a tip. He was feeling generous all of a sudden.

A man sat down across the table from him, holding his own paper cup. He also carried his own atmosphere swirling around him, smells from another world. Indian spices like Garam Masala and Cumin that tickled the nose, also something that reminded Richard of midnight mass at his childhood Catholic church. This new man was dark-skinned but very dirty, black hair curled and pressed down on one side as if he'd just risen from sleep. Maybe he had. The homeless, especially on hot summer days, tended to crouch in the shadows and sleep when the world around them was at least a little bit safer.

"Came to the sidelines," the man said, raising his cup. His voice was torn from too many cigarettes or too much shouting. A new smell drifted from him with the words, slick, like shoe polish. Before putting the cup (which looked stained and quite empty) to his lips, he stuttered, "Inside the traffic circle cone," then pretended to drink.

This gentleman, Richard decided, was plainly nuts. Unless speaking a language so far removed from sense it sounded like *gobbledy-gook*.

Another of his father's amusing words.

Over the few remaining minutes of his life, Richard W. Phelan tried to understand why he said what he said next. *Never interact with the homeless* was a rule most New Yorkers followed as religiously as their crosswalk laws. He raised his own cup and tipped it slightly in the man's direction, said, "And may the force be with you, my friend."

If the expression on the stranger's face had been something akin to a smile previously, it was now gone. Not angry so much as utterly blank. Some of the lines which had carved themselves into odd shapes across his face smoothed out.

The intruder leaned forward. Richard did not feel threatened by him. Even with a sudden realization that in the man's left hand, partially obscured by the unraveling threads of his shirt sleeve (a flannel shirt too warm for the season but which likely covered track marks) was a blade. There didn't seem to be a handle, only the blade, fingertips worrying over holes towards the back where a handle had once been fastened.

Richard himself was not physically strong, nor fast, but this place, this triangular coffee shop sitting across the street from his sin - from his *hole*... his sin? What was he thinking? - was somehow neutral territory.

Holy ground, Highlander, a voice from an ancient film whispered back.

The man, still leaning over the table, cup in one hand and barely-concealed knife in the other, whispered, "The hole is the sin, the sin is the hole but not there," a spasm of the head, in reference to the street behind him, "but here," and the left arm shot out, blade pressing lightly against Richard's tie. In a moment, just a blink, it would press in and pop his heart like a balloon.

Still, he felt no fear, knowing without a reason that this crazy person would not press the blade any further.

Finally, the vagrant's words registered. Richard whispered, "Wait, what? What did you say?"

The girl with the dreadlocks behind the counter said in a loud, shrill voice that surprised him out of his confusion, "Faisal, put the toy away and stop scaring my customers. Manny's going to throw your butt out of here for good if he sees *that*."

Richard narrowed his eyes and looked back down at his guest. Faisal giggled and pressed a little harder. There was momentary pressure before the blade curled sideways. It was rubber. He raised his brows as if to say, *Did I scare you?* Richard only shook his head, but smirked for reasons he didn't completely understand, except perhaps at the reminder one should never underestimate an opponent.

His visitor leaned back. "We all die in sin under unicorn blankets." The fake blade was gone somewhere up that ragged sleeve. Faisal looked back to the waitress, eyes pleading. "I had to give him a note from the Big Guy." He pointed to Richard with the cup hand, one finger extended. "Hole man."

She glanced at Richard for a moment, then whispered to the other, "Yea, I know who he is. Now leave him alone." When no one moved, "Go on."

Faisal smiled and got up, but not before holding out his cup across the table. Richard saw that indeed it was empty. Still, the man waited.

"Go on," the young woman said again, though Richard sensed she was speaking to him now. "Pay the man for his message."

Was *everybody* nuts here?

Richard reached into his pants pocket and grabbed a handful of coins, dropped them into Faisal's cup. The man was suddenly out of his chair, scurrying to the door. The interior of the shop was brighter than the twilight beyond so Richard lost sight of him as soon as the door closed with the tinkling of its bells.

Hesitantly, he looked up at the counter. On closer inspection the woman was older than he'd thought. Late twenties, maybe thirty. She leaned on the counter, both elbows supporting her, and stared at him with a new, calm expression.

Richard held her unwavering gaze long enough to know she was not going to stop so he stood, as well, and lifted his own cup. "Should I pay for this?"

The woman shrugged. No name tag on her uniform. "Don't worry about it. You can pay by either filling in that hole out there, or building somthin' on it."

"I'm not a builder," he said, putting the coffee down onto the counter long enough to slip his arms into the suit jacket. "I invest. That property is an investment."

The woman nodded, glanced beyond him towards the dark street. "Well, I do hope you make lots of money on that investment. Just remember…" and she walked away, letting the statement linger. Richard smirked and finished adjusting his suit jacket. It smelled like sweaty garlic, he knew. In fact, he recognized his own repulsiveness more in this moment. That gave him pause. Why was he beating himself up at all?

She was back, hold out a fresh paper cup with a lid to him. "Here you go. It's hot but enjoy it soon. Our coffee has this thing about cooling off really fast." He glanced around. No one there but a silent Black man reading the paper, one hand gently stroking a long gray beard with his fingers, lost in what he read or simply pretending not to listen. Probably the latter.

Maybe trying not to choke on the foulness of the fat man standing at the counter.

Stop it.

"You're not as bad as you think you are, or like to pretend you are."

She said this while holding the cup further across the counter. No threat, not mocking. He finally reached out, took it, and felt shame. So much shame.

"Why are you giving me this?" He tried but failed to keep the pathetic wavering out of his voice.

The woman with the dreadlocks smiled warmly. His hand holding the new cup (cups, really, she'd doubled it up but the heat still found his fingertips) was shaking. He didn't know how to stop it. She reached out again, touched his shoulder. Richard flinched but didn't pull away. He couldn't. He didn't want to.

She was not making fun of him.

"Why," he said again.

She gave his shoulder a squeeze then released it, shrugged. "Don't know. You looked like you needed it." Her look hardened to a seriousness which smoothed out her cheeks and forehead. "You are not as bad as you seem to think you are. In fact, God thinks you're wonderful."

He opened his mouth, closed it. "What?" Was she hitting on him? No, no, it didn't feel like that.

She leaned both arms on the counter, hands splayed. Her shirt was stained with a hundred coffees and pies and rice and beans and whatever small dish people wanted that she had to carry to the few tables around him. There a spot of something white on her left arm, a bit of flour or sugar or maybe a scar. He looked into her eyes. Bloodshot. She'd probably been here all day. But those eyes looked at him with something he did not understand. They saw him... wrong.

She said, "We are all fearfully and wonderfully made. Like Dukie, behind you." The man with the paper whispered, "Amen, sister. Preach it."

"So's Faisal. So am I. And so are you." She straightened and reached for a dirty towel tucked into the front of the apron wrapped around her waist. She plucked it out and began wiping the counter, moving away from him. "Sometimes we just forget that, or never knew it to begin with. How could we, unless someone says?"

He watched her finish, wanting to leave. "I'm not any of that."

"Yes, you are. God says it, so it's true." She wasn't looking at him, but continued wiping the coffee machines. "Might as well accept it. True is true."

He slowly shook his head.

These people were off their rockers.

"OK," he said, wanting the last word in the conversation. She let him have it, and Richard left the shop, wanting desperately to say something else but having no idea what that would be. The bells tinkled above his head as he opened the door, in accompaniment to the girl's voice shouting, "And don't forget to fill in the-" and then the door was closed.

That was all she wanted. The hole to be filled in. His hole, his *sin* as the crazy bum had called it.

His sin. Maybe it was. Richard sipped the coffee which he hadn't thanked the girl for - the woman, whatever - and crossed the street. There weren't that many cars around. He crossed diagonally, technically jaywalking. To his right, above a row of stores glowing yellow in the early evening, five floors of apartments with blankets and laundry hanging from windows and the occasional balcony railing. On the left the J train rattled past with its metal screams of pain.

And here he was, a sweaty, uncaring tub of a man sipping

free coffee and looking into a plot of land he'd bought for a ridiculously low amount of money, a hole he'd blackmailed Mac Wrensen to dig for him. *Build something on it*, the girl had said. Actually, she said *somthin'*. *Build somethin' on it*. Or just fill it in.

He took another sip, then another step, until he was standing at the edge of the hole. Part of it collapsed under his shoe but he did not fall. He should put up a fence. The cost would eat into his eventual profits, however.

Yet another sin tossed like trash into the hole, that last thought. His head hurt. His head and his neck hurt. Richard reached back to rub the nape and a few drops of coffee found their way from his mouth onto his shoe. What was a cup doing ... what was a cup ... what...?

Something felt loose in his skull, and he needed to sit. No, he needed to go home. His head was already feeling better, only a dull throb circling inside his skull. He walked along the edge, trying to remember which direction was home. He should ask someone.

Richard looked up, turned, but no one was there. Everyone was inside, having dinner, or wiping counters that didn't need wiping.

The apartment building across from him dropped from sight. His head hurt so much.

Richard W. Phelan landed and rolled into the hole, stopped in an arm-twisted pile near the bottom. He opened one eye. The other was pressed against the damp earth beneath him. It smelled familiar down here, like oil, like the street. He could see the slanted wall of his sin rising towards the road. He wasn't all the way in. That was good. He could find his way out again.

He moaned from new pain flaring around him then the world, the neighborhood, his hole, the top corner of the coffee shop above him and the apartments across the street lit up. All of it so bright, in so much detail. He knew, in a detached way, what was happening and prayed suddenly that the girl had been right. That the meaning of his life wasn't simply to die in a grave of his own crea-

Then he was gone.

No one had seen him fall, nor noticed his body lying in the shadowed recess of the hole except the rats. The smell did rise up, but smells find their way through the city all the time. What was one more?

An Introduction to "The Roof"

Who are you, Lord, *that you should care for us?* This line is the one most-often quoted from this Psalm. Not knowing young Mateo was making a comeback, I saw only someone standing on a roof, staring at the moon and stars and wondering about this question. It didn't take long to realize who that *someone* was, and which roof he was standing on.

Like Behram in Chapter 2, we all have a relationship with the Creator in our hearts, but another we show to the outside world. Behram faced moments when he learned over time that these two realities must be reflections of each other, never contradict. Children are less prone to hiding their wonder and curiosity about God, though these tend to be hidden more often the older they get. My youngest son (as I write this, he is seven) asks me a lot of questions about God and Jesus in his burgeoning faith. Like so much in childhood it's fragile, and can be overpowered by fear and uncertainty.

What does it mean to be called by God? When does something like this start, and when does such a connection grow to the point that one's direction in life might be set with the answers to only a few simple questions? I did not know, writing the opening scene, where any of this was going. Only that I needed to stay out of the way and let this young man find his own way.

Psalm 8 - The Roof

O Lord, our Lord, your majestic name fills the earth!
  Your glory is higher than the heavens.
You have taught children and infants
  to tell of your strength,
silencing your enemies
  and all who oppose you.

When I look at the night sky and see the work of your
 fingers—
  the moon and the stars you set in place—
what are mere mortals that you should think about them,
  human beings that you should care for them?
Yet you made them only a little lower than God
  and crowned them with glory and honor.

Psalm 8:1-5 (NLT)

"*Son dos —*" he hesitated, only for a half a breath but once he changed the words she'd know what he was doing, "It's two floors up, Mama. No different than going downstairs." He pulled on his oversized coat, shoved the scratched binoculars into one pocket.

His mother looked at him with that sad, wet stare which pulled her beautiful face so low. Neftali squirmed in her arms, grabbing at her shirt and crying, demanding to be fed. His baby brother was already more like Papa than Mateo. That fact, too, pulled down his mother's beauty. "If anyone is there, you *do not* linger. Come right back down."

"I will, Mama." He began zipping the coat, knowing she

would not let him leave if he didn't.

"And test the door at the top of the stairs to make sure it won't lock on you. With our luck *Senor* Flores would have changed the locks since the last time."

Stuffing gloves in the other pocket, "He didn't."

"Check."

"Mama!"

"Check!"

"Yes, Mama."

He grabbed the door and heard his mother's quieter, but no less intense reply, "One more thing, Mateo." He wanted to pretend not to hear, but he'd already hesitated. She knew he'd heard.

When he turned back and looked her in the eye, she gestured towards his bulging coat pocket. The baby continued grabbing at her shirt with impatience. "Those *pristmaticos:* you owe Bruno Angelo nothing for them. *Un regalo es un regalo.*" She was always wary of any gifts given to her from the men in the neighborhood, especially since Papa left. More so, any given to *him.* Mateo understood, but sometimes wished he didn't.

"*Entiendo, Mama.*" That, spoken in Spanish, was a gift he hoped she recognized. "*Debemos de agredecer a Bruno Angelo. Pero no mas.*" He'd repeated her golden rule back, to prove he understood. *We owe people nothing but our thanks if they choose to help.* Never feel indebted to anyone, especially Bruno Angelo and his posse.

She considered the reply, then whispered, "*Te quiero mucho, mi hombrecito.*"

"Love you, too, Mama." Back to English, gifts given then taken back.

*   *   *

The final flight of stairs leading to the roof was wonky, its fourth and sixth step a little taller than the others. Everything felt slick, too, even on the driest day. Thankfully, the lighting was lousy so he couldn't see why. When Mateo opened the door to the roof, winter reached out and slapped him. The wind was fast, whip-like, but he was ready. The hood of the parka, lined with fur that smelled like cigarettes from its unknown previous owner, blocked the wind as long as he didn't face it directly. All the while Mateo leaned on a door trying to close itself behind him. Not yet, not until he checked.

It almost got away from him but he held it with one crooked leg. The outside handle turned easily, the door latch moving with it. *Senor* Flores was wonderfully predictable.

Mateo backed away and let the wind slam it shut. The sound was like the roof shouting, *Now I have you, young Mateo Antonio Velez.* He listened, turning very slowly (if he moved too quickly it would guarantee someone or some*thing* would be behind him). No one else up here. Who in their right mind *would* be? If anyone knew he came here they'd question his thinking. Mateo the Mental Case.

He wasn't *loco.* He wanted to see God.

And there He was, floating above the building. Not God, not really *Him.* But something He made a long time before Mateo or anyone in his family were born, before anyone in the whole *city* existed. Before everything. The moon was full tonight. According to Mrs. Jordan, a half or crescent moon was better for seeing shadows and details on its face, but he could see more of the Moon when it was full like this.

When the wind buffeted him again, Mateo moved closer to the center of the roof, towards the large, candy-cane vents. They rattled with the wind but served as decent shelter against it. Always, towards the center. The idea of wandering too close to the edge melted the bones in his legs. He could be blown over, crushed onto the sidewalk and left for someone to find in the morning, like the dead man last year in the hole across the street.

It made sense to stay away from the edge.

The gravel on the roof crunched under his boots.

The wind pushed and battered him. Mateo imagined, sometimes late at night and especially if he awoke after midnight, that the wind was really *El Diablo* trying to keep him from seeing God, from wondering why God even cared when He could make things like the Moon and all of those stars. Mrs. Jordan said stars were actually suns like the one that rose over them every day. Uncountable suns, heating uncountable planets.

Did God make all of those, too?

The vent beside him rattled and *thwocked* but that was fine. He wasn't trying to hear God right now. Just wanted to *see* Him. See the Moon, at least, which Mrs. Jordan said was a quarter the size of the Earth. That meant half of half. Mateo had asked his Madre about this and she showed him a dollar, then four quarters to replace the dollar. "*Todavia es un dolar, ninito.*" Then she took one coin and said in English, "One dollar is the Earth; one quarter is the moon."

Then it all made sense. The white ball floating in space above him was a really big quarter. This thought made him smile. He'd said this to his Madre and she looked so confused, wondering why her son's head was so thick, until he burst out laughing at his own joke. Even managed to make his mother smile with that one.

He watched through the binoculars, having to shift his head occasionally so the long blur caused by the crack in the right lens didn't obscure any details. The air was cold but he was warm out of the wind like this, bundled in the hood, parka and gloves. The bumps and shapes were mountains bigger than any down here. There were flat spots, too, where monster asteroids had plowed into the moon before Jesus was born.

"God," he said aloud, now that there wasn't anyone around

to hear him, "are you up there? Or somewhere you can hear me?"

El Diablo slammed his pitchfork against a vent. It sounded like a gust of wind but Mateo wasn't fooled anymore. "Do you really, really hear me?"

Mateo heard no words, but something happened in that moment. Something quiet, and warm. Maybe he was making it up.

Nevertheless, he accepted the answer. For now. If the devil didn't want him talking to God, then perhaps what he felt *was* real. He kept his eyes locked against the binocular eyepieces as the magnified moon slowly glided away to his right. He told the Creator of the universe about Bobby Ramirez and Jakob Minsk picking on him at recess, and who spelled 'Jacob' with a k anyway?

The warm feeling, the sense of being *listened to,* did not fade.

*   *   *

"I know it's almost Easter, Mateo, but that doesn't mean we should go to church. In fact, it's a reason we *shouldn't* go." Early April, Easter was coming in a couple of weeks and Mateo decided this was as good a time as any to start attending. He didn't understand it all, not yet. He'd been listening to that Voice, the one that was mostly knowing Someone with an uppercase S was listening. The Voice urged patience. For three months he'd talked, in whispers and occasional shouts on those increasingly rare moments when his mother allowed him back onto the roof. As the weather grew warmer, she allowed this less often. Better weather meant more chance some *loco maniaco* may be waiting for him. It was time to move things to a new level, anyway.

Time to visit God's house.

"Mama, you used to go to mass every week when you were

a kid. Abuela said so."

"Your grandmother said a lot of things to make me feel guilty, God rest her soul." She made the sign of the cross so quickly it seemed like a twitch. The irony of the action was not lost even on her eight-year-old son. "Besides it's always too crowded on the holidays. Neffy wouldn't sit still long enough, especially if we had to stand up the whole time." She mumbled something else in Spanish as she turned around to grab a shirt from the laundry. His Madre was always doing something, laundry, cooking, cleaning up food from Neffy's tray. She never rested.

He'd been waiting for her to use this excuse. The next part of his plan needed to be quick, yet casual. Walking to the window for no other reason than to make his next statement more like an afterthought. "This Sunday is Palm Sunday, according to Saint Erasmus's website. Easter's the weekend after that. On Palm Sunday, they give leaves or something like that at the beginning - "

"*Ramas de palmera*," she replied absently, making it sound like her mind was on other things, not listening. *But she is listening, Mateo. She just corrected you. She's listening. Keep going.*

Assuming this was the Voice speaking, he garnered the courage to push a little more. Logic would win the day. "Neffy can play with them, then."

"They can get sharp."

Enough.

Something came over him. A tired, exhausted moment of not wanting to dance this dance any longer. He was her son, a teenager in a few more years, asking to go to church. What was *wrong* with her? He stopped fiddling with the curtains and walked up to his mother. She was folding a pair of his socks. Mateo reached out, gently took the socks from her and put them back into the basket before taking both of her large, warm hands in his. She did not look at him. "Mama," he whispered, reaching out one hand and touching her cheek. "I'm asking to go to church. You need to say yes."

"*Estoy tratando lo mejor que puedo, Carino. Es que no confío en el.*"

"You don't need to trust anyone, not right away, and I'm not asking to have a sleepover there, or to be one of those kids that swing the chains with the smoke around."

"*Incienso. Monaguillos.*"

"OK. Right." *Altar servers,* whatever. His heart was beating fast. This was getting weird. He was the one trying to bring them into a place only grownups probably should be in the first place. He didn't understand it.

Trust me. I'm here.

Someday, he hoped he could find some proof that this Voice weaving through his head was more than his own imagination. It felt real, so he would trust it now.

"Mama. This Sunday, we'll go. Sit and listen. Be with God." For some reason his face turned red at the mention of God's name. *Such a baby.* "Like a family. Then we'll come home."

She shook her head, not a definite no, he didn't think. "*No sé.*"

"Mama," he said again. She needed to know he was getting mad. And there was no room for arguing. He would win. "We are going. I need to be there this Sunday. I don't understand why enough to explain it to you. But I need to. So, we're going." He straightened and took a step back, puffed out his chest like he remembered his Padre doing. "If you don't want to go next week or the week after, fine, whatever. But this Sunday," he hesitated just a moment, made sure her eyes were on him. His stomach hurt. "We're going."

One eyebrow raised. Some mental nudge pushed him to repeat, "*Nos vamos.*"

She actually smiled that soft, butter smile that slid up her cheeks like a secret joke. It wasn't a big smile. But it was real. Her hand touched Mateo's face.

"*Mi hombrecito se puesto grande*." She sighed, then nodded. "*Nos vamos.*"

* * *

The outside face of Saint Erasmus was like most other Brooklyn churches they passed on the way to the bodega or the train. Brick and white stone face, narrow stained-glass windows which somehow never got broken nor vandalized. Not that their neighborhood was very rough, not like the eastern sections of Bushwick or Brownsville. This morning it looked all the more like a local parish with the squat, Latino pastor (Father Osvaldo Garza, they would later learn) greeting people with an exuberance and smile that seemed to want to rip itself free of his face. He was genuinely happy to see the Velezes when they stepped up to him. As Mateo expected, his Madre greeted him coolly, yet did not pull away when Father Garza reached up and tussled Neffy's already messy black hair. The baby laughed and reached for the man's robes, green and cream-colored with a dark, frayed edge where he likely had worn it down trying to pull the sleeve up his forearms all the time. He ended up doing this a lot during the homily. The man's otherwise brown and curly hair and beard were peppered with gray. Older than his mother but not by much. Mateo could never guess how old an adult was. Not that it mattered.

The church's interior was narrow but very long, with rows of benches Madre later explained were called 'pews,' which made him laugh. They formed a double pattern of rigid attention on either side of a middle aisle. Each row sat five or six comfortably, though he guessed if need be, they could squeeze in a couple more attendees next week. At the far end, raised a step higher than the rest of the church, the spot where the priest would sit and stand and speak, adorned simply with an altar and a statue of either Jesus or Joseph or maybe Saint Erasmus, whoever that was.

The large room exploded in light that tore through the high windows, the very tops of which curved into simple stained-glass images of a cup, Communion, an olive branch, things like that. Translucent skylights ran the length of the ceiling. This morning everything shone in sunlight and all of it lifting his chest high as they sang songs he'd never heard before, the words old and printed in heavy books stuffed into miniature shelves on the back of every seat. All of it, he knew, meant nothing compared to one factor which Mateo hoped might endear all of this to his mother.

The entire mass, from Father Garza's greeting at the entrance to the smiling words of a pretty, dark-skinned nun standing just inside the door (who handed them each long green palm leaves) to the words of the homily itself, was spoken in Spanish. More to the point, Puerto Rican Spanish.

That, he saw, made an impression. Nothing wide-eyed and obvious in his mother's reaction. Mateo saw it in the way she nodded slightly, acknowledging their words, even a couple of mumbled recitations of prayers throughout mass. She'd gone to church as a child every week and now she did not. Something had happened. Another good sign happened when Father Garza asked them all to go in peace but first, please, join them downstairs for a few minutes for coffee and refreshments. When it was their turn in the narrow procession, absently waving fronds and moving towards the double doors and daylight, she turned right with a subset of other parishioners towards the stairs leading to the basement hall, doing so without a word. He didn't dare hope, only followed and offered to hold Neffy. She pretended she hadn't heard.

They'd milled about the long hall downstairs, Mama talking to whoever introduced themselves, sometimes in Spanish, other times English, always holding his brother who seemed to relish all the attention. Mateo recognized a couple of people who lived in their building. Rarely did his mother look at him, lost in her own exploration. This moment, seeing the quietness (was it a form of peace? he wondered much later) in his mother, was something he remembered much later as one of many which directed Mateo eventually into the priesthood, and wove a thread of doubt and concern throughout the rest of this life.

"*Dios de bendiga, hijo*," Father Garza said, tapping Mateo on the shoulder. The graying man's smile was as wide as when they'd arrived, though he noticed during their time downstairs his expression oscillated from joyous openness to more remote and knitted somberness as he moved among different conversations.

"*Bendicion*," he replied. The priest was wringing his hands, perhaps still uncomfortable with so many people preferring not to shake since the pandemic. Mateo added in English, "I liked your sermon."

Garza's expression brightened at that. In his own accented English, he said, "Thank you! I haven't seen you here before. Is this your sister?" He glanced quickly at Madre. She'd been listening, because midway through whatever she'd been saying to an older, bearded white guy she turned her head in their direction and said, "Oh, please, Padre," then finished her conversation with the other man. Something about Neffy's diaper habits.

Father Garza chuckled. To Mateo, he said, "What's your name, my young friend?"

"Mateo Antonio Velez," he said automatically. Then, simply, "Mateo." The priest nodded and repeated his first name. Perhaps because other people might have needed to talk to him, he continued, "*Que bueno concerte y a tu madre*, Mateo. I hope we get to talk again." He began to turn and the boy saw a series of events, the priest leaving for other conversations, his mother gracefully ending her own then leading them upstairs, outside, perhaps grabbing a bite to eat since they were out anyway, never speaking of the moment again. Never coming back. All of it for nothing.

"Padre," he said, having to take a couple steps towards him to catch up. He laid his fingertips on the man's mysterious flowing sleeve.

The priest looked back down, his smile less dramatic and wide, yet somehow more real. "Si, Mateo?"

In English again, a habit he fell into not to make his mother sad but to fit in more with so many who let their native language fall away. He lowered his voice so his mother would not hear, though somehow he knew she would. That was all right.

"Padre, do you hear God? Has he ever spoken to you? If he has, how do you know it's Him and not just your imagination? I hear Him all the time, though it's not really in words, more like a feeling, like I know…."

He let himself trail off. He'd been rambling, not making sense. The priest's smile had faded a little more.

"You hear God's voice, Mateo?"

He shrugged. "Like I said, not really *words*-words. But," his face was red. This was stupid, but the guy was a priest! If anyone would understand, it would be Padre Garza, wouldn't it? *Yes.*

Yes! The feeling of not being alone filled him again. He needed to use that sensation now, for strength. Before his sudden need to pee got worse.

"But, Father, Padre, yes, it's like He speaks to me, in thoughts. I can't explain it well, I'm sorry, but He does. I'm sure of it. I just don't…" he looked around as if the words he needed might be on one of the old slogan posters on the walls, "…I don't know for sure. I just do." Here he raised his arms to his sides, let them drop. The man would know what he meant, or would not. His face burned in embarrassment.

Garza looked away a moment, his hands having mysteriously disappeared into the folds of his robes again. There were others lingering about and Mateo sensed they wanted some time with him. Silently, he begged the man to say something, offer him a morsel of advice before these people stole him away.

After an eternity, the priest turned fully to face him, even knelt on one knee so that he was more on Mateo's level. The boy cursed his shortness sometimes. "I *do* know what you mean, Mateo. And first off, I am overwhelmed at how strong you have proven your faith to be for coming here and asking me this."

Mateo's chest swelled in response. How could such men know just the right thing to say? He whispered, "Gracias."

"I," Father Garza looked down suddenly, at the floor, considering. "I have never, that I know of, heard what I *knew* to be the voice of God. Even something as -" he waved a hand in the air, juggling an unseen thought, "as ephemeral as a certainty of his presence like you describe. But I do know that God is real, and I'm certain of my calling. I always have been."

"But, you're a priest, Padre. God is more than just *God Up In Heaven* to you, right? Wouldn't he need to be so real for you to give up so much? He'd have to be like a real friend."

The smile came back, but it was not right. Something was sideways about it. Without looking directly at him the man replied, "Like a friend? Why Mateo, that's simply beautiful." He swallowed. Still not making eye contact, focusing instead on some point on the far wall, and probably not seeing *that,* either. "Like a friend. You see God, Jesus, as a friend? That is such a gift."

Such a gift? What did that mean? Didn't anyone who stood there and gave sermons - *homilies,* they were called homilies - didn't they need to know Jesus like Mateo knew his Madre or even Neffy? "You believe in God, don't you, Father?"

The question surprised Garza out of his reverie. "Oh, of course I do, Mateo. Like I said. More than anything. I simply live out my faith on, well, *la fe*." His old smile was back as he straightened.

"I'm sorry if I said the wrong thing, Father."

Garza stood up slowly, then leaned down and tapped Mateo on the top of his head with two fingers. "You most certainly did not, my young friend. I envy you. I truly do. You will do wonders for the kingdom of God with a heart like that. In whatever form that might take."

Then he was gone.

I envy you. The worlds would remain in the front of Mateo's mind, as he continued speaking to God, and from that day forward praying for Father Garza to learn how to hear God's voice. For everyone to learn.

"Are you ready to go, Mateo?"

"*Sí, Mama.*"

They left the church and into sunlight and silence, his Madre still carrying his brother as if the baby was an extension of her own body. He supposed he was. Lost in his thoughts, Mateo barely heard his mother ask, "Did you find what you were looking for?"

He let the question settle as he considered an answer. Finally, "I don't know if I was looking for anything, really. I just wanted to go to church to -" He couldn't finish.

She finished for him, "To see where your friend lived?"

A sob, short and surprising, found escape, but he masked it with a cough. He said nothing, only leaned into his mother's arm as they walked along the road, the trees around them bursting into life, blossoming into Spring.

An Introduction to "The Sign"

Although it felt as if Mateo's story was not completely told, I could not let any of that lead me astray. The primary rule — of sticking to the image that comes to mind from reading the Psalm – must take precedence. Here, it was a wooden sign hanging on the wall. On it a paraphrase of verse 20. I could see it hanging in a forgotten corner of a church hall. That was all. As well, the other verses depict God not only as a judge against the actions of the world, but avenger. Of what? The example the Psalm gives us is murder.

I should explain one aspect of the following story that sort of bothers me, but I left it in with this clarification: the sign itself is not magic. Nothing in the text (I double-checked) says this, but it could be inferred. Don't infer that. Did you ever read a verse of scripture at some moment, some day or time or phase of life, and it spoke to your circumstance directly? The Bible – whether printed or on your phone – is not magic. It is a vehicle through which we learn the nature of God; for His words to flow to us. After all, Jesus is called the Word in John's gospel. In the next story, the concept that the Holy Spirit placed *those* words on *that* sign, to be passed around the world to speak to *this* person or *that* in order to change the direction of their lives, well it was a challenge. How to show that?

The answer eventually sent the next story back in time to a remote Alaskan town I'd never heard of. How did I choose Sitka? I don't remember, except that it had to be on the opposite side of the world from Brooklyn, New York. Honestly, sometimes in writing this book I felt like Phillip being told by the Spirit, *Go here, now go here.* At least I didn't have to spend any time running beside chariots. Enough banter, let's checkout "The Sign" and the words burned onto wood, like a trap set by the Spirit waiting to be sprung.

Psalm 9 - The Sign

But the Lord reigns forever,
 executing judgment from his throne.
He will judge the world with justice
 and rule the nations with fairness.
The Lord is a shelter for the oppressed,
 a refuge in times of trouble.
Those who know your name trust in you,
 for you, O Lord, do not abandon those who search for you.

Sing praises to the Lord who reigns in Jerusalem.
 Tell the world about his unforgettable deeds.
For he who avenges murder cares for the helpless.
 He does not ignore the cries of those who suffer.

Make them tremble in fear, O Lord.
 Let the nations know they are merely human.

Psalm 9:7-12,20 (NIV)

Let Us Know We are Merely Human

Sheila Wan Murphy stared at the words on the sign, one hand clenched against her chest, lips moving in time with how she heard their cadence in her head. No one bothered her. When something caught the old woman's attention it was best to let her process, let her mind run its course.

Not everyone knew this, so Billy Nbutu wandered over like a blind man into a minefield and tapped Sheila with two fingers on the shoulder in greeting. He looked surprised at the sudden tensing of her thin muscles beneath the fabric. Normally, she would have unfurled her arm and slammed the intruder in the mouth. Well, at least threaten to. Everyone - everyone who *mattered* - knew not to bother her. In her opinion, most likely, the young priest would have deserved being struck, good intentions or not. The much older priest watching the encounter from across the room might argue that, but never to Sheila's face.

The old woman was too wrapped up in considering the sign hanging halfway between the hall's entrance and the rectangular serving window to let her attention be diverted this way. This place was a spot *between* things, where signs and notices were often overlooked.

Father Mateo said in warning, "Billy." The humor in his voice should have been obvious but, he hoped, also the urgency. "Here, a moment, please." Maybe it wasn't too late to save him. The seminary student smiled wider and began to walk his way. The woman's arm shot out, hand unclenched long enough to wrap around Billy's buttoned shirt. She pulled him close.

It would take Mateo a few moments to get himself out of the chair and across the room, so he began the process now.

"What does this mean," she whispered into the young priest's right ear. For his part, Billy looked alternately between the old woman and his pastor. Sheila's grip was tight, ruining his newly-ironed shirt. (He ironed his shirts every morning – an enviable habit in some ways, but mostly an unnecessary waste of time, in Mateo's opinion.)

Billy said, "What does what - "

"The sign, the sign, the words," she shook him until he looked up, noticing the wooden sign perhaps for the first time.

"I don't " -

"Don't tell me you don't know until you've read the words and asked for understanding."

Billy raised an eyebrow at that, then obediently read the words, looked back to her, and hesitated. His shoulders relaxed.

Father Mateo slowed his approach. Something was happening. Something always did around that strange piece of wood. Not often, being where he'd positioned it nineteen years ago in such an indifferent location. Waiting for moments such as this. The first had been a couple, long-married and searching for children of their own while the air between them cracked with self-recrimination. They'd come in for therapy, as they had twice every week to patch and repair walls which should never have been raised around themselves. The husband had stopped momentarily to read the sign. Then both read it, and something opened. He remembered, even now, how the relationship changed between them. Details of that time were blurry, even considering nineteen years was but a blink for someone his age. The words, though, or the Spirit behind them had opened some unknowable door to the couple, allowing them to see in a different light.

If something happened now, it would be the fourth time that he was aware of when the aforementioned Spirit took hold of people through these carved words.

Billy Nbutu straightened and read the sign a second time. Sensing a change in him, Sheila loosened her grip. Never quite let go, however. He was fully focused on the words, or considering what he'd read.

What do you see, Mateo wondered? Much as his knees ached standing there in the middle of the floor without his cane, he waited.

Billy said, "Sometimes God needs to remind us that we aren't, well, God."

Good boy.

The young priest glanced down at the woman, a softness falling across his dark face. "I mean, we all know that, but sometimes we have to accept what *knowing* really means. Sometimes," he licked his lips, a student hoping to recite the right answer to his teacher, "God needs to do something to shake us up, remind us who's in charge."

Mateo was grateful to be close enough to hear Sheila's reply, words spoken like a shaking, whispered mist. She still hadn't let go of the ruined shirt. "Like tearing away my baby the night before she was going to be married, and killing my Vin with grief so I would spend the rest of my days on this damned hole of a planet by myself?"

Not accusing. More words than the priest had ever heard her mutter in one breath. He began to step towards them but Billy casually, hardly making the gesture at all, raised his left arm with opened fingers towards Mateo. Clear enough. *Leave me to this, Father.* Billy never took his eyes from her face, never changed his soft voice.

"Yes. That's right."

Shelia nodded her head, her face turning inside itself a moment, building to a sob but as quickly smoothed out. Looking down at the young man's feet, she nodded one more time. "Help me to a table, Father, and eat with me. It's what we're supposed to do, yea?"

Billy smiled and glanced quickly at his pastor, then back to her. "Yes, ma'am."

Mateo Velez never stopped being amazed by the moments that came from this spot, this middle ground between one place and another. Had this happened thirty years earlier, he would have raced forward the moment Sheila grabbed Billy's shirt, assuming he knew what God's children needed more than He. Doing so might have pushed this broken woman deeper into her darkness, or at least never let Him finally bridge the chasm which had fallen between them.

Mateo stayed where he was and watched the couple walk in that awkward half-embrace across the room towards the dining section. Most of the thirteen round tables were populated with an assemblage of locals, two young couples he knew to be homeless at the moment, living in their cars while waiting for a spot in the shelter on Montin Ave; a few families struggling on a single income since Jaba'als Fabric closed in February; quite a few elderlies who simply enjoyed coming out for the company and a free meal. All of them, oblivious to the Holy Spirit Himself standing in the room ... or Herself; Mateo always imagined the Spirit to resemble his Madre when she'd been young and beautiful and always holding his idiot brother in one arm. Young and lithe, loving her boys to a depth beyond understanding. God had spoken tonight to Sheila Wan Murphy and that young man, through a sign Mateo obtained forty years ago when he'd been assigned as parish priest in a long-ago town in Alaska. Given to him by a woman who had just been arrested for murdering her boyfriend.

* * *

When he'd come to Sitka, Alaska at the transitional age of forty-two, the town felt like another planet. Father Mateo Antonio Velez had silently closed his heart and accepted that the rest of his days might be spent in a town with less people than most neighborhoods in New York. He was raised in a city where a person could be alone while surrounded by nine million other people. Here, ninety miles south of Juneau, the official population barely exceeded eight thousand - considered large for Alaska. By noon most knew what he'd had for breakfast. That's what Father Hendricks jokingly told him the day Mateo arrived as the new pastor of Saint Robert Bellarmine Church. It took less than two weeks for him to understand the retiring priest wasn't kidding. Like many of the other Christian congregations in Sitka, a surprising variety of denominations, "Saint Bobby's" was a close community which

Father Mateo had come quickly to love.

Now, nine years later, he walked past the gate on a sunny July day, pulling his Starter jacker tighter against himself. He should have worn the parka, but it was Summer and fifty-two Fahrenheit. He wanted to enjoy the pretend-warmth the season promised (but rarely delivered), especially downtown on the water.

Tomorrow he was leaving. Such was the life of a Catholic priest. They'd picked him up by the scruff less than a decade ago and dropped him here. A nowhere world full of life as diverse as Rose Rock's fishing swells in late Spring. Every person was hardened and weathered and waiting for the moment when there would be nothing for them to eat. Yet everyone worked, everyone ate, even in the lean times thanks to a plethora of government services. Of course the cruise ship tourists spilling into town when the weather was nice also helped. Perhaps because of the latter, Sitka was surprisingly modern. At least it surpassed *his* expectations.

There was love here, too, a thick-skinned kind hidden under layers of emotional blankets. It filled everything and was probably one of the reasons he'd counted thirteen churches in the area just last year. Stubborn people, after all, rarely agreed on the best *way* to love.

The wind slapped his face. Mateo closed his eyes and leaned against the railing overlooking the Lincoln Street moorings. Moments like this reminded him of his nights on the roof as a child, looking for God among the stars and Moon. Finding Him, too, or being found; he was never sure which. A little of both. The Spirit was alive in this place. He would miss it, felt tears from the wind running down his cheeks and pretended they were real.

Yesterday, after his last visit to the town's park, with its totems and old Tingit fort, he'd had dinner with Pastor Gareth from Assembly of God and his family. The man's church was one of the largest Protestant parishes. Mateo connected with them often, much to the Bishop's displeasure. He wondered if this was the reason for the transfer. Perhaps he'd become too tainted by the yeast of other denominations. Or maybe it was his own negative attitude towards such strong Marionist views in the diocese. Either way, the people were wonderful and he would miss them. He wouldn't miss the weather - not at all - but he would miss *them*.

One last appointment at four-thirty, ironically with a parishioner named Marion and her sister. Normally he tried to connect women with other women, but it was his last night and together the sisters were a joyful pair of gossipy energy. They cleaned the church two days a week and had him occasionally over to their house on Lake Street for tea and interrogation (they called it "conversation" but Mateo knew better).

People were throwing him a surprise party at five o'clock in Saint Bobby's hall, and the sisters were a diversion to allow time to set things up.

He turned away from the wind tearing off the water, wiped his face as dry as possible with a handkerchief kept for just that purpose, and walked across the street. Only two o'clock, not too many people for a Wednesday. The next ship wouldn't dock until tomorrow morning. Then, the place would be hopping.

Something tickled his leg. Phone vibrating. It might also be ringing but with so much wind he couldn't hear. He pulled the phone out, saw *Alaska State Police* as caller-ID.

"Hello, Father Mateo speaking. Could you wait one moment? I won't hear you until I get out of this wind." He ran the next six steps, phone pressed to the side of his face, and ducked into the sheltered RIDE bus kiosk, smiling at Tapeesa Kunuatok, one of his parishioners. She was a sweet but quiet woman in her thirties, apparently waiting for one of the small blue buses serving the region

He said into the phone, "That's better. I apologize. How can I help you?"

"Good afternoon, sir. This is Trooper Edward Gilbert and I'm acting in conjunction with the AFTF. We have a prisoner who has waived her rights to an attorney, provided we allow her to speak to her parish priest."

Mateo pressed his free hand against his other ear. Someone from his congregation had been arrested. It wouldn't be the first time. He had no idea what AFTF was. It didn't sound good. "OK, I understand. Sort of. But what do you mean she waved her rights? I'm not a lawyer."

"Yes, sir, we know that, but she has agreed to give us a full confession if allowed to confess to *you* first." There was an unmistakable tone of irritation. Mateo's priesthood was punctuated by quite a bit of anger directed at the Church, some of it justified.

"Very well. May I know who this person is?"

"Not over an unsecured line, sir."

Nothing was private these days, but he didn't push it. He began making mental notes on what he'd need from the rectory for a confession (some people were sticklers for ceremony, so he should bring the sash and a physical Bible), when something occurred to him. "One thing I should mention," he said, glancing at Tapeesa who was being very careful not to look like she was listening. "Anything spoken in the confessional is, by law, protected. I won't be able to tell you what she says."

"Understood. She is being detained at the DPS in Sawmill Creek. Do you know where that is, sir?"

No "Father", only "sir". Angry atheist or bitter lapsed Catholic, probably. Either way he would be walking into hostility, at least with this man.

"Yes, Officer, I do." He didn't want to move his phone to check the time, but there shouldn't be any need to call or cancel anything. Not yet. "I can be there in about twenty minutes."

"Understood."

The line disconnected. He remained with the phone still to his ear and closed his eyes. He prayed for the woman, whoever she was, asking for peace and calm until he got there. Then he prayed for Trooper Ed Gilbert, asking forgiveness for whatever pain he might have received.

*   *   *

Though a Catholic priest was not an uncommon sight in police stations, the looks that turned his way were odd at best. Not angry - thankfully this place wasn't full of shoulder-chipped ex-Christians - but confused. He was led by a glaring Trooper Gilbert through the main entryway and past a few desks, to a back hallway. People often asked for priests after being arrested, but he couldn't remember this ever being in lieu of their lawyer. Usually, one dealt with legal and financial issues first, their soul second.

It made him optimistic about the state of this mystery women. Names and faces passed through his mind, people in pews listening to his homilies, saying hello as they left church. A few settled to the top of likely law-breakers. No one he might consider a person of interest for the Alaskan Fugitive Task Force (he Googled the acronym as soon as he'd taken the phone from his ear).

The small interrogation room contained a table with two unoccupied chairs on one side, a third opposite. Here, an unfamiliar women sat with wrists shackled together on the table. The cuffs were chained through a loop screwed into the top of the table. No sign of a two-way mirror here. There *was* a video camera propped on a tripod in the corner beside him, microphone mounted on the table in front of the woman.

His heart was beating faster, now. This was starting to feel serious.

This person was definitely a stranger. Middle aged, somewhere in her late fifties with wild tufts of ginger hair. Her scalp had intermittent bare spots. She might be older, but he guessed her appearance was from a particular lifestyle aging her beyond her years. The sleeves of her black sweatshirt rode up to her elbows, left arm in a cast, the handcuff on that wrist looped around the cast itself. A peeling Iron Maiden logo across the front of the shirt (so many folks up here were musical prisoners of the eighties).

"Father," she said, her voice and teeth eroded from decades of chain smoking. "Thank you for coming."

He glanced at the camera, then to the large man beside him. Gilbert shrugged. "I'll turn the camera off only if it becomes an official confession."

The woman shook her head. The chains jingled quietly through the table's loop as she fidgeted in her seat. "Oh no, Father. I'm not Catholic."

He wanted to look again at the trooper but had a strong suspicion the other man had no idea what any of this meant, either. Instead, Mateo stepped forward, pulled out one of the chairs and sat. "I'm sorry, I've been trying to remember your name but it's escaping me."

The woman smiled. It was tired, but genuine. No obvious deception in her eyes. Of course, she was chained to a table in the center of an Alaskan State Trooper barracks. Not a glowing recommendation for her honesty.

She said, "My name is Alice Cumberson."

Behind him, Gilbert muttered, "No, it's not."

She only shrugged. "For this conversation, officer Gil-bare," she used the French pronunciation of his name, "it is."

Gilbert sighed, muttered a curse but said nothing else. Sounds from the hallway implied he hadn't closed the door to the room.

"I'm sorry," Mateo said again to the prisoner. "Do we know each other?"

"No."

"You asked for this guy by name, you loon."

"Officer, please," Mateo said, raising one hand slightly, hoping he wasn't crossing some line. "Alice, what can I do for you?"

She shifted a little more, sending the cuff and chain rattling again, and looked down at her lap. "Well, before I tell these fine gentlemen what they're itching for me to say - and I will, Father, I made a promise and I keep my promises," Gilbert snorted at this but said nothing, "I was told to give you something."

"Me?"

"Yes. And to say I'm sorry. I killed him. Indirectly but yea, I killed him. And I'm really sorry that I did. I mean, hell looks pretty damn scary."

Mateo kept his eyes on her, the sensation of weight pressing into his gut had grown since he stepped into this room. Everything was a little left of *strange* already. Ironically this confession helped to lessen it enough for him to keep his composure.

"How do you know who I am?"

"You're the parish priest of Saint Robert Bellarmine downtown, right?"

He nodded.

Another rattle of the chain. "So, well, I owed Telly that much."

Telly. Telly. The name rang a bell, slight as it was, but not with anyone he'd ever interacted with at the church. He waited, hoping for clarification. She said, "Maybe you could still give him last rites or something."

"I'm sorry, Telly who?"

She seemed taken aback, then leaned forward and spoke

his name slowly as if he was hearing-impaired. "Telemachos Galanos."

That triggered a memory, a name and face from his first year in the diocese, the day that Father Hendricks left for his retirement back east. A wiry, twitchy man had come to the rectory door and Michael introduced him. The man had offered a fist-bump and his full name.

Telemachos Galanos, but everyone calls me Telly because they can never remember my real name. Greek as they come. It was a short conversation. Mateo had forgotten the name as soon as it was uttered, asked the older priest later so he would remember. But there had been no subsequent need. He'd never come back.

In this moment, he also understood his own betrayal of that man. Hendricks had made a passing comment after Telemachos left, and he only recalled it now in this frozen moment. *Keep an eye on this one as you go along, Mateo. Check on him now and then.*

Alice Cumberson tilted her head, perhaps wondering about the priest's silence. Realizing he must look as guilty as she did *not*, he cleared his throat. "I remember him, now."

She smiled her yellowed smile. "Good, good. He wasn't much of anything but he did make an impression."

"I didn't know him well."

She shook her head. "No, he stopped attending after you replaced the old guy, and you never bothered to check up on him."

No, he hadn't. Too self-absorbed at the atrocity of his assignment to what he'd initially considered a wasteland. Where God had sent him. Too indignant and proud to be focused on people like Telemachos Galanos.

Her smile shifted. He didn't think she was mocking him, nor accusing. He could do that enough on his own.

"What," Mateo began, then only closed his eyes and tried to put the man from his mind for the moment. "Is that why you wanted to talk to me? To give his body the last rites?"

Her smile was gone. She looked right, then left, as if afraid something might come through the walls. "Not quite. He told me to give you something."

"Telly?"

She shook her head. "The angel. Officer bonehead here has it on his desk, I think. He needs to give it to you."

Beside him Gilbert only rolled his eyes. Looking back Mateo asked, "Give me what?"

"A sign. It's mine, and I like to bring it with me, wherever I hang my hat," she added this last part in a tired, singsong voice, without any humor. Her eyes still scoured the walls for something. Drug withdrawals, maybe? She added, "I'm supposed to give it to you."

Slight snicker, or just an expulsion of breath from the trooper. Mateo breathed in, held it without speaking then let it out. It helped.

"What kind of sign?"

She didn't reply. Only sat back and gestured with her jingling arms to Gilbert and said, "He knows." Then, louder, "he promised! You need to have it in-hand and out the door before I sing."

"Sing?"

Alice smiled. "I like old gangster movies." She slumped fully in her chair, looking up at the trooper, or perhaps beyond him.

It felt like the end of the conversation.

Mateo mumbled his thanks, for what he wasn't sure, and rose from his seat. He was almost out the door when Alice said, "Father?"

He looked back in silence.

"Telly. And the others. I'm sorry for what I did. I guess maybe that could be my confession."

He tried to smile but his chest was heavy with the reminder

of his failure towards that forgotten man. "I guess it could be."

Then he was down the hall following Gilbert, without once giving her a blessing of absolution, too wrapped up in keeping his thoughts empty.

Regardless, ten minutes later he was waiting in the lobby, thinking of the bent old man who was proud of being Greek, who never came back to the church, then faded from everyone's memory. Ed Gilbert emerged from a back room holding an arm-length wooden sign.

"We checked this as much as possible. As far as we can tell there's nothing hidden inside it." He handed it over. It was heavy. Real wood. Engraved, using one of those burning pens to form the words, *Let Us Know We are Merely Human*. Gilbert added, "Any idea what it means?"

Mateo stared for a while. It might have come from a Psalm but he would need to search for the words to be sure. "Not at the moment, but it somehow seems fitting."

"I suppose." Gilbert was also looking at it. "Sometimes people seem more animal than human. That that crazy b— " he caught himself. "That woman. What she did to that guy."

"What *did* she do?"

He shrugged, never taking his gaze from the sign. Mateo made it a point to keep it facing him. "Let him die, slowly, pretending to be looking after him." He shook his head slowly. "Just another grifter, siphoning old men from their disability checks, marrying them, or acting like their girlfriend, whatever. Kept most of the victim's insulin, giving him just enough to survive on, barely, for years. Sold the rest on the market."

After a pause Mateo asked, "That's how he died, then?"

"I suppose. Pending autopsy, but the task force has been closing in on 'Alice' for years. She's done this since she was a teenager. Not sure how it took almost half a century to catch up to her."

Father Mateo looked away and thought of the man he'd

met nine years earlier then never met again. Never tried to meet again. *Keep an eye on this one….* He died alone. Mateo assumed he would be battling a guilt he never knew he had for some time to come.

It wasn't his fault, of course.

He should have known.

How could he?

All that.

It took them fifty years to catch up with Alice because her victims had already been forgotten by everyone.

"Father?"

He looked up, noted the use of the title but said nothing. He never actually liked that term, anyway, and he suspected its use had some deeper meaning with this man. Right now, though, he didn't have the emotional energy to read into it any further.

"Thank you, Ed. Can I call you Ed?"

The trooper smiled, more a slight twitch at the edge of his mouth but it was something. "That's my name."

He nodded, and said, "Hold this a moment?" He shrugged deeper into the parka, zipped it up, hat, gloves, then accepted back the sign. "Call me if you need me. For anything."

"I will, but I hear you're being transferred."

He pressed his lips together and grunted. "That's right. I am. Such is my calling. And, I suppose, life in a small town means even the Staties know."

Gilbert laughed. "I guess. I appreciate you coming out, and enjoy…." He stopped.

This time Mateo's laughter was louder, and genuine. "I will, Ed. I love parties."

An Introduction to "The Forgotten Man"

First off, let me apologize to my wife. She gets so annoyed with some of the names I give my characters. I admit to pulling some out of thin air (in my *Vast Array* series one of the main characters, Gendrick, is a perfect example). Now, here. I researched old (and obscure) Greek names before choosing Telemachos. But he was so proud of being Greek, he needed an equally proud name.

I thought I was done with Telly and Alice. I thought "The Sign" was mostly Alice's story. Telly was just an eccentric character she exploited and, through premeditated neglect, murdered. Until I read Psalm 10, and felt the Lord clearly tell me (nothing audible, but clearly nevertheless), *Alice was able to do what she did because Telemachos had been forgotten by the people around him. Don't let him be forgotten. Make him real again. Save him.*

Now, since Alice was arrested for murder, there was no physical saving of the old man. That wasn't what needed to happen. *We* needed to remember. How many people in our own neighborhoods or churches have we forgotten about – never called to check on, never offered to clean their yard or shovel their sidewalks in winter; never brought a meal or simply spent time with? I can name a few in my own church, my own neighborhood, whom I've neglected through sheer procrastination or, yes, apathy. Now imagine someone like Telly brought into your life. They might be eccentric, say weird things, maybe they smell or fill in whatever blank might be the cause of us turning away from them.

This is one of the hardest parts of following Jesus. Turning our whole selves towards the forgotten of our world and remembering that they are as fearfully and wonderfully made as everyone else.

Come with me for a little while; let's sit with Telly in his final hours and make sure he is remembered with love.

Psalm 10 - The Forgotten Man

Like lions crouched in hiding,
  they wait to pounce on the helpless.
Like hunters they capture the helpless
  and drag them away in nets.

Lord, you know the hopes of the helpless.
  Surely you will hear their cries and comfort them.
You will bring justice to the orphans and the oppressed,
  so mere people can no longer terrify them.

Psalm 10:9,17-18 (NLT)

Sitka was a borough of eight thousand people located southwest of Juneau, Alaska. Its downtown, harbor and scattered islands was a modern affair, including a McDonald's amid locally-owned coffee shops and restaurants. Spiritually and emotionally, it was locked in time, running from echoes of its orthodox Russian heritage.

To the East, beyond this tiny metropolis the hills rose, homes became scarcer until there were only mountains, forests and glaciers hovering over the town. Sitka was on the edge of what was, in truth, an island, the westernmost of an archipelago. Beyond it, to the west, the Gulf of Alaska stretched towards the ocean. Occasional cruise ships docked and disgorged tourists whose tired eyes stared, wonderstruck, at the region's beauty. They milled about the stores, acting as the commercial lifeblood which kept the region alive with money and interest. The relationship between fishing, tourism and retail kept Sitka spinning for the eight thousand who called it home. Most ignored these *cheechakos* as they moved through town, acknowledging with reluctance this symbiotic relationship but having no desire for more than that.

Tucked at the northeastern edge of town, the small red house squatted without pretense among its neighbors at the corner of Pherson and Bastille Roads. These were quiet neighborhoods, though sometimes Wilson and his wife Racket - her name was Lucille but Telemachos called her Racket - had parties in their house at the end of the road. These dragged on until nearly eleven some Fridays, until folks complained about needing to get little ones to sleep - a hard thing to do with metal guitars and drums rattling everyone's window panes.

Alice never minded the noise, when she was over. More than once she'd wander down the street, ostensibly to complain but then stayed for hours. Telly's girlfriend enjoyed hanging out with that type of people. He suspected other things as well but what could he do? Why should she stay stuck in the little red house with a sick old man all the time? She was young - younger than he was, at least - and healthy. She had needs.

Telemachos Galanos took in a shallow breath and wondered if it might be better to drop onto the floor with his blanket and pillow. It might be colder there, however - whatever heat the radiator's occasional ticks implied traveled upward, right? The couch cushions had something bad in them. Mold, maybe. Alice rarely visited these days, said the whole place stank. He'd seen her cleaning sometimes. But *this* smell was more like a presence. Definitely mold. Her increasing absences meant something more, too. Telly didn't want to think about what, not at first. After all, she'd been taking decent care of him for so long; wouldn't let anything go too far.

He'd watched a TV special a couple of years back, when

the television worked, about someone living in a place not much bigger than this house. The woman had been dragged outside because too much mold had been growing in the walls and over the furniture. They told the screaming women she'd die if she kept breathing it in.

Telemachos raised himself up, looked again. An unmistakable white haze over the couch and chair legs. Some of it was black, too. Black seemed worse.

He could hardly breath, couldn't remember what he was supposed to do about it. Go to the floor, that was an earlier thought. Or was that only for fires?

Alice would be here soon.

It was time for his shot. She'd come by at some point with his dose, said she kept it all in the top drawer but when he'd gone to the dresser himself the other morning (*Yesterday? Last week?* What was wrong with his brain?) there was only the one needle and two doses (and one of those was only half-full).

She was taking his medicine.

No, that didn't make sense. *She* wasn't diabetic. Alice was healthy, even vibrant. That's what drew him to her in the first place.

Full of life.

She didn't need insulin, was probably getting more at the CVS right now. Telly had filled out the forms to make it legal for her to get his medicine, even go to the bank and make deposits or withdrawals with his APA checks. They weren't much, hardly enough to support the two of them let alone two *homes* since she lived closer to the center of town now, over on Indian River. They were married but... not *really*. Worked out better for the benefits if they didn't make it legal. She said that, and he agreed.

The first time they'd met, it was Alice who'd struck up a conversation with him at Kanaag's. Telly had been coming downtown twice a day, in keeping with Smitty's old walking schedule. For fourteen years he'd done the trek with that wild-haired mutt. First in the mornings, to the waterfront and back, both of them pulling the salt air into their lungs and, if he had the money, stopping at Sue's Breakfast and Lunch just south of creepy Saint Michael's Cathedral, the one that looked like someone dropped an old rusty church on top of a customs house. He preferred Saint Bobby's simplicity, and Father Hendricks' bad jokes. Their second trip of the day was usually just before suppertime, either a quick route through the neighborhood or, if he needed something, or had to grab his meds or a new carton of Camels, they'd make the trek to Kanaag's grocery. A lot of folks from church took the bus to Juneau once a week to shop at Foodland, but that was a waste. Even with a rolling hand cart you could only carry so much onto a bus.

When Smitty the dog finally bit the dust, Telly still made both trips, still followed the same paths every day, pulling fresh salty air into his lungs alone. What else was he going to do, weed the garden? The small plot out back was doing fine on its own without him pulling and planting and making things worse.

The rug pressed against his face.

When did he come down here? It smelled better, though. He'd been thinking about Alice, maybe dreaming. The memory of her was fuzzy like the couch's upholstery. *Kanaag's.* Yes, that's where he'd seen her. She was so happy, so much energy for a woman in her mid-fifties. He learned that later. A woman never told the first time, said she. On that day he was seventy-one. Four years ago. It all started so good, too; they had plans.

Something ticked along the floor by the hallway leading to the bedroom. Smitty needed to go out. He moved his face along the carpet. Yes, it definitely smelled better here. Like cigarette smoke. He needed a smoke, now.

And Alice. He was thinking about Alice. But he needed to

get up, get his medication. Telly took in a breath, crouched, and managed to get onto his knees and elbows.

That day, she'd asked him some question or other about the store, said she was new to town. He'd answered and listened and smiled when she made a bad joke. On that day his heart beat to a rhythm he'd long forgotten. On a whim the two asked Melissa working the register if he could leave his groceries by the window so they could go for a walk and, with a sideways eye to the stranger, she'd agreed. Good kid, Melissa. Someone said she had a baby last year. Must have been Alice who told him. He didn't see anyone these days.

Wasn't Melissa wondering where he was right now? Wonder why he didn't come downtown anymore for smokes and Pop Tarts?

No one came.

Alice took care of things.

He walked on his elbows and knees towards the hallway. Smitty wouldn't be there. Smitty was dead. But his meds were there. He paused at the end of the living room. Something was wrong. Glancing up, trying to decide if the light switch was something he could realistically reach, or if he really needed it with all the passive daylight coming in from the open bedroom door.

That was when he noticed the sign. Rather, the empty rectangle of wall where Alice had hung it years before when she and he became something special. Had it fallen? Telly blinked, slowly. Shut his eyes, *wait, open them, look again*. He was just being a confused old man.

No, he wasn't. Like the sun coming through clouds, or an explosion, his mind cleared enough to truly understand what was happening. It hurt, this sudden lucidity that squeezed his heart. Alice hadn't come by and given him his medicine for four days. *Four days*. When was last time she'd given him a shot even *two* days in a row?

The worst part: she'd taken the sign down. Her sign. That meant she was gone.

He stared into a spot on the old wooden floor before him, not wanting to look up again, then crawled into the hallway. The floorboards moved like a molasses river. Didn't smell as bad in here. Everything tilted like a cardboard box leaning to one side. He used to play in boxes with his foster brother Cam. He missed Cam, thought of him now, held onto the memory while everything else fell away.

*　　*　　*

The ride to Juneau was uneventful. This was the scary part, the escape. Breaking free of whatever town she'd ingratiated herself into without being noticed. An *Uber* pickup at Geodetic Way, by the cemetery. She'd come up with a reason for this location if the driver was someone she knew. He wasn't, and the ride into the city was quiet. Twenty minutes staring at her phone pretending to be immersed in whatever she was reading, occasionally entering a series of random characters in her Notes app to make it seem like a text conversation. It was all for naught. The driver couldn't have been less interested. He dropped her off in front of an ancient IGA supermarket and here, since someone could trace her to this point, was where her trail would become cold.

Alice left in an Uber to Juneau, got to the IGA. That makes sense. She'd been going there pretty regular these past few weeks after having that strange argument with the manager at Kanaag's. An argument she'd started under a false pretense about not having enough variety, loud enough for others to remember it later. *After that, she simply disappeared.*

Eventually the feds who had, she assumed, been on her trail for years, would grind their teeth in irritation and realize she'd slipped through their net again. But just barely. She'd noticed the woman walking along Lincoln last month, casual but too well-dressed for someone who'd just stumbled off an Alaskan Cruise mainstreamer. Definitely too fancy for a local. The woman was a stranger, and too quietly observant. The kicker, of course, was her phone. Appearing to take the usual flurry of tourist snaps, it was too often aimed towards people rather than the usual trappings of the cathedral or the boats wobbling about in the harbor.

Facial recognition had come into play and was going to make Alice's way of life a lot more difficult. She kept an eye out for overly-observant strangers, wore sunglasses more often and accelerated the old man's isolation. If he was with her, that would be a sure sign for Miss Well-Dressed, if she was with the government and looking for someone Alice's age walking around with a bent stick man.

From the IGA parking lot, the walk to Cope Park took less than fifteen minutes. Then a call on a newly-purchased trash phone to the Checkered Cab company, one of the few old-style cabbies left and one which accepted cash. After a fifteen-minute ride to Juneau International Airport, she asked the dark, brooding driver to drop her off at the short-term parking across the street from the terminal. She wasn't sure why, just an impulse as they drove past the main entrance. In the end, it was how she was finally caught. Outside the cab, she pretended to fumble in her bag for keys. It was cold, but around here *this* cold was considered summer. Next stop: Arizona, via a connecting flight at San Francisco International. Madison Collins, a name that belonged to someone decades younger but that was the point, right? - would eventually land in Phoenix to start a new, warmer life. Plenty of old people down there. She shrugged the single carry-on higher over one shoulder as the cab drove away. The bag was heavy. Besides her sign and laptop, two changes of clothes, everything else was left behind in Sitka. All of it had belonged to Alice, and Alice was officially dead.

As she stepped into the crosswalk towards the terminal, the cab now out of sight, an image of Telly flashed across her mind. She didn't let it linger. Last time she was at his house he'd looked up at her from that disgusting couch, asking when his next shot was supposed to happen. Brain beginning to slip. She'd looked away, thought of the sign, the heavy thing her father had given her on that dark, embarrassing morning with a shrug and guilty glance, the morning before he left and never came home. The stupid *We're Only Human* sign, as if that gave him the excuse to do what he did, then leave her alone with -

The driver never beeped, never even saw the woman crossing the road. Alice hadn't been looking either, too focused on her father's distant face. The hood of the car echoed her impact, one arm, thumb hooked under the strap of her bag, slammed into the windshield, spiderwebbing the glass. The look of the teenage girl driving as she looked up from her phone was almost comical, until Alice's head continued forward into the windshield.

*   *   *

She hovered over an abyss, above swirling hurricanes viewed from space, except the storm raging below her made *so much* noise, more fury and rage than she'd ever experienced in her broken life. It was like being caught under a screaming train but multiplied a thousand times. Roaring wind howled and reached and tried to pull her down into its gravity.

Mixed with the sound were screams, a few individual voices she could make out through the torrent. More came through, until there was no way to tell one from another. Millions and millions shouting and wailing and Kinsey - for that was her real name, one she hadn't said aloud in forty-three years - was suspended over all of them, feeling the front of her t-shirt pressed tight against her breasts and belly, making it hard to breath. What air she managed to take in was whisked away by the chaos below. Below, then around her for she was suddenly dropping, lowered by whatever held its grip to the back of her shirt into the maelstrom below.

She cried without a voice to the unseen hand, begging it not to let go. Her body dropped closer to the screaming death, then closer still. Her shirt was ripping. Swarms of arms and legs broke through the clouds only to be chewed up again. No faces, though sometimes the back of a head or shredded back. Tiny, insignificant shapes tossed and rent by the storm. She screamed but her voice was no match for the roaring eternal machine around her. Kinsey realized finally she was staring down into eternal death. *She* was dead and there, below, waited her reward.

A voice, angry, almost growling, whispered over the wind into her ear. Its voice - *his, hers,* she couldn't tell - was clear and pointed. "Give your father's sign to the priest of Saint Bobby's."

She cried, "What? Who?"

The hand holding her over eternal damnation shook violently. It was time to let her go. Throw her away.

"Please no! Please don't!" Her protests were nothing against the hell she was falling into.

In her ear again, pounding dents in her brain, "Find a way, and tell them everything you did. You have sinned against the Lord and His children and you - will - atone!" She was shaken again and finally set loose, falling and tumbling and down into the storm of arms and legs and pain and hopelessness. She rolled and glimpsed the owner of the voice but it was too much to accept so Kinsey shut her eyes and tried to forget but could still see every detail of the damnation around her, all of it reaching inside and ripping her apart, her scream joining the countless leagues of souls who thought they had one more chance.

She woke up with a shout, but only until the pain in her head nearly threw her out of consciousness again.

"Ooouuch," she finally moaned, falling back against a pillow. An hour later, after drifting in and out of dreamless sleep, Alice again opened her eyes. Hospital room, arm in a cast, something wrapped around her head. She stared at a single spot across the room, a bulletin board, then down a little - her carry-on bag leaned against the wall by the door, zipped closed but bulging.

Sounds of beeping.

Voices.

A woman's voice beside her bed said, "Ah, you're awake, good. I've got a few questions for you if you're feeling up to it." Alice didn't need to look in that direction to know the woman would be well-dressed, a little *too much* so. Her arm hurt. She only stared at the bag, so close to escape, and knew there never would have been any, not in the end. In her bag, the bulge, most likely the sign. *Oh, Lord in heaven*, she hoped it was still in there.

*   *   *

Eyes opened again.

It was cold. The heat was out. The oil people let the tank go dry again. He moved his head, enough to see into the bedroom.

What was he doing on the floor? Shaking so badly he curled into himself. *Help me, God, please. Jesus are you there?* He hadn't prayed in so long yet there Jesus was, right there in the bedroom wall beside the dresser where his needle and bottle of insulin were waiting. Where they *should* have been waiting. Something about Alice. Where was she? Not here, but Jesus was. The silver metal Savior hung like a sack of potatoes on the old cross Telemachos' mother gave him for his Confirmation a hundred years ago. Father Hendricks - maybe he could call the oil people, get the heat turned back on. Wasn't it summer? It shouldn't be this cold, not in summer. Not *this* cold.

Why didn't the old priest, or Donna Ipsie who always answered the church phone ... why didn't they come and help?

He pulled himself along the floor, tried to at least, managed to draw closer to the bedroom, the dresser, the top drawer, the metal Jesus dying forever on the cross. Telemachos was shaking. *Help me Jesus, I'm sorry I stopped going to church. I didn't want to meet new people. No more new people.* Alice had been new. Alice was going to pour sunshine into his world. His shaking turned into twisting. He eventually lost sight of Jesus on the wall.

*   *   *

Melissa Chin wiped food off the floor and tried to keep the phone pressed between her shoulder and ear. Ryan wailed his indignant rage because she hadn't given him the next spoonful of carrots and, really, he was supposed to be holding the spoon himself now, wasn't he?

"Cuppy, please," she said into the phone, "we don't need overtime that much. I need he-" but Cuppy began talking, sharing one of his usual pride-filled explanations about how it was so hard to get these shifts and they should be grateful to have a blah blah blah blah.

The baby reached out with both hands for the small spoon and she scooped a little extra from the jar in her other hand. He sucked it greedily. "Never mind," she said, dropping the spoon into the jar and taking hold of the phone. "Just make sure you stop at the store for the stuff on the list." Before he could say *What list* because he absolutely *was* going to say that even though she *saw* him snap a picture of it on his way out this morning, Melissa thumbed the *hangup* icon and tossed the phone onto the table. Another scoop. Ryan was calming down.

She suddenly thought of Telly. He'd been coming to mind more recently, usually when Melissa thought about going back to work at the store. She'd quit when Ryan was born, no way they could afford daycare though maybe if she worked enough hours they might. Cuppy didn't understand spending any money she'd make for someone else to watch the baby. Didn't understand she needed a break. Be around grown-ups sometimes.

Another scoop.

Telly had stopped coming by about a year or so after she'd let him and that woman leave their groceries on the window sill. Benny had scolded her for that, said not to let people leave paid groceries anywhere but their car. She guessed folks used to do that all the time, not wanting to carry bags around as they sight-seed, sight-saw, whatever.

After he stopped coming in, Melissa only saw the woman. Never got her name but old as she was, still seemed a little young for the guy. Not that Melissa thought much about Telly before then. In fact, he usually smelled bad and always left his mangy dog tied outside when he came in, never picked up its poop.

Still, lately she couldn't help wonder if he was all right. Something had felt wrong since that woman showed up.

Ryan threw up across the front of his shirt and Melissa did not think again about the odd little man until she read the story in the paper a few days later.

*　　*　　*

Father Michael Hendricks had a hard time enjoying retirement, dirt poor as he was. Granted, there had never been much in the way of income when he'd been a parish priest, but the congregation had supported him in those years (he'd be hard-pressed to call what they gave "tithing"). Of course, he got his share of the ever-decreasing diocesan pension plan, seven hundred dollars into his account each month. Enough for gas and take-out food now and then, an occasional movie. He would never be able to live where he wanted.

Instead, he leaned back in a wooden chair on the porch of Our Lady Of Perpetual Bliss. (He used another word, in private, since he seemed to go to the bathroom every hour these days ... joys of being old). The Boston-area conference center was light-years from Alaska. One major difference was the people. Maybe it was *all* of New England, but Boston natives minded their own business. Far more than Sitkans. There were a heck of a lot more Catholics here, too, and Father Yahaya, senior pastor and administrator of the center, was on him every - single - day to help with visitations, administering Eucharist for the shut-ins, whatever else he didn't want to do himself.

That wasn't fair. The man was busy. He needed help.

Still, Michael thought retirement was about reading an entire book every day and getting discounts at fast food chains, not do *more* of what he'd already been doing.

It was getting chilly. Still August, but Autumn had its tendrils snaking through the world, getting ready to take hold and seize everyone in its grip. It could try. He'd lived in *cold* for over twenty years so could handle any sad attempts *this* region threw at him. He wrapped his arms around himself anyway and considered getting up and grabbing a jacket.

Deep in the house behind him Yahaya was calling his name in that baritone Nigerian accent. No peace. Not a minute's peace. Might as well never have retired.

A face he hadn't seen in over nine years interrupted his mental whining. Bent, smiling with such terrible teeth. Telly, that was his name. He tried to remember the man's actual,

Christian name, something Greek and starting with Tel ... but damned if he could remember it. Why was he thinking of Telly now? What date was it? He grunted audibly, hoping Yahaya didn't hear. The young Puerto Rican priest who'd replaced him in Alaska was leaving soon. A few days, maybe. Marion's sister Rebecca called him the other day to let him know they were setting up a video link during the younger man's going-away party. Michael had no idea how to connect with anything like that. Even during the pandemic, he let other people handle Zooms and chats. Today, he just wanted to relax and complain about things.

But there was Telly again, returning to his thoughts. The man was annoying. He and his dog, whom the guy tried to sneak into Mass sometimes, of all the crazy things. Michael had reminded him that God's house wasn't a manger. He smiled at the memory. He could be condescending when the situation called for it. People loved him for that. A curmudgeonly white priest managing a small congregation filled with eccentrics like old Telemachos. *That* was the name. He should call Marion tonight, ask if she's seen him -

"Ah, there, you are."

Father David Yahaya was a tall, thin man with skin as dark as, well, as someone born in Nigeria.

"Evening, David. How can I help you in my wretched old age?"

"Stop, Michael," David said with a smile. "If you only used that rage for good, the devil would have no foothold in the world."

Michael nodded, forgetting for the moment about his old congregant. He would be reminded of him again in a couple of days when Rebecca called with the news.

*   *   *

He wasn't cold anymore. Someone had turned on the heat. A hand on his head, gently caressing and fixing his hair. "You're OK," the voice said.

Telemachos took in a breath, deeper than he'd remembered taking in years, let it out. It felt good, rejuvenating, but still he kept his eyes closed.

"Everything's OK, now."

He knew the voice, tried to remember where from, but his life, the people who'd come and gone were only vague shapes, drifting away in an unfelt breeze. This familiarity of the voice wasn't from any particular face or moment, only the feeling of knowing that he knew.

Wanting this illusion of health to continue, Telemachos breathed in again. Spices, scents long forgotten, his mother's face so close, holding him. The memory was sharp. He opened his eyes, stared along the floor of the small red house then up to the dresser and the cross on the wall. The metal Jesus was gone. None of this kept his attention longer than a passing consideration; none of this mattered. Only the hand still caressing his head, and the dog sitting beside the bedroom door, tongue hanging out in joyful exhaustion after a long walk.

"Smitty," he whispered. *Thump, thump* of its tail on the floor, then his old dog, young and healthy, stood and trotted to him. Telemachos sat up quickly and wrapped strong arms around the animal, accepting its kisses, crying with a joy he could not remember feeling before.

"Oh, boy, I missed you so much. You're such a good boy, yes you are."

He sat there for an eternity before the dog finally sat back on its haunches. The hand which had been on his head rested quietly now on his shoulder.

"Time to go," the familiar voice said, and Telemachos Galanos turned around and looked into the other man's face for the first time.

"The Hole"

Part Three: The End of All Things

An Introduction to "The Arrow"

Welcome to the future. As of this writing, the first book in my science fiction series *Vast Array* has been released and its sequel isn't far behind (though it's been fighting me like a petulant child). I understand sci-fi isn't everyone's cup of tea, but bear with me for the next few stories. Again, when initially beginning these, I did not know they would be connected (not to the previous stories, but to each other). In fact, I couldn't see how they could be, until they were. I know, writers are weird.

When reading the following Psalm, I did not see an arrow flying through space. In fact, I thought John Roy was simply a man who'd suffered too many slings and arrows of the modern world's hysteria and ran away to the mountains. Then everything changed. As soon as the story morphed into a science fiction piece, the "arrows" aimed at our character were no longer metaphors but an actual entity emerging from a hole in space. I almost stopped and started over, then remembered my rule: go with what the Spirit is driving you towards. He hadn't let me down yet. I look at the next few stories in this section and honestly shake my head, wondering where they came from. Sounds vain, but it's not. It's simply marveling in wonder at how the Spirit works through us - *when we let Him.*

Like "The Snow" earlier in this book, "The Arrow" is somewhat open-ended. Whether this unconsciously drove me to connect these people to subsequent stories or not, I don't know. But we end up with a series of short vignettes in a future wasteland where God is an unknown entity. If you think that sounds bad, well, it is.

But before we have to face such a scenario, let us boldly move out among the stars.

Psalm 11 - The Arrow

I trust in the Lord for protection.
  So why do you say to me,
    "Fly like a bird to the mountains for safety!
The wicked are stringing their bows
    and fitting their arrows on the bowstrings.
  They shoot from the shadows
    at those whose hearts are right.

The foundations of law and order have collapsed.
    What can the righteous do?"

Psalm 11:1-3 (NLT)

For most of his life, John Roy's dream of retiring to this place had moved out of reach, if not financially then at least practically. People were leaving Earth and not going back. With good reason. His home world had become broken and dying, and the new Earth-like planets discovered along the growing *Array* of Holes were like gifts waiting for humanity to discover and unwrap. If he'd been a man of faith, he'd agree with those who said they were from God.

He did not have faith in such things, yet here he was at last. Everything nearly as perfect as he imagined it could be. He would, now, truly retire from work, and people. From everything about his old life.

He would be fine. No one would miss him.

He wouldn't miss anyone else.

John closed his eyes and leaned back against the log cabin,

checking first to make sure there wasn't anything untoward on the wall waiting to bite or sting. Only the dampness of the summer morning. This high in the mountains, the air was a constant cool against his cotton shirt, thin coating of moss on the wall for comfort. There was moss everywhere.

He let forgetfulness fall over him like the dew that covered everything in this utopia. John waited for the rising sun to dry the world, setting his worries to rise like steam into the air until there was nothing around him but joyful peace, and wilderness.

Life in this place awoke in a cacophony of birdsong and the *rat-a-tat-a-tat* of the woodpecker five trees over, which began its drumming every day looking for breakfast. The wind cut through the trees, sounding like a ground vehicle approaching but slowly, in its time, becoming what it was, the world's breath exhaling and inhaling, oblivious to everything but its own motion. The wind was his daily companion, moving not with violence but a graceful dance with every branch and needle. It lighted across John's bearded face. He leaned forward when it came, tilted his head as it teased his hair, almost felt like he could lift from the ground if he let go of this world a little bit more. Even here, he was bound by gravity.

As the sun painted the distant mountains with soft violet sweeps in the distance John pushed away from the cabin. The breeze cooled his back, wet shirt stuck to skin. The Sierra Nevada range was a rising and falling cornucopia of foxtail, ponderosa and sugar pines, enduring against weather which would, in a few short months, turn harsh and deadly. All of it was now washed in summer, exploded in greens and yellows glowing under the bluest sky.

If his first winter in this place, when it came, was to be his last, if he found himself crushed under its weight, then he would die happy.

And free.

The walking staff leaned against the wall just inside the door. John reached in, grabbed the leather jacket atop it, fur lining removed for the season - it could be re-buttoned when temperatures changed. Shaking the coat a few times to be sure nothing had made a nest in the sleeves, he pulled it on, grabbed his staff and closed the door. The sun had risen above the farthest range. This cabin was built on the edge of a rocky promenade facing east; the mountain its foundation. Posts had been hammered slowly, carefully into the ground, finding purchase and gripping so deep that the cabin would never be moved. It was an extension of the mountain, welcoming the rising sun every morning.

As he followed a well-worn path into the woods, the temperature within the canopy of trees better reflected the previous night's cold.

He walked, and watched. Movement in the shadows deeper in. John remained silent, became an extension of the wind playing across the branches. He touched fingertips to laurel and pine and rocks and moss - *there* she was, a deer with her two fawns giving him no more than a passing glance. There were bears here, too, though he hadn't seen any in some time. When he did, it had been down the eastern slope, around twilight. That was how John told time in this place, not in numbers but in moments when evening touched down. When Autumn began, the darkness would arrive quicker. Time would accelerate during the day, slow to near hibernation at night.

Captain!

The trees disappeared, replaced by the cold starkness of his cabin. They returned just as quickly, though more muted, less real. *Don't think, be here. Be fully –*

"Captain to the bridge, please." The voice fully shattered his world. Min's voice. John's eyes were open, looking across the room to the red light beside his door. He groaned and pulled the earpieces free. "Gimme a minute," he murmured into his pillow.

John Roy did not want to come back. Even knowing it was nothing but a subliminally-induced dream, it was one he tried to return to more often the farther they ventured from the real place. It was a reunion, and parting, that offered equal amounts joy and pain.

*   *   *

"We're under attack, sir," Min said, his expression calm. The short man rarely showed much emotion. A good quality for a pilot but too cold and mysterious in casual settings. John never knew what the guy was thinking. Maybe he didn't think anything, except what mattered in the moment.

The command room of the *ISS Gotottur* always felt too small for the three of them: John Roy, in charge of this current mess, Lenten Min, expressionless Nav officer and Alana Rodriquez staring down at her screen in Comms. At the moment she was silent, long hair hanging across her face. Protocol was to keep hair in a braid, so she'd probably been asleep not long ago.

The anomaly flowed on the far wall's viewscreen. It had appeared while he'd been sleeping - itself not a big deal considering these holes in space had begun popping up for the past two years in this system's outer rim. Nothing ever emerged from them, but more significantly no probe sent inside ever came back. It looked like an artist's rendition of a mythical black hole, subtly-spinning corona of dust and light around a nucleus devoid of color. There was no change in gravitational pull to indicate these might actually *be* black holes, with no oddities on any spectrum including x-ray. It was just … there.

This one, however, was different from the others in one significant way. A long, pointed... *something* of light emerged. Like a sword, but no more tangible than the edges of the anomaly itself, a swirling twist of light and perception.

"What am I seeing?"

From the speaker built into his chair, Nylah Bagdonas said from down the hall, "First guess was the anomaly breaking apart, the edges distorting. I don't think so, however, after what happened while you were out."

Memory of trees on the mountainside, silent perfection.

"Explain."

His First Officer was speaking from Second Bridge, an equally small room one hundred meters down the ring from where he sat. "This is the second one. The first broke through and nearly cut us in half."

He blinked. The real world had gotten a little more interesting while he dreaming.

John was tired of *interesting*. He wanted simple. "Solid, then," not exactly a question.

"As far as we can tell, yes. We launched a probe after it passed us, but at the moment System's projection for its destination is nowhere near any planet or known ship's location."

"It missed."

"That's our best guess, yes." *Best guess*. A common condition out here. She continued, "Missed us, and just continued in the same direction."

He asked the woman beside him, "Anything coming out of there at all, Alana, besides the next arrow?"

"No, sir. Nothing."

No signal, no blip or flash that could in any way be construed as communication. No one was talking, only throwing sharp things at them.

"Can we get out of its way before the next arrow breaks free?"

In front of him, Min said, "Working on it. Moving away now, and accelerating - the image on the screen is enhanced so we can see what it's up to. Based on the speed of the first arrow, though, it'll catch us eventually."

"If we're the target."

No one responded. Everyone assumed they were.

The unspoken next question was: how far from the nest did they need to get before the bees stopped trying to sting them?

On the screen, the arrow stretched as if making one final press through its celestial amniotic sac, then was free, shining like steel or liquid silver. It occasionally swirled with colors, but the enlargement of the video probably exaggerated or even created the effect. There was no time for speculation as it twisted, turned then suddenly filled the screen.

When it hit them an hour later, the crew was as ready as they could be, given the complete lack of knowledge about what might happen when it did. Their ship was a massive, kilometer-long ring, always spinning around a central hub in order to create an artificial sense of gravity. The arrow punctured the inner curve of the ring just shy of the fitness and med wings, then passed through the wide corridor to emerge partway through the outer hull, which was actually the *floor* from a false gravity perspective. Then it stopped. Atmosphere tore out of the breeches, triggering emergency hatches on either side to close. Trapped inside were Doctor Bosede Numbi and his PA Henny Schmid. Wang Jun was also in the wing, having stopped by to treat a persistent headache which plagued her whenever she was forced to suit up. Like everyone else, they'd donned their bulky environment suits as a precaution, but Jun removed her helmet long enough to drink the concoction Bosede put together. He'd intended to inject it into her suit for her to drink through a straw, but as the two physicians stared at the screen in horror, Jun removed her helmet, sucked the liquid from the plastic syringe but never managed to get the helmet back on before impact. Pulled violently towards Medical's open entryway, her body remained rooted to the floor when the ship's AI system activated everyone's magnetic boots. Her helmet, however, continued into the shattered corridor and tumbled into space.

By the time Numbi and Schmid recovered enough to turn around, it was to see the frozen, bruised body of their patient floating before them, boots firmly planted to the floor, eyes unseeing. A few minutes later they understood they were trapped in that section of the ring.

*   *   *

First Bridge felt more claustrophobic with everyone wearing environment suits. John listened to reports coming through the speaker, first from Min sitting in front of him. Their momentum away from the anomaly had stopped with the impact. Now, they were moving back *towards* it.

The ship no longer had gravity, the ring's rotation having stopped. Aside from Medical, oxygen levels were normal. He ordered everyone to stay suited up, but allowed for visors to be raised. No sense wasting suit oxygen until it was needed.

Beside him Alana Rodriquez confirmed no obvious communication, nothing visible on any light spectrum between the arrow embedded in their hull and the anomaly. She maintained her theory that something nevertheless connected them - making it a harpoon rather than an arrow if they wanted a better analogy. John didn't.

Nylah Bagdonas, along with Kim Cho and Dietrich Wahl from Internal Systems positioned themselves on either side of the closed bulkheads, trying to find a way to reach the surviving crew in Medical without doing an EVA along the outer bulkhead. That option hadn't been ruled out, however.

Doctor Numbi reported from the corridor. One of the cameras still worked, showing PA Bosede's shoulder and a massive silver rod taking up half the image, wide as the man was tall. It had torn through the upper corner of the hallway and into the floor through a jagged tear in the hull. A few stars could be seen through the gap, unmoving now that the ring wasn't spinning.

"It's smooth," Bosede was saying.

"System, split view to show his suit camera." The ship's computer divided the large screen between the corridor video and Bosede's suit camera, mounted just below the faceplate. The doctor's gloved left hand ran along the surface of the harpoon (may as well use Alana's analogy, John decided without humor). He considered, only for a moment before dismissing the idea, to tell Bosede not to touch anything. What did it matter? If he was trapped in there, might as well learn what he could. The doctor continued moving his hand along the surface towards the break in the floor. "No blemishes or scratches, even after slamming through the hull. Henny anything?"

His assistant was out of frame in the corridor view, standing on Bosede's left. "Nothing abnormal, reflecting light on all spectrums, temp and radiation levels are consistent with surroundings. And ...," a pause. As it tended to do, the ship's AI assumed what people might want and added Schmid's suit camera to the screen. He was raising the spectrometer towards the tear in the upper hull.

"Keep away from the sharp pieces," Bosede whispered. Henny responded with a curse-laden acknowledgment of the obvious, before adding, "No radiation or signal beyond its tail, or whatever you'd call it. It's one, autonomous unit but there's nothing connecting it to anything else."

"But it nevertheless seems," Nylah added, "to be towing us closer to the anomaly and we can't do a thing about it."

"I tried," Min said from his station, frustration clear in his voice. "Whatever is going on, it's faster than we could safely accelerate to with our thrusters."

"We know that," John said, not wanting to sound placating but also not wanting to get into a whine-fest with his navigator. "I just wish we could tell if whatever it's doing, stops." He paused, considering. "Doctor Numbi."

"Sir?"

"Apparently touching the thing doesn't melt your brain, so would you and Doctor Schmid please see what you can do about dislodging it from our hull? Just don't touch the sharp pieces."

Henny laughed over the speaker and Numbi acknowledged the request, though with some reluctance.

Silence for a few minutes, then Rodriquez's voice beside him and over the comm said what everyone had been assuming. "If we can't get it free it's not going to stop until we're inside that hole." The first window of the three-way image showed the unenhanced view of space before them. In the center was a bright, fuzzy ring, small but growing. The anomaly's mouth, opened wide, waiting to swallow them up.

What that meant, no one knew. Nothing sent in ever returned, likely because nothing survived the passage. These things weren't black holes, but as far as anyone could tell, neither were they remotely like the Holes humanity had been using for over a century to move between habitable solar systems. Even now, no one understood how *those* particular wormholes worked, either, whether they'd been created through some inexplicable act of nature or a more intelligent design. These smaller aberrations in space were a recent mystery and thus far, treated with more caution. Now they had a justifiable reason for that fear.

"Time to contact?"

The dispassionate computer voice of System answered, "At present rate, fifteen minutes, twenty-seven seconds."

In fifteen minutes, then, they'd all find out. Their situation and position had been communicated to ISE command, but no one would reach them in time. In fact, at John Roy's recommendation the region would be officially quarantined for the foreseeable future. They were on their own with this, though Command would monitor.

"We're not going to have any time to extricate the two of you from the ring, Doctor. See what you can do, with obvious caution, but if you have no luck in the next few minutes take the rest of the time to get secured inside Medical."

Bosede Numbi acknowledged with surprising calm. "Yes, sir."

"Nylah, Cho, Rick, get back to Second and strap in. System, how much external suit oxygen is on hand, and how long would that last us if we abandoned ship?"

Min and Alana both turned towards him, the idea clearly horrifying them. "Just asking," he added, already knowing the answer because he'd checked the levels manually on his personal monitor, not wanting a panic. Everyone needed to know it was not an option.

The answer was disappointing but also a relief, based on how the others seemed to relax. They wouldn't last twelve hours if they divided the air between them. With any possible help at least two weeks away, all of it would merely be a delay of the inevitable.

Voices buzzed inside his helmet, but he ignored them. John closed his eyes and imagined morning outside the cabin. It was an experience fabricated by his mind which had shockingly taken place less than three hours ago, but felt like a lost memory of his youth. The air had been cool; he'd stepped away from the warming rays of the sun into the forest's deeper shadows. There was a deer and if he'd been given more time perhaps John might have spotted a fox. Woodpeckers would continue rat-a-tat-a-tatting for their meals, and birds, so many birds, chirping and squawking and singing their language of "mine, mine, mine," and "here, here, here." Proclaiming their presence, and their importance to the universe.

Everything had been as it was supposed to be and he could imagine that all of it was real, had happened, a too-perfect rendition of his home world. Three hours ago he'd been plucked from of that paradoxical world of beauty and ugliness, of consistency and change, and forced back here into the vacuum, into the eternity between stars. His home planet, broken as it might be, was a living, breathing creature. Everything outside the walls of this *new* home was empty and suffocating.

He refocused on this real world again, for no other reason than to give the crew whatever anchor he could offer. Less than eight minutes until impact. Min was trying maneuvering thrusters, with some luck. The Docs reported the arrow had slipped a little. Then two minutes of misery and pain as they tried to manually wrestle it free, gaining more ground. The thing, whatever it was, must have understood what they were up to and suddenly charged up the section Henny had been gripping. It burned him into ash before he had time to scream.

John did his best not to consider they'd been doing that under his order. He couldn't think about that, not when they only had six minutes left. Doctor Bosede howled over the speakers for a full minute, then deactivated his comms. John was grateful for that. He'd liked Henny. Everyone did, but no one had time to mourn, nor comfort the man who'd been standing beside him but remained unharmed.

Eventually, the doctor could do nothing else, so he retreated into Medical to pray.

Five minutes.

John closed his eyes again and wished for some sudden enlightenment, some magnificent words to share with the rest of his people. Some comfort, or clarity.

Everything fit together, if you let it. The stones underfoot in the mountains exposed by melting snows, water finding its way into the frigid rivers he and his brothers would play in during the too-brief summers in the northern Canadian District.

Why shouldn't the rest of God's creation be the same? The rest of His universe? If there *was* a Creator, wouldn't the rules be the same for a skittish doe staring at him through trees and a swirling hole in space that defied human understanding? Both were part of existence, even if mere mortals like himself couldn't see how. Both could shoot, or be shot by, arrows.

The thought blinked his eyes open. He hadn't realized they had closed. Alana was in her chair beside him, bent over, her prayers like static in his helmet's speaker, petitions to a God John still wasn't sure existed, who worked His plans behind all of this emptiness and violence.

He glanced at the screen. The anomaly filled the frame. *Time to impact, 4:21.*

The timer changed to *4:20,* then *4:19* before his brain caught up.

He considered asking a question over on the comm, get his people to focus, then decided it would be a disservice. Let each face the unknown in their own way.

From his station in front of him Min said quietly, "They managed to loosen the thing a little, sir, but not enough. Integrity of the hull in that section is failing too much for me to risk firing thrusters."

"Trying to escape at this point will tear us apart, you mean?"

A pause, then, "Yes, sir."

"You did your best, Min. Proud to serve with you." Louder, he said, "System split views between Med and Second."

The screen, which had become ominous with the growing image of the anomaly, split into three images. The hole in space remained, but smaller now, and the quiet, standing figure of Bosede Numbi whispering his own prayers through the comms. He'd apparently turned his mic back on. John wanted to order him to get seated and strapped in, but in these final moments what Bosede was doing might be more important. An odd feeling for the Captain, but one which he wrote off as a purely emotional response.

The third image showed Second Bridge. Like his own, it was overcrowded with three fully-suited adults strapped into their chairs. Nylah was center-screen, with Cho beside her typing something furiously on her monitor. Maybe writing home one last time. At the back, the large chief engineer stared between the other two at the screen, eyes wide in terror. John could pretend it was an expression of wonder but that would only be to make himself feel better.

He focused instead on Nylah's face. She looked back at him, or maybe at the anomaly or Doctor Numbi. He hoped she was looking at him. He nodded slightly. She nodded back. That brought some comfort. John stared at her face, understanding that the universe had suddenly expanded before them. New experiences, new truths unfolding as the seconds wound down. Dark truths, yes. Violent. Years before, he'd privately hoped coming out here would reveal some new part of the wonder of the universe. This was ...

He stopped thinking. Didn't matter. They'd all be dead in another minute or they'd evolve within whatever celestial carnival waited for them.

All of this, simply, was. If there was more, so be it.

1:22.

"Visors down," he whispered. Everyone silently obeyed. He searched, and found Nylah's eyes behind her visor, tried not to notice how the anomaly was all-encompassing inside its window, the mouth of a whale larger than their entire ring leading them to oblivion or something else which he now hoped or prayed - he envied Bosede in these final few seconds - was something other than death. That maybe there had been some point to his existence up until now. To all of them.

0:39

He suddenly didn't want his life to end alone in the woods on a mountain under heavy winter snows. He regretted that obsessive urge to escape so often; wanted life to mean something more. To have had an impac-

0.

An Introduction to "The Truth"

The opening words of Psalm 12 project such anguish and disillusion. It made me wonder, what would a world be like without those who are 'faithful' and 'loyal' to God? There's a popular End-Times interpretation of scripture which expects the Church to be raptured to heaven before Satan rises and takes over the world, at least for a time (think, *Left Behind*). What a frightening, Orwellian world would result from such an event? Have you ever wondered: would God truly leave those left behind to suffer? Perhaps He'd find a way to leave His Word behind, like a Holy forbidden treasure, one which spreads like metaphorical yeast through society, rekindling a sense of faith in a dark world.

Yes, all that came to me as soon as I read this Psalm. Whether the story itself does justice to such a revelatory question, you, Dear Reader, can be the judge.

And, to my wonderful wife Linda, I apologize in advance again for all the weird names. There is a method and meaning behind them . . . I just can't remember what that was, now.

Psalm 12 - The Truth

Help, Lord, for no one is faithful anymore;
  those who are loyal have vanished from the human race.
Everyone lies to their neighbor;
  they flatter with their lips
  but harbor deception in their hearts.

And the words of the Lord are flawless,
  like silver purified in a crucible,
  like gold refined seven times.
You, Lord, will keep the needy safe
  and will protect us forever from the wicked,
who freely strut about
  when what is vile is honored by the human race.

Psalm 12:1-2,6-8 (NIV)

Kaylin glanced out the window, but only briefly, not wanting to seem as if she cared whether anyone else looked in. In fact, she didn't, and kept trying to convince herself of that. Secrets beget Forces at the door, tearing up the floor or knocking out walls for the thinnest of rationales. Suspicion of sedition, as they liked to announce whenever someone disappeared, sometimes for no reason other than someone reported you were hiding something, at some time, on some day. Always, the turned-stomach fear that the rest of her family will be taken away, that she might be raped or killed here in this filthy box the Government called Housing Unit 515-11. The five hundred and fifteenth unit on the eleventh floor of a block-sized wedge of concrete, pressed behind a hundred others.

Kaylin was tired. More so these past few weeks. In the not-so-distant past, everything was exciting, especially when she and Derek received the voucher for their own place. The future that dangled before them was the same for all young families, possibilities that were only prefabricated deceptions. People were nothing but parts in a machine. Serving a purpose then discarded.

"Down," she said to the little ones banging and playing around the table, a half-shout, hardly caring, "no play on table. Hurt you. Down." Kaylin waved a hand, wondering if they knew they would never see their father again. Wondering if they cared. Dalek was ostensibly named after his father though Derek wanted him to have something unique about his own. He was the oldest of the three, enough for Basic Grades. Most of the useful schooling, however, was learned on the block itself. How to read simple things, get along, understand life. How to fight. How to stay alive. Dalek was cruel, both to his friends and ten-month-old brother Malcolm, though her youngest already stood his ground against the older boy, without fully being able to stand yet.

Dalek practically worshiped Bree, however. His sister would come to no harm in three years when she, herself, reached Basic age. By then, Kaylin imagined her oldest son would have established his place as an Alpha in his level. He'd keep an eye out for his sister's well-being. It was all Kaylin could wish for her family's truer, darker future. One without Derek. Her heart and body ached for him, for anything resembling a hope that he might touch or simply speak to her again.

The Forces had come to the door four months ago, while dirty rain splashed against the plastic curtain outside the window, the sound a chaotic chorus echoed by thousands of others in such weather which for a time drowned out the constant backdrop of rage and hurt pouring from the units around them.

Three knocks, then a passkey turning before Derek could come fully out of their bed in the corner. As rehearsed, when the volume of strange voices in the unit rose, the older two children scrambled from their blankets to sit beside their mother as far from the door as possible. Derek, meanwhile, dressed only in his pajama pants tried to placate the soldiers.

They had come for *him*, she'd understood quickly. Not her, nor the children. Not yet. Derek glanced back quickly before focusing again on the lead solider, a heavyset, narrow-eyed man in a black combat suit. Her husband knew to keep the visitors' attention on him. Meanwhile, Kaylin had carefully reached back, wrapped her hand around the punch weapon wedged between the mattress and wall in case they came for her or the children. Malcolm kept blissfully silent in his crib beside the bed. Derek's final glance as they strapped his wrists together had been a worried stare into her soul, full of love and always, always, the edges of rage at the world and her *pretend God* (words he never dared never say aloud, only in semi-affectionate secret whispers on quiet nights long past). All of it, he was convinced, were tides pushing back against their family's forward motion. Everything in the universe was a force moving against him, pressing down, drowning the human race in selfish cravings and addictions.

My life pushed into dirt, he once said. *When I try to plant trees.* He was obsessed with trees, the thin spindly sentinels lining the roads down-below, good for nothing in Kaylin's opinion besides catching the trash as it blew along. The Garden of Eden had bigger trees. She imagined finding a door into that universe someday, a way to bring her children into its perfection.

The glow of the forbidden words offered that promise;

God's promise for a day after life ends. They burned under her now, four months later, inside the kitchen chair's cushion as the kids fought in front of her. Nine sheets of paper stacked and folded and clipped to make a booklet. Words, so many, in careful script, telling of the God whom Derek probably now hated; how this God came down from far away to help his people. She didn't read well, could make out some words, but Derek had been able. Neither of them knew how he'd come into the booklet's possession. It was simply in his backpack when he crawled home off-shift one evening.

These words are True, the text began. *Learn about God, and share. This one part. More of Truth outside with others. Don't let them know you have it.* Derek had read these words to her in whispers, hesitated before saying, *"This is what they are calling movement of lies. We die get caught with this."*

In that moment, the children asleep because he'd been blessed with the common sense not to examine anything new in view of their excited gazes, he and Kaylin stared at the small, bent book before turning to each other not with fear, but a spark of hope. If the government said these words were a movement of lies, they must have some truth in them. They must *be* Truth.

Derek whispered the entire booklet that night, haltingly, though the language was easy to follow, like someone speaking to them through the window, but in Derek's voice. The Garden and the fall, God's people scattered then brought together through one family, becoming slaves, freed, growing powerful then falling again, becoming slaves again. Throughout, God promising to one day come to Earth to save them.

"Where Earth?" she'd asked, and Derek had only shrugged, said, *"Where Eden, or land that this happen? Far away, other side of world, maybe."*

"Maybe other world," she'd whispered, excited by all of it.

He'd only shook his head and said, *"Baby stories, those. No one come from sky. They fall and go splat on ground."* Kaylin had to cover her mouth to suppress a giggle.

They'd fallen quiet then. Derek absently tapped the paper, considering, perhaps planning. Kaylin finally said, *"Did God ever visit them at Earth?"* Too loudly, he answered, *"How I know?"* Quieter, gentler, *"Maybe another book say."* He'd slowly moved about the unit then, searching and settling on hiding the papers under one of the chairs, slipping the booklet into a tear on the underside of its cushion. It was a good hiding place, not easily noticed.

Over the next few weeks, a sense of hopeful expectation fell over Kaylin, but Derek became more agitated. He'd asked, casually, around his shift if anyone knew anything about the *lies* going around, hoping for more, learning nothing. Instead, he began to see shadows following him home, eyes watching through walls, falling into rages with little prompting. Afraid, he refused to take the book out from its hiding place to read again. It remained there, a fond memory more than anything real in their life.

Then the Forces came and took him away, either because of his earlier inquiries or they sensed his fear and hoped it would lead to something more. Kaylin didn't blame the Truth that had come into their home. That was how she thought of it, as the Truth. Near the end, the hope of the words gave her comfort. *How* they did so, she didn't understand, for they'd equally brought such fear and dread to her husband.

One day, she worried, the wood of the chair might ignite from the Truth inside. Its existence would bring back the dark-clad Forces to take away her children. Maybe they would toss her out the window as they had Rose Sinclair two months ago. Rumor spoke of Rose daring to speak against a soldier who was dragging someone *else* away down the hall. So many choices these Forces had, whom to take, to spare, day after day.

The soldier released his captive, taken Rose who was ten years younger than Kaylin herself, barely grown, and dragged her into her family's unit not to rape but push her through the unit's only window. That had been two floors higher. Thirteen levels of Rose's rage-filled scream. Rumor, all of it, about the scream. Angry, not frightened. Everyone was angry. Fear hardened that way over time. Kaylin turned the memory, false or not, over in her thoughts. At least Rose was able to scream that rage, if briefly.

A part of Kaylin, a dirty part, wished Rose had given her life to save Derek instead of the other nameless victim who - in her own, unsubstantiated version of the story - had escaped the Forces. Maybe the nameless figure was even now hopping along rooftops fighting for the people.

That fancy pulled her mind back to the words she could not read, hidden in the pages under the chair. They ended with comments which echoed in many ways the booklet's opening lines, always in Derek's whispered voice, *Learn these words, and share with others. In secret. Do not let your right hand know what the left is doing.*

Kaylin considered those final words, then slapped her eldest child on the head.

"Down from couch, Dalek, now. We not rats."

The boy glared for a moment, as if daring his mother to assert her power again, yearning for a chance to become a part of the violence around him. But he looked away quickly and bounded to the floor, no trace of the rage because it was not real. Too long her in her own head, she knew; too long seeing her fears come alive. Malcolm squealed and followed his brother toward the cracked vid screen and its cartoons.

*　　*　　*

He walked slowly, to not draw attention, never be seen as

a threat. Just an old man walking from one place to another, pressed down from the weight of the world and stumbling closer to death. Morbid thought, true, but it sometimes pushed his expression upward, almost to a smirk. Sometimes, all of this was so completely ludicrous he would come to the edge of hysteria, one blink away from an outpouring of terror and amusement, of resignation that where he was, what he had been through these past twenty-nine years made so little sense it could not possibly be real. There had been moments in his old life, times of stress, but also long stretches of peace when he would sit back and soak in the warmth of life with little care, when he was certain the Light would always be there, the safety and certainty that *all will be well.* It would never leave him. It always did, of course, for a time. The old quote, he'd long ago forgotten its source (likely one of those 'anonymous' attributions on someone's wall or virtual signatures), said, *If you want to make God laugh, tell Him your plans.*

If this was God laughing, Bosede would hate to see him angry. Maybe the old stories of a vengeful and destructive *Yahweh* were more accurate than of Jesus' loving Abba. It felt that way, since the moment he and the others fell from the sky.

Over the decades on this world, or this time (his current working theory that this was some dark version of Earth far in the future, though it could as easily be or some city on a planet yet to be discovered) - their arrival had become whispered legend. He could count on one hand the moments he'd encountered anyone else from the crew. It encouraged him, knowing he wasn't the only survivor. Therapy, this talking with someone who'd lived in his past, a reminder that he was not mad. Two people had so far been absent. None of the others had seen them, either. The Captain, John Roy, and first officer Nylah Bagdonis. Dead, maybe, or next in line to accidentally stumble upon a chance meeting with him in this dead, concrete world. For all he knew they could be on the other side of the planet. Whatever this planet was. In the meantime, he rehearsed their names, all of them, so he would not forget where he came from.

Bosede Numbi might still be mad, of course, and those previous meetings mere illusions drawn in his mind, part of the masquerade. They helped Bosede to keep on surviving, however, living this new life. These encounters were never repeated, either, at least never with the same crew member. There were no devices, no electronic paper or k-watches to keep in contact, share information. In fact, he hadn't seen an actual pencil in a week, search for one as he might. He needed another and was starting to suspect their disappearances - even from private shops - had a nefarious reason.

The noose was closing in. The governments in this strange land were scattered and unorganized. Now and again, however, they threw darts that connected with the intended target. He needed to be careful.

Blowing air across his lips and rolling his eyes in the manner that suggested he was considering his options, he finally said, "Noodles and pie, yellow."

Cairns laughed from the other side of the window where Bosede sat on a wobbly stool - it would come loose from its moorings soon and be stolen if the man didn't tighten it. Cairns had dark skin like himself, but head shaved smooth. Suspiciously smooth, no nicks. Good razor. Everyone was suspect. He wished he could trust more. Especially this man who always had a smile for his customers.

"That some breakfast, Bo Man. Want me give you beer to wash it down?" He laughed, not expecting an answer. Bosede smiled, the written summary of Jesus' ministry burning between the layers of his backpack. Five weeks of careful transcribing, considering. His were not perfect Gospels, but then, neither were the originals. All, copies of copies. Stories passed on from original eyewitnesses. Drops of light in this inky blackness of a world.

Cairns dropped the plate before him. "Here go, my friend. Gave bigger piece."

Bosede tapped two fingers to his head in thanks and pointed with those same fingers, to add emphasis. "Yellow show pretend fruit, can pretend good for me. And noodles good to digest."

"Who say?" Wiping his hands, still that smirk in corner of his mouth.

Bosede took a mouthful of noodles with sticks, like the old Asian style back home, and spoke through his food. "Me say."

Cairns laughed his usual deep rumble and clapped his hand on the counter in appreciation before walking to another customer. Bosede ate, thought of the man's cleanly-shaved head. Again, too much so, smile too healthy. The words in his pack would stay for a while longer. Someone else, then.

It had taken years to feel this inconspicuous, wandering the streets, living off a system eager to build human dependency on itself. He'd eventually found a job as cleaner in a chrome-heavy finishing plant for the few small automobiles skittering to and fro through the overcrowded city. They called them "districts" here, all in a broken, basic English. Sometimes Bosede wondered if what he heard was not English at all – that perhaps his brain had been rewired through the hole in order to understand the words. The implication of *that* was too staggering to accept. Whatever the anomaly that attacked his ship had been, if it had somehow scrambled his brain into some organic, universal language translator, then it was created by an Intelligence, not some bizarre natural phenomenon.

All of it, for a purpose. Some of the crew scattered around this endless maze of concrete thought he'd lost his mind. They might be right, might be avoiding him now. He might also be the only one who seemed able to grip the tattered ends of his faith and stay sane in this reality. The others, former navigator

Lenten Min especially, had a look of low-burn terror and confusion. They were wild animals suddenly caged, pacing back and forth looking for a way out.

Min had asked why Bosede didn't simply find a job as a doctor. Bosede had long ago decided, however, to remain below the radar of authorities. An undocumented citizen suddenly able to perform neurosurgery or even sew an injury cleanly would point the wrong attention his way. For reasons he did not fully understand - but accepted as necessary - the rest of his life would be lived in anonymity down here.

Wherever 'down here' was.

In the meantime, amid all the uncertainty, the dream he'd had nearly six months earlier and *its* comforting surety drove him on, even as pain in his side grew. *It's nothing,* the doctor at the clinic informed him, when his appointment had finally come. She'd glanced at the scan and added, *Looks like you had a fall, got a bruise on your side.* Bosede only nodded, looking at the scan as she held it out. The doctor wasn't able to tell a bruise from the ominous shadow along the side of his lung. His breathing wasn't labored, not yet. He wondered if the cancer might be along the pleura surrounding the chest cavity. He'd find out soon enough. The woman had pulled the flexible sheet away as he stared then dropped it into a folder. She muttered something to an aid and left with no further word. The aid laid a gauze pad across the ribs on his left side and attached it with tape. It was the wrong side, but Bosede hadn't bothered to correct him. After all, he was an old man and had lived out his usefulness. Time for them to move on to the next patient.

Already, he wondered if the government had been made aware of his condition. His room, hardly more than a ten square foot cube which he was very grateful to have considering the alternative, might now be on the pending availability list. The doctor might have seen the truth, understood what the image showed her and decided he did not need to know. What would be the point? They would never expend the energy or resources to treat him.

So much darkness.

After his noodles, Bosede moved quietly through the market, bought a few things then returned to his cube. He sighed and sat at the table, pulled a bag from the sack containing a half apple and an oversized protein flat. The apple was a rare treat. Fresh fruit rarely lasted long on the shelves, if they appeared at all these last few years. Bosede's loosening teeth were a testament to that. The noodles would suffice for rest of the night. Tomorrow he would cut the apple into manageable slices and eat half, force down the flat, then finish with the remaining apple. It would be a decent dinner. He put them aside in the plastic storage box, protected from any rodents that found their way onto the counter.

Then, as he did every night, the old man who'd fallen from outer space moved to the larger chair and closed his eyes, asked for peace, then for guidance.

I've done as you asked. Three summaries of the Old Testament as best I can remember have been given, are out there, somewhere. I trust You to guide them along. The one in my pack seems so much more incendiary. Jesus' name is always controversial, even in my world, my time.

Where am I, Lord? Why am I here?

He blinked, realized his thoughts were straying again, back into the usual whining.

No matter. I'm here. Show me whom to give this new work to. Then I'll begin the next. And the next, until you call me away from this place. Wherever this place is.

*   *   *

Sky managed to carry both bags from the Stream to her front door without incident. It had been touch-and-go near the end. The public market - specifically Oron's Spice Booth - was the only place she could find Mahlepi, and have it actually *be* Mahlepi. But the human rats were everywhere in that place. Refresh was always the first Tuesday of the month and the desperate and dirty came in droves, scuttling among the Clean like herself. She was shielded from theft, displaying the insignia of her class on the front and back of her shirt as a warning to anyone assuming a lone woman in public was fair game. Not that she mightn't still be, for those desperate enough. But the penalty for any crime against her kind was instant death. The Forces were everywhere, especially on days like today.

She nearly stumbled coming inside the townhouse. The extra, odd-sized step leading to their front door had been Berna's idea. A way of fooling any would-be burglar into tripping over themselves before they reached the door. Her husband was paranoid. Sky didn't think having this stupid extra step was worth any sense of security Berna thought it provided.

She reached inside her bags as soon as they were on the counter in the kitchen. Two armfuls of vegetables, even some decent pasta. Of course, the Mahlepi. She never dared buy any flesh at those places. Meat went bad outside and the masses had their hands all over it. She preferred paying a premium for delivery. *Freshness guaranteed* and all that.

Everything she'd procured at the market was accounted for. The woman who'd bumped into her might have planned to take something, but unless Sky was losing her mind in middle age, nothing was missing. The rat had been apologetic, trying to keep her three dirty children in sight. She'd seemed sincere, but Sky knew better. It was a common diversion tactic. She'd lost sight of one bag for just a moment.

She stared into the bag now, mind tumbling through options, trying to process what she was seeing.

Nothing was missing, but something had been added.

No, she thought. Her throat tightened. *Don't look at it any more.* She turned away, trying to remember what the stranger looked like but all she remembered was pale skin covered in smears, eyes downcast, mumbling voice. Sky had been too intent on keeping hold of her groceries and glancing around for a solider she actually needed in that moment. No one. Crowds and noise. Soon the woman and her minions were gone.

Sky looked back into the bag now, read the words on the topmost folded sheet. Every one of them was illegal. Should she call the Forces and get involved? Her name would forever be on someone's register. Better to fold the words away and burn everything in the fire. She casually folded the paper bag which could have been reused another dozen times, but no one would know that, and tossed it into the fireplace along with a two pieces of kindling. There was a chill in the air. She was simply treating herself to a small fire to warm up after being out among the lower classes. At the same time, she was righting a wrong done against her.

Everything she was doing, everything, was proper. Igniter in hand, she pointed it towards the crumpled bag with the vile lies (she assumed) inside of it. Sky hesitated, wondered why the government hated whatever words were there. What *was* it?

It didn't matter. Her life with Berna was comfortable, less so than it had been, perhaps, for her family when she was a child, but far more than many, many others. Curiosity was not something she could afford.

Still, she kept the flame away from the paper. There was no surveillance in this room. Berna always checked.

For the first time, she wondered *why* he checked.

Slowly, as quietly as possible, she extracted the bag from under the wood, opened it and glanced inside. She would only read the first page, no more than that.

These words are true, the words began.

An Introduction to "The Scorched Earth"

Following Jesus, especially during the admittedly unique twist on the Apocalypse my futuristic stories and novels tend to reside in, isn't always *Hallmark* and *Veggie Tales*. Sometimes it's Gibson and Tarantino.

My goal with this next story is just that: to try and see faith the way someone like Job, or the writer of Psalm 13, or the early Christians under Roman persecution must have seen it. To suffer to the point of death, or to the point where death is a relief, yet struggle to hold tightly to the threads of one's faith. Don't think that if the Enemy has been working to turn our eyes from Jesus, it would simply let us die in peace at the end. When better to hit us, but when we are down?

Never one to stop at the edge of a literary cliff, let's ask what would it be like for someone at ground zero of Satan itself rising from hell. This also serves as a bit of background to the previous story, and the one coming after.

A warning, this story has some violence in it, off-screen as much of it might be, it's still a bit disturbing. I promise, this overall volume of stories will end on a happy note. Until then, let's get a little dark for Jesus.

Psalm 13 - The Scorched Earth

How long, Lord? Will you forget me forever?
    How long will you hide your face from me?
How long must I wrestle with my thoughts
    and day after day have sorrow in my heart?
    How long will my enemy triumph over me?

Look on me and answer, Lord my God.
    Give light to my eyes, or I will sleep in death,
and my enemy will say, "I have overcome him,"
    and my foes will rejoice when I fall.

But I trust in your unfailing love;
    my heart rejoices in your salvation.
I will sing the Lord's praise,
    for he has been good to me.

Psalm 13 (NIV)

One hundred and seventy-four years before
Bosede Numbi began his final ministry in the concrete
dystopia that had once been known as Pine Bluff, Arkansas,
but on the same day that the *ISS Gotottur* was being pulled into
the maw of the anomaly, an old man named Alejandro
Gutierrez Cruz wondered if Satan truly would rise from the
ground like his captor said would happen. An honest-to-
goodness physical *being* rising from Hell. He imagined
something like that would be a terrible sight to behold. The
fallen angel's appearance might be horrific enough to kill

millions with only a glance. The zealot who was now the choreographer of the old priest's pain certainly relished and promoted that idea.

If this expectation, dark and bizarre as it was, came to pass it might fit with everything else that had happened in the last hundred years. As if the human race had been given just enough time to inherit a myriad of new Earths, habitable worlds within the recently-discovered network of wormholes they called the *Vast Array*. Each new system was like all-new heavens above them. With these second chances for life established, the old, abused ball called Earth orbiting their original sun could finally succumb to the evil eating away at it ever since Eve listened to the serpent, and Adam was too passive to suggest otherwise.

Alejandro didn't blame them; what did either Adam or Eve know? They'd never been lied to before; had no idea someone could hint and cajole through deception to gain more for themselves. If God was going to hold that single mistake against them, then Alejandro wondered how good a Creator he served.

I'm sorry for that, Lord. It just hurts so much.

He screamed again.

The pain in his head should have pushed his brain into unconsciousness, but they'd shot the old priest with a stimulant to keep him awake while they blinded him. The darkness that now filled Alejandro's world burned as if they'd shoved two small suns into his skull.

*   *   *

"Sinclair Lewis."

Earlier that day, the middle aged, well-groomed man who'd spoken offered a half-bow in greeting. The priest returned the gesture.

"Like the author?" Alejandro asked.

Lewis straightened and blinked. "I'm afraid I'm not familiar with that person, Father." His accent had the skipping lilt of someone native to the region, an Afrikaner's hint of British, but long-mingled with an older, heavier Zulu.

Alejandro explained, "He was from a long time ago, somewhere between now and Shakespeare."

His host, perhaps annoyed how the conversation had begun, waved the words away and gestured for him to follow. "I'm surprised you came, aside from the risks inherent with such long travel given your age, no offense ..."

"None taken." *Establishing dominance*, he thought, a lion circling its rival for control of the pride. Lewis was not incorrect, however. Alejandro turned eighty-one only three weeks earlier during a trip that was, at times, excruciating. He never enjoyed spin gravity. Nor did his knees.

Lewis continued, always a half step ahead. "I thought you and your ilk's obsession with spreading your beliefs into the universe would keep you moving forward, not back to this forgotten hellhole. Excuse my language, Father."

"Please, call me Andro. I'm honestly not comfortable with the archaic title of Father."

"I couldn't do that, Father. I've too much respect for your position."

Alejandro shrugged, not taking the bait by getting into a philosophical discussion on Matthew 23. He'd always disliked the honorific 'Father' for someone in his profession. Many people still felt the need to use it, ironically, *except* Church leadership. His denomination had changed much over the years. The shattered post-War Catholic church had merged with a number of more moderate Protestant denominations, partly for reform and partly for survival. The Apostolic Christian Church had emerged from the ashes of humanity's near ruin during the Final War as a driving force for the

Christian faith, even with its constant bickering over inane matters as calling its priests "Father," or for that matter still using the term "priests." Neither was required. People still used them.

He suspected this man, walking a half-step in front of him, used it as an insult.

The corridor was sparsely-adorned. Aside from anonymous doors every four meters or so, nothing hung on the walls except a single adhesive label outlining the emergency exit route. The building was a composite of five single-story structures radiating from a central reception area. From the sky, it looked like a giant snowflake. Closer in it was worn and dirty and fallen to disrepair like everything else on Earth. Even the air was infused with what could only be called *dread*. Ridiculous, of course. Biases against the broken world of his childhood, after spending nearly a half century serving the faithful *out there*.

He didn't want to be here; had grown to think of those *other* places as home; Earth was only a memory.

Now that he was back, something definitely felt wrong. Not just in this neglected office structure. That sensation of dread had woken him more often than usual last night, brought him to his knees in prayer. He sighed, knowing he was thinking like a worried old man. Alejandro wasn't the only one who felt this way, however, even among his peers.

Whatever was happening, *if* anything was happening, it had brought the priest unknown light years back through two interstellar Holes from his current home on the planet Toojay, to sit with this man in a fading office park in the South African township of Boksberg. The town was a confusing jumble of new and aging structures, its population having skyrocketed with neighboring Johannesburg's rise as one of the world's major ports, as had many regions in the southern hemisphere untouched by the devastation of the War. In its aftermath, global re-population and rezoning had redrawn borders in Africa and South America as the new, unified human government rose to power to bring populations together. It succeeded, more or less, over the past hundred years. Especially once the Holes were discovered and humankind moved beyond its original, shattered foundation.

All the while, something was happening here, back home. The people left behind had grown angry, bitter towards anything to do with the old ways of things. Faith in God, especially. The Government still enforced its primary law: persecution of religious beliefs was punishable by imprisonment or death. It had been a way to stem the increasingly bloody conflicts spawned by those using *religion* as an excuse to kill. This had been one of the reasons for the Final War, after all. The law worked, until now. The iron grip holding Man's innate need to be an idiot began to loosen when the seat of human power moved farther out into other planetary systems.

"Please, Father, have a seat. Our transport has been delayed but is expected to arrive within the hour."

They entered an office. He took in a long breath, tried to concentrate.

Like everything else here, the room was plain, though Lewis had posted a few pictures on a nearby shelf, presumably of his family. A large screen was mounted on a movable base by the door, positioned to face his desk. On it were a myriad of windows with text too small to see from this vantage, pictures of rocks and one lone tree. In the center of the screen one image drew his attention: an open field of scrub with a massive circle of dark soil in the center. It looked like mud, but Alejandro knew better from the reports he'd been reading.

"That's it?"

"Yes. A mostly open field known as Gordon's View, twenty kilometers from the center of Benoni along the northeastern border."

Alejandro half-turned in his chair, watching as if something might suddenly happen in the window to explain everything, including why he was back on Earth in the first place. "How far is it from *here*?"

"About forty-six kilometers." The man tapped his desk and said, "Veleni, please bring in the sandwiches and drinks for our guest."

A woman's voice replied, "For you as well?"

Sinclair Lewis seemed to consider, then, "Yes, why not? Two of whatever you have."

Alejandro wondered where she was, one of the rooms they'd passed or another wing. Lewis tapped something else and nodded to the board. A ground-level image of the region in question filled the entire screen. The darkening land surged upward a half-meter, settled down, rose again.

"Looks like it's breathing," he whispered, feeling the dread settle deeper in his chest. *Lord,* he prayed, not for the first time, *if the theory of the Rapture is more than wishful thinking, I have* no *objection to being taken now. Anytime, in fact.* He knew better; knew for reasons he would never understand this side of eternity that this pale, sad room was to be his Garden of Gethsemane. Months ago, as he prepared to leave the planet Toojay, Alejandro understood one primary truth: if he went back to Earth, he would die.

Lewis rose from his desk and walked to the board, eyes alight in its afterglow. He touched his fingertips gently onto the image. The board's AI System understood the gesture was not a command. Forty-six kilometers away, the ground continued its labored, dark breathing. "This planet has been discarded by your God, Mister Gutierre, or Cruz, which ever it is, and has been given to the beast."

Your will be done.

"I don't know about God turning his back on you, Sinclair.

But there is something dark about that plot of land." His heart was beating fast. Alejandro tried to remind himself there was no fear in love. It didn't work, but had been worth a try.

The man spun towards him so quickly the old priest leaned back in his chair. "Not just that plot of land, you pathetic worm. All of this," he gestured to the room, the sky, the world itself, "is infected with my master's presence now. You felt it. I'm certain you would have *had* to."

Alejandro, for a heartbeat, considered arguing the point. It wouldn't matter. "Yes."

Sinclair smiled. "Good boy." He reached up and actually patted him on the head, pressing down the thin gray hair and moving his palm around as if smearing something into it. "You understand, don't you? I assume that is why you're here, at least in part?"

Alejandro nodded, not fully understanding any of it at all but playing the role he'd been given, then reached up and, gently as possible - which was not as gentle as he intended, one final act of defiance - pushed his host's arm away.

"Good, good." Unphased by the gesture, the well-dressed man walked back to the board. "I had a dream, Father Alejandro Gutierrez Cruz, that you would be sitting here in the final moment when the master rises and takes his throne." At that they both stared at the image, as if that would cue the ground to suddenly swell upwards and explode in demonic rage. Neither happened. It continued rising, falling, rising again. Lewis seemed disappointed. The food arrived, a welcome distraction.

Sandwiches, freshly made. Wrapped in paper, not bioplas, as everything had been on the months' travel to Earth. Two glasses of water. Alejandro had to assume the water was tap and not sterilized, but he'd had his shots so hopefully any repercussions from local microbes wouldn't be too incapacitating.

They ate and drank in unhurried silence. His host occasionally tapped his desktop which was lighted with dozens of windows. He would read one or another, then swipe it aside, ignoring his guest. Alejandro was content with that, glancing casually at the messages and news vids passing under his plate as he ate from the corner of the desk.

In this way they finished their meals, before Lewis wiped his left palm across his face, beginning from the forehead, slowly down the nose and mouth until the small tuft of beard at his chin was pressed flat and cleaned of any crumbs. To Alejandro, it felt like he was slowly donning a mask through which he smiled politely, then rose from the chair.

"Well," the man said, almost reluctantly, "you've come all this way, let's hop into the shuttle so you can see the place for yourself."

Alejandro stood, glad he'd come wearing normal, civilian clothes and not the usual ceremonial robes of his ACC priesthood. Where they were going, where the earth had been scorched and darkened for no reason anyone was able to discern, already had a history. On that site, years before, a mob attacked a small church which had setup inside a diner. The diner itself was gutted by fire. Three people, including one of the attackers had died. The young pastor escaped losing part of his left arm. It was a scene echoed in various flavors throughout the heavier-populated regions of the planet, as if whatever sense of control, of communal brotherhood holding the post-war society together for a hundred years was quickly and violently unraveling.

God's Spirit has left the Earth to its own destruction. Someone said this to him during the last connecting flight here. Muttered apprehensively by a middle-aged security consultant. He was traveling for one last gig before retirement. The closer they got to Earth, the darker the man's mood became and the more he felt the need to talk to the only religious person on the ship. At one point the consultant announced to anyone who'd listen that he was staying on the ship and buying himself a ticket back to his family, rather than ever "set foot below."

Alejandro hoped he had.

The dark spot of land he'd come to see, and possibly die at, had begun in the place where the diner once stood before it was demolished. Everyone assumed it was *literally* scorched earth. Nothing grew there again. Like ink dropped into the center of a glass of water, the black began to spread until it was a near-perfect circle twenty-seven meters wide.

And, apparently, now breathing like a cancerous lung.

The shuttle was not the flying kind. Round wheels, solar panels on top. The trip over well-paved roads took an hour. Sinclair parked by a set of three modular buildings thirty meters or so from the spot's periphery. Outside, on a foldout deck and already perfecting their posturing, angry glares, four men and one woman waited. Alejandro would have laughed at their absurdity if the threat wasn't so real.

*   *   *

The pain dulled to an insistent throb in the center of his head. The headache had burrowed too deep to ever be rid of. Maybe, when they'd taken his eyes, his tormentors hadn't been careful and scorched an actual part of his brain.

Over the past couple of hours, the ground under the building rocked and swayed as if he'd been abandoned in the keel of a ship at sea. Either they'd dragged the modular unit, his prison, across the scorched zone or the dead, breathing area had accelerated its expansion.

They would be back, to kick or hit or pluck more from him. Days and nights had no meaning. There would be no more light for him this side of the veil. His captors were making certain his new life here, in darkness, would last as long as possible. Sacrificing him in painful increments to whatever dark power they believed existed under the earth.

He was beginning to believe it was all true.

Lord, what purpose does my existence serve now? Why have I come; what does any of this mean?

One statement alighted on Alejandro's mind. It could simply have been his own fevered brain grasping for reasons. The statement, however, carried a certainty the old priest had come to recognize as the Spirit's voice.

Witness the end.

"End of all things," he muttered, a mixture of excitement and deep sadness washed through him. A little disappointment, too, if this meant the obsessive, literal translations of John's Revelation, or the prophecies tacked to the end of the book of Daniel, might be true. Some cases in recent history had made it seem so, like the Final War. Not that *every* World War hadn't been attributed to end times. Now, though? The ground darkening, breathing, a pervading evil in the air, a sense of abandonment by God Himself, even among whatever elect remained. The Church, on this planet, reviled and rejected by the population.

"Stop," he muttered, wondering if anyone else was in the room but also no longer caring. He was being an idiot. Witness the end of what? Everything? All of the planets along the *Array*, the series of new Earth's God had given His people? All of it, gone?

No, the inner voice which might be his own mind replied. *There are more doors than these to open. But this planet has been too long poisoned by sin.*

It was an exciting thought, if true. More worlds, and more beyond them. But here … man ruined what he'd been given. Jesus was weeping for it even now as He'd done to Jerusalem thousands of years ago.

The floor tilted again.

Maybe his captors had fled.

A laughter bounced through the room, deeper and more hateful than the jeers of the men and woman who'd surrounded Alejandro at his arrival, who used pipes or rope, no weapon that might kill him too quickly, hitting, ripping at his clothes, causing new levels of pain each time they struck. In those early days, their sounds were rage and pain set loose against an anonymous target. He had become a goat to be dragged out of the city gates. Their laughter during more recent beatings had been tinged with fear and perhaps a great sadness. Not so, this new sound which now drifted blessedly away. No fear or hurt in that laugh, but all of it -

"Stop it!" He curled his broken and naked body tighter into a ball, the act painful and exactly what he needed to clear his thoughts. "Do not play into this. Do *not*."

His mind was failing. Hopefully, his body would follow soon. Every corner of his compressed universe screamed in agony. He screamed, too, gave the pain a voice. Better than to dwell upon the illusions he'd been building inside his head.

All of it is real, said a voice biting at his ear, digging into his shattered head. He lashed out with one arm but connected with nothing. The room tilted again, and again until his body filled with a nauseating vertigo. He rolled along the angle, crashed into a wall which then fell away from him. Outside suddenly, Alejandro rolled through mud and broken fiberglass and plastic. Something bit into his arm and shoulder. He crawled away, felt for the first time in too long the fresh, cool air around him. The ground rose, and he rolled with it. Damp in this place, cool. Night maybe, but he would never be able to tell again.

Witness. This thought, calm. He was covered in mud, crawling away from wherever he'd been, knowing this might be opening old injuries but what did that matter?

At least he was in motion.

What could he witness with no eyes?

A nervous rumbling began around him, then the breaking of stones. Were those trees falling, as well? Hard to differentiate sounds, only what images each brought to mind. The ground beneath him split apart and his right leg dropped into a crevice. Mud and dirt shuddered around it as the earth closed over it and pressed and pressed until Alejandro no longer felt true pain. What was left of him to suffer?

Under the rumbling and dying of his immediate world, the deep laughter returned, threaded with a background chorus of screams. The two sounds twisted together like wire. There were other voices, too, other screams more distant, perhaps wailing against whatever was happening. What were *they* seeing?

Newer voices joined in the chorus, but these shouted praises once reserved for God alone. As the crevice closed completely around his leg, he distinctly heard a "hallelujah" and "praise you." They were *not* praising God.

Alejandro's body twisted in time with the shaking Earth then everything rose up again and tossed the priest into the air. He landed on a reasonably flat surface. For a breath's time all was still, then the planet seemed to explode around him. Showered in rocks and dirt, he was struck by something large and heavy which rolled away to his right.

The old man shouted, "Enough! I have had enough!"

Something settled beside him, a rock or fallen tree trunk. He grabbed onto it and with his remaining leg forced himself to stand. The only sounds of existence were the grinding Earth and tearing roots, something like metal screeching and falling aside. The sky had fallen then was tossed back up. Everything that happened played out in whatever images his adrenaline-spent brain could cull from the noise surrounding his shattered body.

Everything fell into silence, a distant rumble like thunder rolling at the end of a storm. His hearing or, perhaps, his entire body was finally failing. One leg gone; he was likely bleeding out, leaning against the vibrating trunk/stone, refusing to fall. If Alejandro was to blindly witness whatever was happening, he would do it now with whatever strength God had left for him.

"I am your, mmm," an unwanted moan escaped as pain shot up his right side. "Blind, I am your witness, Lord," *whatever it will serve, let your will be done.* He hadn't strength to say these final words out loud.

Something massive rose up before the broken old man standing against the altar-like boulder in the dimming twilight. He saw none of it. Within his own, personal darkness, he witnessed the final departure of the Spirit from this shattered place, and the freeing of something dark and malignant, rising to complete its purpose in the world.

Finally, gratefully, Alejandro Gutierrez Cruz was set free.

An Introduction to "The Fall"

I firmly believe that every time we read Scripture, even words we've read before, Jesus has something new to say through them. This happened for me earlier with "The Forgotten Man," where the Spirit told me that the story of Telemachos Galanos needed to be told. Here, the words of Psalm 14 said to me, *We are not done here; you have two more stories to tell.* First, I need to show one of the crew actually falling to Earth (until now I wasn't actually sure if they'd literally or figuratively "fallen" into this dark world). Second, I imagined a refuge of sorts in the middle of all this chaos, a throwback to the mountains John Roy had been dreaming of in Chapter 11. Not to get too Matrix-y, but a Zion.

The timelines in this next story might be a little confusing, but bear with me, it'll all come clear by the end, I promise.

Psalms 11 through 14 follow a theme for me. I actually broke a lesser rule and peeked ahead to Psalm 15 to see if its tone was different. It is. Phew. *So*, said I, *fine, we'll return to this dark place one more time.*

God's never done until He says so, anyway.

Psalm 14 - The Fall

Do all these evildoers know nothing?

They devour my people as though eating bread;
   they never call on the Lord.
But there they are, overwhelmed with dread,
   for God is present in the company of the righteous.
You evildoers frustrate the plans of the poor,
   but the Lord is their refuge.

Oh, that salvation for Israel would come out of Zion!
   When the Lord restores his people,
   let Jacob rejoice and Israel be glad!

Psalm 14:4-7 (NIV)

Nylah blinked; nose pressed into the soft mattress. For a moment she forgot where this mattress had come from, how she'd gotten here. It was comfortable, and part of her didn't want to remember. She thought about the fading dream instead. Home again on Eden. The Mother planet of all human life since her kind's expansion through the Array. She hadn't dreamed of home in over a year. Eden had been — still was as far as she knew — a planet lush with forests and life, a gift from God after humanity nearly destroyed the original planet they'd been given. New doors opened for them just in time, doors leading home to Eden, and beyond. She'd been born there, her great grandfather one of the first generation to settle. These memories brought others: friends' faces drifting past....

Something dinged beside her.

Nylah Bagdonas blinked, struggled to hold onto the dream, memories of grass in her yard, fields leading to forests with paths, small animals running about. Smell of shonteys blooming outside her bedroom window. Her mother loved those plants, grew them everywhere. In Spring, Nylah would be overwhelmed by their cloying scent, more prominent in the mornings as dew settled and triggered their unique pheromonic responses.

Ding again.

She rolled over, saw the room, the table beside her and half wall separating the sleeping and living sections. Her gilded world crystallized and erased the smell of the flowers. Nylah pushed aside the blanket and swung her legs over the edge of the bed, tapped the black box on the table so it wouldn't ding again. The box was plain, featureless, but could display the time or show an image from outside as a hologram, talk to her in a soft female System voice if she wanted to catch up on the news. She did not, nor ask what day it was. She'd done that yesterday. The last thing Nylah wanted was for Constantine to realize something was wrong with his Attending. She had a household to run, even if her Alpha more often directed his attention to the younger ones. There'd been two other Attendings when she'd fallen from the sky, but they'd long ago disappeared and been replaced with these younger women. A common occurrence for anything, or anyone, Constantine had no further use for.

Nylah was his secret pet, the angel who'd lost her wings and fallen into his arms from the abyss. She'd played along in those early days, confused and disoriented but clinging privately to what had come before, what *must* have come before - Eden and school and the academy and her rise to First Officer alongside John Roy aboard the... she blinked. *Remember, you have to remember.* Like previous mornings, she'd lost the ship's name. Most names of the crew as well. Not John's. Nor Jun Wang's ... no, wait, Jun had preferred Wang Jun, keeping the pattern of her ancestral line, family name first. Jun had died.

Jun had died.

An image wedged like an old photograph into her brain, Jun's body a swaying reed attached to the floor by her magnetic boots, no helmet, staring into some void only she could see. So many other moments and pictures and names falling away. Enough that Nylah wasn't certain how many she'd lost.

The box beside her bed dinged again. *I will rise, and not be afraid. There is no fear in love. I love nothing, am losing everything, have lost everything. Except you, Lord. Be with me.*

These secret words, or those like them, were a mantra recited to push her from bed every morning. Ironically, in her old life she'd been apathetic to the concept of God. Now, the universe into which she and her crew had been harpooned and dragged against their will might very well be hell, itself. Only when she'd fallen into this nightmare did she begin to earnestly cry out to Him.

The *anomaly*, they'd called it, in that brief, final hour of their old lives. Its heavy darkness had choked and crushed her to the point she'd no choice but to scream to the God that so many in the old worlds believed in without question. They'd been brought here, condemned by some Power to this this insane, dystopian world she suspected might be a version of Earth, long separated from the other planets, taken over by a darkness beyond anything she could have envisioned in her saturnine youth.

At least, Nylah assumed the others had been dragged here. Thirty-seven years, and she'd never seen another person from the ship, no reports of others falling from of the sky. Not that reliable news traveled well, especially to this place, nor had she personally interacted with more than the dozen staff here in The Kingdom and whatever dark, leering guests Constantine might invite to *pay their respects*.

Maybe the anomaly had been created by some force or technology here on this world. If so, she'd seen no evidence of it. For all she knew the others had been deposited somewhere entirely *other*, some hitherto unknown world. That idea frightened her more than being the only one who'd survived. Not that her specific corner of *this* world was completely dark. It could be wonderfully light compared to most others below, if she only would let go of what she knew.

What she knew seemed to be falling away a little every morning, anyway.

Her mind was failing. But she dared not tell anyone.

Constantine would eventually discover that his secret toy had a few new cracks. Unlike her, the man never aged, at least not as quickly as Nylah and the other Attendings in his Kingdom. That was what he called this place, this comfort-draped prison, *The Kingdom*. Rumors of him drinking human blood, giving his soul over to the demon or whatever was ruling down on the surface. Only rumors. He was too spiteful to age the way people expected him to, and would never, ever, give his heart or time to anyone around him who might *reflect* his true mortality. If one held onto possessions too long, they became a reflection, and her *own* reflection showed her mortality more every year.

"Are you feeling well?" asked the dispassionate female voice inside the box. System had probably noted Nylah was still sitting on the side of the bed.

"I'm fine, thank you." Better move now. Get back into the routine.

What *was* her routine? Pee. She needed to pee, clean her teeth then everything else would come back. It always did. And would again, until it didn't, then she would disappear like the others, fallen angel or not.

*   *   *

Thirty-seven years earlier, John Roy found himself also falling from the sky. Everything that had come before, the seconds or years spent inside the madhouse that was the anomaly where his mind and soul reeled in disgust and terror, all of it forgotten as he suddenly appeared in bright sunlight above the trees.

Wide eyes desperately tried to fix on the world spinning around him outside the helmet's visor - blue sky then ground then a flash of what might be a mountain then clouds rolling over then more blue sky. Something like a massive arm grabbed him in a sharp, momentary grip, breaking its fingers as well as something inside John. He bounced away and fell again. A tiny part of his mind, which had mostly shut down during the transition into this place, understood that he'd landed in a tree, falling and snapping along its branches, tumbling again without obstacle until he hit a new branch large enough to shatter most of the helmet's visor and send long shards into his face. He felt nothing, considered all of this as a bystander in this numb moment of panic, including the realization that this last impact would have crushed his skull if he hadn't been suited up. When he landed across the next branch everything exploded in pain and light then blessed, welcome darkness.

He awoke later to this pain, face-down, cheek pressed against a jagged remnant of his visor, forehead resting on actual ground. He raised his head enough to realize that he was able to do so. No spinal injury, not enough to paralyze him completely. His right arm was twisted behind him, but his fingers could wiggle, feeling inside the gloves. He couldn't feel his legs, or tell where they were. Maybe his back was shattered....

Eyes opened again, the lighting had changed, a shadow

stretching longer than before from what seemed to be a deep red maple tree. Time passed. Still no pain. Tired, though. Sound of footsteps, light, tentative. Wolves, maybe, or whatever would pass for them on this planet. The steps were cautious, unsure what had brought them this meal but moving forward out of hunger. He took in a deep breath, felt fire in his chest, let it out, moaned aloud, not caring if the things heard him. Closing his eyes for the final time, he prayed to a God he suddenly craved to believe in that he would not wake while the beasts ate him.

The agony when he *did* awaken later was as fierce and terrifying as he imagined. Neck, legs, stomach … everywhere, they tore into him. He screamed, unable to lash out. One of the animals shooshed him and told him he was lucky. John wanted to tell them being eaten alive wasn't considered luck where *he* came from. He drifted into one valley of jagged pain after another, realizing that nothing was actually touching him, nothing was tearing him apart. His body was doing that fine on its own.

And he'd been turned over, onto his back.

He risked opening his eyes. Sunlight flashed in the distance, low to his right beyond the cracked rim of his helmet. He was moving, or the trees were moving. The motion made him nauseous. Neck muscles screamed in protest but he had to turn his head, craned his neck as far out of the broken suit as possible, then the vomit came. It splatted on someone's hand and legs. That person cursed and raised a dripping hand as if to strike him, then fell back, out of line of sight. John closed his eyes, having seen enough. Wolves didn't carry their prey on stretchers. The world, wherever this was, moved above him. Sunlight like his home's flashed beyond his lids, and soft mutterings of voices danced in circles. Not English, or maybe he was too broken to process their words. Was he home?

He wiggled his toes, finally able to feel them inside the

boot. One boot. The other foot was bare, cool air dancing between his toes. For all he knew he had no feet, everything merely phantom sensation. More mutterings, flashes of sunlight, when an idea came into existence which nearly sent him crying in either relief or despair. All of it, his entire life before the arrow dragged them away, had been a dream, albeit a vivid one. An hallucination suffered from what apparently had been a bad fall from a cliff or a plane. Failed chute perhaps. He'd free-fallen into the woods and imagined everything else, rising from his chair as they entered the anomaly, his mind and body squeezed into a single, terrified scream. In the Holes, the normal passages between planetary systems in the Array, this effect lasted only a few seconds, connecting his mind to everyone's around him. Here, he'd been alone, no connection and no end to the hallucinatory swirling colors and compression and racing at speeds beyond comprehension until he wanted everything to end and tear him apart because he should not be going this fast, the terror of a flying nightmare gone wrong, vertigo at levels beyond understanding. And the face, the face that was not a face but light and explosion and power and knowledge and he had screamed in silence knowing he was not truly screaming but dying -

John Roy jerked awake on the cot.

Dream, only a dream.

All of it.

All of what?

He would remember. In time.

But this here, now, was not a dream. Based on the bursts of pain that broke through his body, his brain had finally decided he was ready to feel the injuries' full effects. Shock wearing off, no more pretending *this* life wasn't real. He would die facing whatever this was as best he could.

"What is he saying?" someone muttered above him. Another voice shooshed the first, said he was delirious. Maybe they were speaking English after all.

He tried to move again, but everything hurt too much. Arms and legs could be forced to twitch but no more. Broken, possibly in many places.

"Calm down. I know it hurts, but try to stay still. We're almost there."

He moved his head despite the pain, could not focus on the face above him. He whispered, "You speak…" but he got no further.

The blurry man seemed to nod. Said again, "We're almost there."

Almost where?

*   *   *

Thirty-seven years later, Nylah Bagdonas was summoned by Constantine himself. This of all mornings, when she'd sat too long on the side of the bed like a feeble old woman. No, not feeble, not yet. Though here, on some miserable dark Earth of the future, she was older than many of the Elevated down below, for theirs was a world of deceit and treachery, everyone jockeying for a better seat. To sit at the table of someone higher, drawing closer to the royalty *they* deserve, at least in their minds. Most methods of social ascension involved the death of someone above, and of anyone who might later come up behind *them*. There seemed a stronger sense of morals and personal selflessness in the lower orders of society. The unwashed masses living in the concrete cities rolling by beneath her.

Nylah had stopped at one of the long windows facing outside. This station was in low orbit, forever circling the globe and never to venture out to the Holes and other planets beyond. There were none, anyway. The gateway to the other systems, including Eden's, had apparently closed at some point in this world's history. Closed, or ceased to exist altogether. No one knew. Those remaining here were destined to live apart from of the rest of humanity which was still expanding among the stars, she hoped, safe from the spiritual infection blanketing everything here.

The station's wide ring spun fast enough to simulate near-Earth gravity, a decent illusion except for the constant feeling like she was falling forward with every step. Her old ship had a ring like this. Outside, the planet spun like a massive glowing ball on an invisible string, circling around, coming back into view. It helped to think this way, rather than the truth - she was the one spinning. It kept the nausea at bay. In Constantine's estate room a half kilometer along the ring, the view outside was far more stable, the Earth moving only enough to register the station's - The *Kingdom*'s - orbit. Video screens pretending to be windows, images manipulated to suit his tastes. Only the best for the king and his wealth.

Outside, a round pod broke off from the side of the ring and raced towards Earth's atmosphere. Nylah forced herself to watch its progress towards the planet, swallowing the occasional need to vomit, until a brief flare of light indicated the pod's entry into the atmosphere.

It was free.

"The king is growing impatient with your tardiness, Angel," the neutral female voice of System announced from a hidden speaker above.

Angel. Fallen Angel. The pet of the king. Nylah looked left and right. The ring's corridors were awash in their usual silence, secretly bustling with servants within its unseen honeycombs, all nervously worshiping their dark deity. If one lingered too long between sections, one hadn't been assigned enough productive work. So spoke the rules of the Kingdom to those laying at Constantine's feet, if only for the chance of another day of existence in his realm.

She'd become long-inured to the insanity around her. Never ceasing to wonder, through all the subsequent years, why she'd been brought here. The act had seemed so deliberate and demanding. They'd been dragged from their old lives to this broken future world, and for what? To be entertainment for the devil?

Nylah resumed walking, instinctively wanting to appease her master, knowing she was moving closer to her death. He would toy with her a while before killing her in some terrible way. He'd long ago lost interest. She'd been showing cracks in behavior, and her reflection was something unwelcome now.

Lord, I know I've given myself to you too late, and maybe you don't even hear me, as much as it's comforted me to think you have.

It was over. All of this nonsense had to end.

If this was all punishment, I accept it. But I have to leave on my own terms, not his. I'll die never understanding why you brought me here.

She could see the feet of the guards further along the ring where the floor curved away. Nylah stopped. When they could see her fully, any option she might have would be gone. She needed to act before her mind betrayed her and any reason for leaving was lost, or muddied. Fear did that.

Show me this one time you're real. Let me leave.

Where? Behind her. She turned around. Ten meters back waited an access ladder along the outer wall. On her left was one of the occasional carpeted stairways leading to the other levels, more wasted exhibitions of grandeur. She turned around and stepped casually back from where she'd come, expecting any moment an arrow or harpoon like the one that dragged her into this world, breaking through her back and chest and pulling her into the devil's cave at the end of the hall. One step. Another. Towards the access port. A simple ladder built into the wall, leading up or down. She went down, one flight, then two, carefully stepping into the gold-adorned Reception corridor.

Everything shone gold here. Actual gold, stolen or purchased with Constantine's earnings from his thriving slave industry. The gold was melted then coated along the walls to impress anyone arriving at the station. The first thing a visitor saw as they stepped from the airlocks would be this hedonistic display of excess.

Since a pod had just left the station, there was no other flight scheduled for some time. She'd seen no transport arriving. Less chance for a full security contingent at the airlocks. Nylah stepped as casually as possible, given the speed at which her heart raced, towards Fremin Stimpson. He was a tall, burly man who'd always had a kind eye for her - *kind*, not lustful or needy in any way.

One sign, Lord. Let me leave. Show me your kindness, your love. Just once.

Nearly every person she'd read or spoken to about God - and those who spoke of such topics were few, and only with derision - insisted He had left Earth to cater to other worlds, had handed over their planet, as promised, to darkness. Nylah would have liked to read the ancient book that presumably spelled all of this out, confirm if any of it was true. That book, however, had been outlawed and purged from all systems, at least those *she* had access to. Until she saw that, Nylah wouldn't accept their arguments. God, at least the one she tried to recreate from snippets heard before the anomaly, was all she could hold on to. Especially as Constantine …

Stop. No more. She was old and beyond her usefulness and would not give him that one final pleasure of dying by his hand. This was all she had left, and the thought focused her vision, set her brows and firmed her step. It would last, this sudden power, only as long as she needed. But it *would* last. *She* would last, long enough to be free. Nylah blinked, mentally stumbling, wondering what she'd just been thinking about. *Not yet. Hold on. You're leaving.*

I'm leaving.

"Morning, Fremin," she said with a soft smile. The man smiled back, though his expression was unconcealed confusion. Was it also relief?

"Good morning, Madam Angel. A pleasure." Didn't matter how often she insisted he use her real name, she was Madam Angel. Nylah wouldn't be surprised if the penalty for calling her anything else was death.

She stood before him, trying to form the right words. Fremin shifted slightly and said, quietly, not that any volume would prevent System from hearing and relaying the words to those in power. "I thought I just heard the master summoning you."

Here we go. "You did." She cleared her throat, keeping her gaze fixed on the guard's - the man's - eyes. "He did, and it will probably be the last time I enter that door."

He looked about to object, then glanced away and nodded. They had all been informed, then, to prevent flight.

To prevent *this.*

"I'm sorry to put this on you," Nylah said. "I need to go in there." She gestured towards the airlock beside him, with the green light glowing over the door indicating the pod was already prepped and ready for departure. A required precaution but insufficient. Given the population of eighty-seven humans on board there should have been eight pods prepped and ready but, like the historic *Titanic*, only the Elevated would have access in the event of a crisis. No one else mattered in The Kingdom.

When he glanced at the airlock door, something changed. Where Nylah had expected fear or consternation, especially knowing it was his life or hers in this moment, Fremin stared back at her, took a deep breath then turned fully towards the panel beside him. He tapped a few commands, followed by a long string of numbers. She didn't understand what any of it meant but kept quiet, and waited.

The airlock door opened. The large man turned back only to press a finger to his lips and nod his head towards the waiting pod.

Could he be sincere? She stepped past him into the small room connecting the ring to the shuttle docked against the outer hull. Fremin's fingers pressed her shoulder. *Go inside*, the touch said, *hurry*. He followed. The door closed. The guard stepped quickly to the inner door's panel. Nylah's ears popped as air pressure equalized. More tapping of commands and characters.

Fremin swallowed, sniffling as he typed. She stepped closer and glanced at his face. A tear ran down his cheek. A dozen possibilities ran through her mind, one of which was that she was doing exactly what Constantine wanted. Fremin was seconds away from tossing her out of the airlock into the cold vacuum of space.

That was fine. This, here, was a decent man. Better die by his hand than …

The inner hatch opened, and the station erupted in red lights and a deafening klaxon.

"Unauthorized access to shuttle *Behemoth* in Bay Seven," System announced, both behind them and inside the shuttle.

"Sit, there," was all Fremin said as they stepped inside. She didn't know where *there* was; with a dozen seats crammed together in the round room. She chose one, buckled herself in. The man shouted over the alarm, "Get ready."

He moved quickly, arms a blur as if these moments had been mentally rehearsed for years. Maybe they *had* been. How could Nylah have assumed she was the only person dreaming of escape? Fremin had always looked at her with genuine kindness. Which meant there *was* genuine kindness in this world.

"Fremin Stimpson," System said, "you are not authorized

to pilot this ship. You will report immediately to Senior Supervisor Duddy." It continued droning on yet seemed powerless to stop Fremin from carrying out his plan. Something to do, perhaps, with that mysterious string of characters he'd entered. An override to System's control.

The kingdom's massive ring dropped away outside the windows. The station rolled away to be replaced with Earth. Her stomach floated in odd ways, arms raised by her sides. No gravity, now that they'd detached from the spin.

She would *not* throw up. Not now.

"Guard!" a new voice screamed through the shuttle's comm system. Nylah flinched and pressed herself into the seat. Constantine's voice was normally deep and preternaturally calm but when enraged, the pitch rose to a metallic harpy's cry. After a long series of unimaginative curses, he said, "Bring her to me, or open your hatch right now and let the interior of your vessel burn. You do that and I'll consider letting your family survive this betrayal."

Fremin reached out and fumbled for the correct icon, shut down the intercom.

Would they kill his family for saving her? As if hearing her thought, the large man shouted over the roaring of the reentry flames outside the ship. "They're already gone," he said. "That monster above us simply doesn't care to know that."

"Why are you helping me?"

He only shook his head, muttered, "Have to help someone," and they were out of the flames and falling too fast towards the world below. Not a city. Their apparent landfall was a flat plain ringed by mountains. In the center spread a massive blackened crater. Nuclear blast site, maybe. They couldn't land in a hot zone, could they?

As the Earth's surface raced to meet them Nylah leaned back, or tried to. Gravity had not only returned but was pulling her towards the viewport. She fumbled along her armrest, found the button. The restraints tightened, pulled her back. She would die in a fiery explosion in the middle of a radioactive hot spot and even that ... yes, even that was fine.

Less than ten meters from impact they leveled out, skirted along the burnt landscape towards the mountains. Maybe her pilot was actually *trying* to escape, not just die by his own terms. She closed her eyes, tried to relax. There *was* no escape, not here, not ever. They'd find her eventually.

It occurred to Nylah, in this single, exhilarating moment, that she was free, all thanks to the kindness of another.

Maybe God *was* real, answering her prayer even now.

The rear half of the shuttle disappeared behind her. The wind roared with an insane, screaming cry and a moment later she was in the air, her and all the remaining passenger seats. Tumbling and twirling yet still hurtling towards the mountains which at some point had come up to meet them. The remnants of the shuttle, and Fremin himself, exploded on impact below. No, that wasn't right. The shuttle was indeed coming apart in a terrible, rolling crash, but the explosion, now far behind her, had been from something else.

The next missile screamed past her shoulder and ignited on the ground. The shock tossed her higher into the air. Only then, as she became entangled in it, did Nylah realized she'd been coasting along with a chute opened from the back of her seat. She fell to Earth for a second time in her life, knowing this would be her last.

*   *   *

John Roy watched the sun rise over the top of the Flatheads, not yet cresting the Great Northern Mountain closer by, and tried not to think about his upcoming trip to Helena. Tried not to think about anything. It had always been a hopeless endeavor for him, not thinking. Still, it was a beautiful morning here in Whitefish. Why he felt a need to leave the refuge, when the most recent supply run had been so successful, he could not explain. It was an itch he would not be able to scratch except *there*.

"Ten minutes," Vincent shouted from the other side of the cabin. John ignored him, was already dressed with coffee in hand. Everyone was allotted one cup per day, a concoction brewed from beans lovingly cultivated by Ramon and Elizabeth in a protected, fire-warmed hothouse at the corner of East Edgewood and Second Roads. Their "lab" was kept a distance from downtown in case government forces ever detected its heat signature and decided to blow it off the face of the Earth. Just in case.

John had fallen just outside of Whitefish nearly four decades ago, broken and close to death. Healing had had taken more than a year, as well as accepting he'd neither died nor fallen into a warped version of his old mountaintop dream. *That* world, including his final hours aboard the *ISS Gotottur* was not real. Only this life, where Vincent Toussaint and his crew had carried his delirious and screaming body into their town. These past thirty-seven years were the true reality, nightmarish and impossible as his home world had become.

No, not impossible. Mankind had fallen this far before, though never on such a global scale.

In his old life, the dream he sometimes found himself in was an isolated cabin nestled in the Sierra Nevada's. Montana was an eerily close cousin during its short summer season. *This* Montana, though broken like the rest of the world, was far enough from any major metropolis that its residents seemed immune to the influence of whatever sickly evil had enveloped everything else. Vincent and his crew weren't friendly, but hadn't become so jaded as to let an injured man die without reason. Of course they'd seen him appear out of a swirling hole in the air thirty-six meters above the edge of the Flatheads then fall through the treetops three kilometers beyond the cabin where he now stood. That wasn't something a person, friendly or not, normally ignored. John considered himself lucky to have fallen so far from the choking stench of any city. The closest of those was miles to the south.

The entire world crumbled under a permanent police state. A cross between Orwell and Faust. Whatever passed for modern civilization was focused within those cities, yet encroached outward a little at a time, or when it was economically feasible. Like a moral or sociological pandemic whose fingers reached even here to the old border of the US and Canadian districts. Whitefish was far enough from Helena and Missoula, and often buried under yards of snow, that it wasn't worth any Forces (loose allies as every power center tended to be) to do much more than sporadic fly-overs or an occasional visit from an official who never dressed appropriately for the weather.

He'd grown up in harsher climates, himself, as far north as you could go without hitting the Arctic Circle. That was another time, possibly another universe. When John Roy's family finally could afford to emigrate to the newly-discovered planet, Eden, the idea that Earth could fall into such chaos was not a fantasy, but a fear. Now, a hundred and seventy years, apparently, after he'd left the planet, Earth seemed ready to shrug humanity off its shoulders for good. At some point his race had assumed the role of feral, endangered species hiding in its burrows.

John sipped slowly and watched the sunrise - he needed to do this as often as schedules permitted. See the innocent perfection nature offered. Living in this climate without electricity, there was always work to be done. Schedules were lighter in the summer, allowing for some leisure, but never complacency. Winter would return, and the government had long ago cut off their electricity. Staying warm when the snow came meant firewood. A lot of it. Generators weren't an option. If rumors were to be believed (and rumor was all anyone had out here), refuges such as this had been nuked for less reason than generating their own energy.

What was one more hot zone to a government built on death?

The sun broke free over the top of Great Northern, illuminating the sickly yellow haze staining the horizon. Beyond the mountains lay a recent hot zone, somewhere near the Fort Belknap district. The best theory anyone could come up with for the government destroying whatever had been over those mountains was that the Forces intended to destroy everyone *here* in Whitefish. Something had gone wrong. The nuke detonated prematurely.

That was fourteen years ago. In sight of this cabin, an unlivable, nuclear hotspot was forever held at bay by the jet stream. He still had nightmares about the light and sound that reached their haven and spoiled the eastern horizon for a generation.

That aside, since he'd arrived among these weathered and decent people, there'd been only a handful of questionable events, and nothing since Belknap.

All these years, and John Roy still did not understand why he was here. Or if anyone else from the *Gotottur* had survived.

He savored the last sip and wondered why now, of all *nows*, he felt an obsession to leave and go southeast, past the Flatheads and Missoula into Helena. At seventy-three he was not up to battling angry hordes of whatever demons the human race had morphed into out there. Helena was on the outer edge of the blast zone, but had been abandoned as a precaution, full of long-spoiled food and irradiated husks of bodies who would not, or could not, leave the fallout-exposed region.

The radiation in that area wasn't lethal in the short-term, but it would cut one's lifespan in half if they stayed long. Many did, and died. So did everyone else, though, eventually. Helena was a city of miserable ghosts.

"We're going with you, sir," said Beal as John stepped back inside. The kid was barely twenty and already scarred, physically and spiritually, from years of labor and weather. He was one of the new generation which knew *only* this place, these people. Beal was lean and hard with long hair braided in some meaningful pattern his peers had developed as a social ranking. They were a calmer and far happier lot than their elders. Both of Beal's parents, however were now dead. His father, Kal, had fallen to pneumonia only last year. Kal and others of his generation, including Vincent and John, had built this corner of the world from a small huddle of revolutionaries and survivors into the protected, growing community it now was.

A new growth, carefully cultivated from a dying plant.

Maybe humanity's time on the planet wasn't ending, but changing, relegated to a minor player beneath the elk, and buffalo, and whatever the God Power behind everything decided to bless the world with after the disease of man.

John put an affectionate hand on the young man's shoulder and gave it a squeeze. "It would be an honor to have you join us." Across the room he noted Vincent's silent concern, then resigned nod of approval. The man had taken Beal under his tutelage after Kal's death, as there were no others in his line.

In all, the crew would be small, five of them determined to bring John Roy to the city, scour the dead structures for medicines and anything else useful (and portable), then back home again. Though no official elections were ever held, John, Vincent and a handful of others were the refuge's *de facto* leaders. Time had softened the oddness of his arrival, yet still added a tinge of legend to it. With his own scars carried from that day, he was seen as an near-reverent figure. There'd been a few cautious questions when he announced he needed to go Helena last night, but no one pressed for a reason, nor would they now.

He didn't know why he was going, anyway.

The journey took a week and a half, along whatever pathways were the least obstructed without exposing themselves to satellites, staying away from the abandoned highways, especially. No cover. They walked for ten hours a day. The fifth day brought explosions and the unmistakable sound of something crashing in the distance. They moved more cautiously after that, but nothing else disturbed their travel, or the peace of the forest.

On day seven, they lost sight of the road they'd been moving parallel to and spent most of the daylight working their way back.

After reaching Helena they slept in an empty roadside motel until late the next morning. That afternoon, Annie Spotted Horse hit the jackpot with a supply of penicillin and other medicines John couldn't pronounce, in a basement of an abandoned drug store.

On the morning they'd voted to return home to avoid possible radiation poisoning, a woman wearing a hoodie limped crookedly from a broken-glass diner on North Beattie Street. She fell unconscious in Beal's arms.

Eventually, the gray-haired woman told her story in a broken dialect most had trouble following without frequent interruptions. This, in the lobby of a half-collapsed Sunrise Glory Hotel. She'd been treated for whatever wounds Annie could attend to with supplies on hand. The language barrier was wide between the worlds she and this group had come from (both spoke an English differently-evolved from each other), so she supplemented her story with hand gestures and drawings in a notebook found behind the front desk.

The woman had been a slave most of her adult life to an Elevated warlord who lived perpetually in orbit. She'd escaped a few days ago with the help of someone in his security force. It was her shuttle they'd heard crash the other day.

John said little, staring at the stranger with such an intensity she finally returned his gaze, and only then, in that moment of full connection, did they both truly understand who the other was.

For an extended moment of confusion and vertigo, John Roy's world was shattered by the confirmation that the life he'd lived before the fall had *indeed* happened. He hadn't understood how much he had written it off as inconsequential, since none of it would ever matter in his personal universe again.

For Nylah Bagdonas, the abandoned hotel's sagging lobby, in a city full of the dead, was suddenly filled with the light of God.

Part Four: Bertrand, Monday and TinTin

An Introduction to "The Promise"

OK, everyone, settle down. I know. The stories got pretty dark for a while back there. Return with me now to present day and a quiet little town called Hillcrest.

Let me tell you what I prayed, before reading Psalm 15: *Lord, let the story you give me this time be light-hearted, even humorous. People are going to need a laugh by this point.*

Here's the problem. I've got a very strange sense of humor. I mean, Stephen Wright-strange (look him up). As I wrote the following story – which is, in fact, a novella or short novel – I laughed out loud more than once. Laughed a lot, actually. I am my own biggest fan, no doubt. I hope saying that doesn't ruin it for you. If so, I was lying. The next story is dumb and not funny at all.

So, one big rule as you read "The Promise": do not take it seriously.

Rule two: yes, I broke the fourth wall (or is the fifth wall?) and made myself a character. If Stephen King could do it in his *Dark Tower* series, so can I (*but, Dan, you always said that's what ruined the series for you* . . . be quiet, random voice.)

Rule three: and this is just for my wife – yes, there are characters named Monday and TinTin in the book. Remember, you're supposed to love me unconditionally.

Rule four: There is no rule four. Just enjoy the fact that no one gets melted or has their eyes removed in the following piece. Celebrate small victories. Again, if you don't think the next story is at least a little amusing, be content with knowing your hapless author felt better getting it out of his system.

Psalm 15 - The Promise

Who may worship in your sanctuary, Lord?
　　Who may enter your presence on your holy hill?
Those who lead blameless lives and do what is right,
　　speaking the truth from sincere hearts.
Those who refuse to gossip
　　or harm their neighbors
　　or speak evil of their friends.
Those who despise flagrant sinners,
　　and honor the faithful followers of the Lord,
　　and keep their promises even when it hurts.
Those who lend money without charging interest,
　　and who cannot be bribed to lie about the innocent.
Such people will stand firm forever.

Psalm 15 (NLT)

I

"So, you're supposed to only hate sinners if they stink?"

"Stink?"

"Smell."

Bertrand took the Bible from him, keeping the page open with his thumb. He looked at the Psalm. It didn't take long to realize what his friend was talking about. He lowered the book, still keeping thumb in place because this conversation was *not* over until he was sure Monday knew what he was planning.

And yes, his friend's name was Monday. A long story that will be explained, eventually.

"*Flagrant* sinners, buddy. Not fragrant."

Monday scratched the stubble of his beard, no more than two days' unshaven but still more than most students in their class. He could pass for someone older, until he started talking.

"Then what does 'flagrant' mean?"

Bertrand - he preferred Bertrand, not Bert nor *Trend* as a couple of cutting-edge wannabe's from Art class once tried (though admittedly, he didn't care much for the name Bertrand, either) - held the book a little more towards him and muttered, "Really bad or something like that. Figure it out from the context."

"No."

"My point," he said, louder, "is that I was elected Senior class president after promising to do a bunch of stuff I never planned on actually doing." He pointed randomly towards the nearest window. "That is, until I was in the parking lot after school yesterday and TinTin Gambrelli shoves *this* at me." With his free hand he pulled a folded piece of notebook paper from his back pocket. With the open bible in his right, he looked like a preacher who used too many notes for a sermon.

Monday scratched his cheek and said, "His metaphors are pretty bad, lately."

It was a simile not a metaphor.

"Yea, whatever, point's the same."

Bertrand glanced around him, as he always did when his best friend addressed the narrator - that's what he called it, *addressing the narrator,* and he'd done it for as long as the two had known each other which was nearly their whole lives, since they were three years old -

"Dude."

…Bertrand pulled a folded sheet of notebook paper from his back pocket and waved it between them.

"What's that?"

"Every promise I ever made to get elected class president."

Monday laughed, but his expression quickly fell. "Wait, seriously? I thought you were going to tell me it was a love letter."

"Please."

"Seriously, she digs you."

"Digs?"

"Yea, I'm bringing it back. So, she wrote down *every* campaign promise?"

"As far as I can tell, yea."

Monday smirked. "Kind of stalker-ish."

"You think? She's in the chess club. What else is someone like her going to do except something like this?"

His friend shrugged but said nothing, instead checked the time on his phone then started walking. Bertrand re-pocketed the paper and kept in step, waiting for a better response. Lunch was over and the first bell had rung.

As they walked, Monday said, "Ok, so she wrote everything down. Are you seriously going to do everything you promised? If I'm not mistaken, you said - totally as a joke, and even *I* knew that - you'd solve world hunger. World hunger! Not sure that's solvable."

Bertrand put a hand on Monday's shoulder, stopping them in the middle of the hallway. High school humanity flowed around them like a Boston molasses flood.

Monday muttered, "Seriously?"

Bertrand held up the bible, again, having to shake it a few times to work it back open to the right page. "I got home, and opened this as usual to read the next psalm and it was *this*. Of all one hundred and fifty David-rants, it was this one!"

Monday smiled. "Have I told you lately how cool it is that you're so into your faith, even in the throes of this satanic high school phase of our lives?" When he got no reply, he added, more seriously, "So God's kicking you in the butt to keep your word?"

Bertrand nodded. "I think so, yea."

"World hunger?"

Bertrand took in a breath, let it out slowly as the second bell went off. "Yep."

Though he was panicking because his OCD screamed at the thought of being late for anything, ever, Monday still took the time to put an affectionate hand onto his best friend's cheek. At the same time, he shrugged Bertrand's hand off his shoulder. "Let me know if I can help with that." Then he was down the hall rushing towards English class.

Not as concerned with the second bell, Bertrand considered the words written before him in the Psalm. He *should* take another look at TinTin's list but was afraid to; pretty sure it included a promise to repair the damage of global warming.

II

Her name was Tina, short for Kristina. After she and her mother moved from California to Massachusetts the summer before high school, she began introducing herself as TinTin and avoided eye contact. Not that she didn't watch everything around her. Her calling, at least in this new phase, was to notice everything and write it down. Tina wasn't sure what she wanted to *do* with all of the scratches in her notebooks (she was on her fourteenth since Freshman year), something between novelist and preacher. She still had this final year to figure out a direction.

The fact that she was able to keep herself in the background of *any* public high school was an impressive accomplishment. Bad as her California years had been, *high school* boys practically drowned in hormones. That, coupled with the unavoidable fact that she was, despite her attempts at hiding it, one of the more attractive girls in her class, made staying under their addle-brained radars difficult on the best of days. She also happened to be one of the smartest in her grade, try as she might to keep her grades tempered. Truth was, deliberately giving the wrong answer felt as much like cheating as copying someone's answer (which in this school would guarantee a lower GPA).

So, she kept herself tucked under a veil of crazed long hair and baggy clothes, eyes cast down whenever someone glanced her way. She spoke only when called upon and joined clubs where, if her secret was revealed, the students would be too terrified to act on it, like the chess club. Of course it also helped that she loved the game.

All of this subterfuge drove her bonkers sometimes. Even in the glow of recent movements to lift women's rights to hitherto unreachable levels, forcing men's chins to face the ridiculous gauntlets thrown at her sex every day, boys *this* age were mostly too stupid to manage any decent awakening of spirit.

Not all of them. There was a smattering of quasi-self-actualized individuals who managed to keep their gender's biology in check, who carried themselves a few notches above Neanderthal. Like Bertrand. His buddy with the weird(er) name was alright, too, but he played football and thus aligned himself too closely with the Dark Side.

But Bertrand. He was sort of good looking, in a gangly, too-tall-too-fast kind of way. More importantly, he carried himself upright, was comfortable in his own skin and didn't care what anyone thought about him. In a good way. There were jerks who felt the same way, but that kind of self-love bordered on sociopathic.

Most of all, Bertrand was comfortable and open with his faith. Tina kept a growing collection of bumper-sticker meanings of life. One of the biggies: *There is nothing hotter than a man who loves Jesus and his neighbor, and doesn't hide either fact.* A person like that truly lived.

So, yea, she stalked him and, embarrassingly enough, pined for him on paper whenever her mind drifted his way while she wrote in her journal. They'd shared classes since Freshman year, but she hadn't noticed who he was, inside, until late Sophomore. Not until recently, during his ridiculous, albeit funny campaign speech in the auditorium last month did she decide it was time to start connecting with the guy more directly.

Time was running out. They were rounding the final corner of high school.

He'd promised so many things during that speech. Anyone with half a brain (which made up half the senior class) understood most were spoken in jest, a way to poke fun at the entire political process. Still, it was a way inside his circle. She'd caught up to him in the parking lot yesterday, a page torn free from her notebook. With the space between them closing, it had occurred to her he might wind up thinking she was more than a little odd for doing this. Tina had nevertheless taken a breath and reminded herself that he *already* thought this, as did most of the school. That had been her plan from the day she moved here, wasn't it?

The tricky part would be to get his attention in a real way, then remove her mask one conversation at a time.

He'd taken the list from her but hardly spoke in reply. Only stared at what she'd written. He was actually *reading* it. She prayed more fervently in that moment for divine intervention than when her guinea pig had been acting sick when she was twelve. Squeaks still died the next day.

Now, sitting at the small desk by the window of her bedroom, staring at the oak tree as it glowed with such amazing shades of orange and red - she *thought* it was an oak tree; it made acorns so that made it an oak, right? - Tina played over the only sentence she'd managed to spit towards him in the parking lot yesterday: *I took notes on your speech; you made these promises and I was wondering since they were* promises, *when are you going to actually* do *them?*

If she'd smiled or laughed like a normal person, he'd be with her right now, *right now!!!,* at the movies or the Jolly Giant eating a vegetarian wrap, and she'd be laughing at his really funny jokes.

Instead, she'd only stared at him in the middle of the parking lot and tried not to throw up.

He'd read the list with a glimmer of scorn twinkling in his left eye - scorn! – then thanked her before walking the rest of the way to his car. He didn't say anything else. She'd impressed herself by half-shrugging and walking in the opposite direction towards her mother's old minivan, one hundred ninety thousand miles of un-coolness which she adored and thankfully had not parked anywhere near Bertrand's Honda.

Tina thought of that glimmer in his eye a lot today. Even now, staring at him on the sidewalk outside her house as he glanced down at his phone then back up.

Oh.

She murmured some unidentifiable sound and thought, *Focus focus focus.* Not understanding what was happening, even as some screaming corner of her brain wondered if she was only imagining him out there. She leaned forward and lifted the window sash, called through the screen, "Are you looking for me?"

Bertrand looked up, and when he figured out which window she was at, raised his other hand. In it was a worn-out piece of notebook paper.

Her list.

"We need to talk," he shouted back, but came no farther into her yard.

III

"What's up?" Monday asked.

Nothing. Just checking in. Giving some literary transition as Tina forces herself into some semblance of composure and heads outside to meet your friend.

"Bertrand?"

Yes. He came by her house.

Monday laughed, slapping the open Calculus book. "He really did it. By the way, she prefers TinTin for some reason."

Actually, she doesn't. Long story.

Monday shrugged. "If this wasn't due tomorrow, I'd say I'm all ears but, you know."

Yea. I should get back, anyway.

"Hey, wait, one question." He looked uneasy. It would likely be the same question he'd asked before and would ask again in the future.

What's up?

"Am... am I broken somehow? I mean mentally? Or maybe I'm a psychic or something?"

I thought you didn't believe in all that.

"Well, yea, I mean if you ask Bertrand, none of that sounds very biblical, but every now and then you just talk to me, and I can hear you. And you still insist you're not God?"

It's complicated, except for that part. Definitely not God. Just doing what I hope is some decent - if not too bizarre - work for Him.

"Everyone else thinks I have the Shining. And you way-overuse dashes. Just saying."

Well, just go with that, the Shining bit, not the dashes. Sounds less bizarre than what this really is.

"Which is?"

Simply and honestly, I'm not sure. Kind of winging this chapter. Things needed to be a bit lighter after the previous sections.

He nodded, not knowing what that meant. Monday wasn't a big reader, though he should have been. It would open up so much for him in life.

"Yea, yea," he muttered. "Homework, need to do now. Lecture me later."

OK. Sorry for the interruption. Thanks for listening.

"Mmm, hmm," he said, already working out the next problem.

IV

"Do you like your name?"

Bertrand wasn't sure how to answer that. The question came too far out of left field for a quick answer. When TinTin had finally stepped from her house, a small two-story job surrounded by a modest yard and one huge tree already exploding in Fall colors, she'd walked up and stood before him, at first only looking down at the sidewalk, hands in the pocket of a hooded sweatshirt. This question was the first thing out of her mouth.

Finally, he said, "You're an odd duck."

She looked up at him, and her eyes momentarily tore his soul free from his body. It felt so overwhelming he looked away and started walking. She muttered, "What's wrong? Should I be following you?"

She did, eventually, walking a step behind until putting on a burst of speed to keep an even pace. Bertrand glanced to his right, but she was staring straight ahead as they moved along the sidewalk. He wanted to see those eyes again, find out what that moment back there was about.

The neighborhood was a typical New England postcard suburb, with Colonials and ranches adorning roads which wound through a neighborhood Bertrand's father always called the *new development* though it had been here as long as he could remember. He and Monday would bike these streets on Halloween and make a killing in candy. Well, they used to. Both were too old for that now.

"We're just walking?" she asked.

"Yea."

"You mad?"

"Mad? No. Nothing like that." He struggled to understand why they were here in the first place, then remembered the list. Where was his head?

"Actually, a couple of things happened after you gave this to me," he didn't clarify what *this* was but assumed she knew what he meant, "and I think you might have a point." Still walking, she suddenly reached behind him and pulled the sheet free of his back pocket.

He stopped in front of a house that was raised on an awkward-sloping hill, then faced her. She stopped, too, unfolded the list, looked at it instead of him.

He said, "Are you always this forward with people?"

TinTin looked up with genuine surprise and said, "Blah blah blah blah." He thought she said that. It wasn't just her eyes. Her face, too, shaped within the dark hair, that small chin. The angel turned her head slightly and smiled.

"Shoop shoop?"

"Did you just say shoop shoop?"

She laughed. "Yes! I assume you didn't hear anything I just said before that."

This was crazy. She was crazy. *An outcast*, everyone whispered about her when she walked down the hall. He himself already tottered along some social borderline at school because he was a believer. He couldn't... *fall*, was he falling?... for the "class hoodie" (one of her lesser-known nicknames). What was happening to him?

A strange look darkened the glow which had, to that point, emanated from her perfect face. "Shoop," she whispered, not actually using the word *shoop* this time, but something far more sailor-y. "Shoop, shoop, shoop, shoop, shoop."

Then she was gone, dropping the list and turning back the way they'd come. She ran and cursed up the road then disappeared around the corner before Bertrand could understand any of what just happened.

Well, he decided, picking up the list and feeling sensation returning to his body, her exit had helped with the sudden panic rising inside of him. In truth, he'd only thought she was eccentric in a slightly annoying way. Now, it was clear she wasn't firing on every cylinder. Whatever happened earlier, whatever he'd seen in her eyes, he'd never think about again. Only focus on that sudden bout of cursing and fleeing.

All he'd done was look at her face. Like some gawking idiot.

"Excuse me!" A voice that sounded like an old person's drifted from the raised front yard beside him. Bertrand looked up. At the summit of a steep set of concrete stairs an ancient woman leaned on a walker - tennis balls attached to its feet to complete the stereotype - hmm, maybe I *do* overuse dashes - and said, "What did you say to little Kristina to make her run away like that?! She's a wonderful girl. You boys have no manners."

He didn't know what to say, only glanced to his left towards the spot TinTin ran off. Nothing was working in his head. And it was getting dark. And he had a list to focus on.

Her list. The thought warmed him.

"Who's Kristina?" he finally said. The old woman shouted, "Gaaah!" and stomped off on tennis ball feet.

V

She wailed in Marilyn Gambrelli's arms for twenty minutes, answering her soft questions with snot-filled nods and shakes of her head.

"Are you hurt?"

Head shake, then, "No." More desperate wailing.

Something changed in her mother's posture. She asked, "Is it a boy?"

Hesitation, then a severe nod and deeper sobs. Mom's grip tightened. "Did he do something to you?" Her voice was fierce. Tina quickly shook her head, sending a combination of mucus and tears across the woman's sleeve. The girl ever-so-slight relaxed after that. "Did he say anything?"

She had to think for a moment, realizing, no, he hadn't. He'd barely spoken. And that was the problem! She cried harder, but shook her head and wailed, "Noooo."

"Tina, baby, here." Mom leaned her back, wiped the girl's face. "Why are you crying? Are we talking about the boy who was standing on the sidewalk?"

She nodded. "Bertrand."

"What?"

Tina laughed a little. "That's his name."

"That's the name of someone's old uncle."

She laughed louder. "I know!" The brief sunshine in her head clouded over and her shoulders fell.

Hands smoothed out her hair. With forced casualness, Mom said, "He seemed kind of cute. Is he nice?"

A nod. No other reply.

"What happened, baby?"

One massive, sky-crashing cascade of sobbing tore from her belly and she pressed herself into her mother's chest. She shouted, "He fell in love with me, Mommy! Right there on the sidewalk!"

"He… he what, baby? Have you two been dating…"

"No! That was our first walk."

An annoying snort of amusement from the woman and a gentle pat on her back. "Why was he here?"

Tina explained everything. Marilyn Gambrelli understood very little of it since her daughter spoke through sobs and snot, all of which were ruining one of her favorite sweaters. But telling the story seemed to calm her daughter down.

"Well, baby," she said, not sure how to help since she still didn't quite know what the issue was, "what should you do now?"

Tina blew her nose, but since the thin tissue was well-used already most of it dripped down her wrist. "Oh, my word, girl." She grabbed more tissues, wiped her up. Something was making Tina cry and so far, the story wasn't giving any good reason for it. "Why are you so upset?"

Tina sighed deeply, then muttered, "I'm too pretty."

Her mother tried very hard not to roll her eyes. Some day she needed to have a talk with this girl about her oddness. Maybe. She'd managed to avoid it for nearly eighteen years, what was another ten? "I know, baby. But it's a cross you need to bear."

Tina nodded and blew her nose with a clean tissue. She settled, neither of them speaking for a few minutes. Finally, "That was sarcasm, right?"

"Yes. Is he a nice boy?"

A half shrug turned to a nod at the last moment. "Pretty *bloopin'* nice, yea." She didn't say bloopin'. "He's smart, honest, loves Jesus, smells nice."

"Well, then, stop being a deranged idiot and go talk to him. And nice Christian girls don't say the *b* word."

VI

It wasn't too long of a list, a half dozen or so. Sitting sideways on the front porch of his family's small salt box, four miles west of *her* house, Bertrand typed TinTin's list into his phone, then stared Zen-like at the seven promises. He started arranging them in ascending order of difficulty.

The first was embarrassing, but the most possible. *Sing the National Anthem at a football game.* When he'd given this promise at the school assembly during the candidate presentations, those who knew him groaned aloud. It was a stupid enough campaign pledge, however, that he'd ingratiated himself with a class that, honestly, couldn't care less who their president was going to be.

The second might take some leg work, maybe a meeting with cafeteria management. Even so, *Better tasting healthy foods at cafeteria* seemed do-able. Had he actually phrased it this way, or did TinTin write it down wrong? Lunch always included one or two healthy components, a fruit and vegetable. What he was promising was getting these to taste a few grades better than plastic models used for advertising.

The next wasn't too bad, either. *Establish a new award for outstanding service at the school.* He liked this one, and meant it. In fact, he'd come up with this for a specific reason: giving a shout-out to Manny Lindberg, the janitor who worked mostly outside and around the Gymnasium. Manny was a lumbering, oft-confused man who would step in and stop bullies from ruining some skinny geek's day. Bertrand had witnessed this twice himself from a distance. The term "saved by Manny" was common among the students. Future senior classes could do whatever they wanted with the award. Manny was getting his due this year.

Get a senior project going which will benefit all of humanity gave him pause. Had he said that? Must have. He'd already pledged some of the nuttier, more impossible items further down the list, so hands had been clapping, newly-converted fans whistling in support so he probably did say this. All caught up in the moment. Every class had a community betterment project that hardly anyone participated in. "All of humanity" implied a slightly larger scale.

But he had to try. For TinTin.

Her real name was Tina, apparently, which, if the angry lady with the walker was to be believed, was probably short for Kristina (or Christina). She was so pretty. Why hadn't he noticed that before?

Focus, you moron.

The last three required something other than normal human effort: *Defeat communism wherever it shows its dark countenance*, *Solve World Hunger* and *Defeat Global Warming*. He left these in the order she'd written them down. They were the result of him being on a roll with the speech; anyone with brains or imagination would know he was just trying to be funny.

He stared at her handwriting. She had nice handwriting.

"You don't really have to do those," the paper said to him in her voice. "I guess I just did it to get your attention."

"Oh, no," he said to the paper since he didn't trust himself to turn around and look at her. "How'd you find me?"

A shadow moved into his peripheral vision. No, a *vision* moved into his peripheral vision. Bertrand growled in frustration.

Tina said, quietly, "To be honest, I might like you as much as you apparently like me, so we should both just get over it and maybe, I don't know, go do something together."

The statement was awkward enough to burst the bubble he'd been trying to raise around himself. Bertrand looked to his left. His future wife stood there, smirking.

The smirk was annoying. Face red, he said, "You making fun of me?"

Her expression became serious. "Sorry, no. I actually like you. I was just trying to smile like a normal person."

"You don't smile normally?"

She laughed, then immediately covered her mouth. Through her fingers she said, "Do you mean if I normally don't smile, or when I smile it's not normal?"

OK, maybe she wasn't his future wife after all.

VII

You're acting like a stupid giggly school girl, knock it off! Tina dropped her hand and straightened. Trying to act like someone she wasn't was only going to mess things up worse. She stepped onto the small porch and sat opposite him, leaning back against the other railing. It was a nice porch, a good place for talking. She said, "This is a nice porch for hanging out and talking."

Bertrand nodded. "I guess."

"Sorry for acting weird. Honestly, I don't talk to a lot of people for more than a few sentences."

He seemed to think about this. "I guess I haven't noticed you walking around with a gaggle of friends."

She shook her head, embarrassed at this truth. "Believe it or not, I was pretty popular at my last school."

"You guys moved from California, right?"

A nod. No secrets in small towns. "Yea. Tiny speck of a place like this one, called Lavish if you can believe that."

Bertrand shrugged, obviously not finding the town's name interesting. He held up his phone.

"I was just deciding what promise to keep first."

Her face burned. "Honestly, I was being weird. You don't need to - "

"But I do. Because when I went home and did my quick devotional for the day it was Psalm 15."

She tried not to swoon. Casually, "You do devotionals?"

"Yea. Every day I read something from the Bible, then write in a journal what I think Jesus is saying to me through it." Tina was astounded that he never once seemed hesitant saying any of that. Maybe Massachusetts *wasn't* the atheist outpost her old pastor had warned them about. He shrugged again, an act she was beginning to understand meant he was working out what to say, then started thumbing on his screen. "Anyway, after you gave me the list I got home and read this." He handed her the phone.

Of course, their fingers brushed as she accepted it and metaphorical electricity shot between them. It was like being stuck in some bizarre Hallmark movie. She read the Psalm, carefully handed it back.

"Wow. Synchronicity."

He said nothing to that. She added, "You think God wants you to actually do these, then?"

Another shrug. "Feels like it."

They sat without speaking more for nearly a minute. Tina felt very comfortable in the silence. Finally, she shifted away from the railing and turned so her back was to the front door, scooting closer to him. "OK, then. Where do we start?"

VIII

"So, what, are you guys teaming up for this Grand Adventure, now?" Monday took a bite of his sub and looked alternately between them. Bertrand shrugged, his neck reddening. Monday felt a twang of pity (and envy) in that moment.

TinTin's actual name was Tina, a fact Bertrand was quick to point out when he and she met him outside *Jolly Giant Sub Shop and Cool Conversation Emporium* (the second half of the name was added by Monday long ago - and seemed to be catching on a little bit within the general population). Monday knew her real name, as did most people. His friend may be smarter than him in some ways, but had always been a little clueless with general life things.

Tina said, "We are." She casually bumped sideways into

Bertrand's arm, an unabashedly affectionate gesture which only served to redden his white friend's skin to the point Monday wondered if he should intervene. She added, "And we assume you're helping, right?"

Either his best friend was completely smitten with this girl, based on all the nonverbal cues since he'd arrived, or was completely horrified at being stuck with her for the duration of this new project. Monday decided to shake the tree a little and see what fell. First, he finished chewing his turkey, ham and Swiss on whole wheat with mayo, spinach and pickles, the same thing every time because it was so, so good. He hoped he wouldn't regret, however, passing on his mother's homemade raviolis to meet these two odd ducks.

After taking a quick sip of soda, he raised a finger in the air, needing their attention.

"So," he said, "are you as crazy as you sometimes act, *is* it just an act, or are you an eccentric who simply hasn't felt the full brunt of emotional oppression the world has thrown upon so many others of your kind yet?"

Tina glanced back and forth, not in a panicked way as if unable to respond, but seriously considering his question. He'd gone wild with as many big words and accusations he could muster, keeping his voice firm as if demanding an answer right then. To throw her off and see how she handled herself.

She put her hands flat on the table and sat straighter, ready to give her answer. She didn't color her nails, he noticed. Monday liked her a little more for that. Something about girls painting their nails annoyed him.

"I suppose," she began, her pretty face all smiles and joy framed within the curtain of her hair, "I am a tad naive, not having been far outside either of my hometowns except for vacations. Even then, these days we usually just go up to New Hampshire or someplace equally non-oppressive. I feel that God made me this way and though I know I'm pretty and could manipulate you lost members of the opposite sex any way I want, I choose to hide myself from the eyes and lurid imaginations of men until such time as I find a boy who shines like the sun when he is anywhere, near me or not, partly because of a strong self-view and partly, if not mostly, a strong faith in God. So, in my own world…"

Monday raised both hands and leaned back in his chair. "OK, OK, you win. And yes, my questions kind of bordered on rude. I'm sorry." He mock-bowed and added, "I concede to your greatness." When she smiled, a half-confused expression crossing her face, he realized her ramblings had been serious, and also that he needed to be very careful because he decided he liked this chick way too much already.

Bertrand, meanwhile, had tuned out and was eating his sandwich, meatballs and sauce with shredded cheese, one of *his* favorites. When he realized no one was talking, he put his phone down on the table between them, pushing some wrappers aside to make room.

"OK, item one."

Monday said, "That the National Anthem one?"

"Yep."

"Done. I talked to Coach Purcell. Though he did express reservations that your careless treatment of the song, which celebrates our wonderful country, might prove slanderous -"

"Scandalous," Tina corrected. "Sorry, go on."

He sighed, wondering why he found himself so flustered at her interruption. "In short, he agreed to go along, if you play the gig straight. No embellishments or stupid outfits or dragging out the notes."

Bertrand scoffed over the top of his straw. "I'll be lucky to even remember the words, let alone sing."

"*Can* you sing?" Tina asked. Monday snorted.

"That bad, huh?"

His friend laughed. "Yep. Anyway, the next home game is

Thursday night. Two more days and your list is one shorter."

"Maybe more than one," Tina said, moving Bertrand's phone slightly to read. "Who do we talk to about cafeteria food?"

IX

Over the next two days they'd come up with a plan for mutual cooperation, sticking Bertrand with the bulk of the leg work needed to deliver on his promises. At least he needed to make a valiant effort to do so. This latter caveat was agreed to since red tape and the inflexibility of any governing body could make delivering some of his less world-altering promises impossible.

Tina combed through the school website Tuesday evening to learn whom Bertrand should speak to in Food Services (the answer: Miriam Nourse). Monday had practice but would talk to his mother and father who were, respectively, Sociology and Philosophy professors at a college in Worcester (he referred to them as "modern hippies"). They could help him think of ways to approach the Big Three at the end of the list. He expected, however, that the three of them would solve everything before his parents even finished debating the emotional implications of their son asking them for advice on such vast, world-changing topics. It was why he usually didn't ask their advice in the first place.

Bertrand went home and tried to memorize the words to, and musical nuances of the *Star Spangled Banner*.

"If possible, sing it without the words in front of you, and try very hard to be serious," Tina had said. Bertrand argued that she was overstepping any authority she thought she might have. She'd looked at him silently, drowning him in those annoying eyes of hers and he'd grumbled something significant back at her like, "Whatever." Monday nodded, giving Tina enough sideways looks that Bertrand began to wonder about his friend's intentions.

That first evening was difficult, both because he had to explain to his parents why their son was singing so off-key in his room (it wasn't just his voice, the song was un-singable), and also who Tina was, after he explained that she'd started this in the first place. Worst was when Dad asked if they were "dating or something?" The man had pretended not to care when he asked, leaning on the door jamb. He always seemed nervous, or upset at some secret slight never shared with the rest of the family. Dad also thought he was hiding this chronic anxiety from everyone. All Bertrand said in reply was that it was an evolving process.

The next day the three of them sat together at lunch, along with the other regulars to their table, Emil Patrisky, Jowell Ellis and Münchhausen (Billy Ferren, who never explained the self-proclaimed nickname).

Somehow Bertrand made it through most of lunch without explaining why he'd suddenly become so magnanimous. Emil, Jowell and Munch were too distracted by the mysterious TinTin sitting in their circle to bother asking, too busy sitting straighter and being oh-so-clever and entertaining.

"So," she said after enough pleasantries had been bandied about and lunch was almost over, "Miriam Nourse is your lady. Her office is right back there." She pointed with her fork towards the food pickup line and the mysterious, brightly-lit world beyond. "Senior Food Services Supervisor for the school makes all the decisions." She shrugged. "So sayeth the website."

Bertrand had found a phone-sized spiral notebook and pen in the desk drawer at home and wrote the name down, misspelling it terribly. Monday snickered. Jowell muttered, "What's so funny?"

"Nothing."

"You seriously need counseling, man."

"I know."

Bertrand tapped his finger on the tray over and over. It was warped and the act sent everything on it, mostly trash and utensils, rattling around in a symphonic cacophony of noise. The newly-elected class president stood suddenly. "OK, no sense putting this off. You've all done well with your quests. I'm off now to save the world."

Emil opened his hands in the universal *what did I miss?* gesture but said nothing.

Monday sent his friend off with a casual wave of his hand. "Saving the world's a bit farther down the list, buddy."

X

Miriam Nourse, Food Service Chieftain, was a sternly pretty woman in her late thirties, with straight black hair and a regal chin. Every aspect of her appearance shouted "executive," distinguishing her from the rest of the white-aproned people milling about with steaming trays and hair nets. No hair nets for Miriam. She had a small desk in a three-walled cubicle (the fourth was open to the goings-on in the kitchen) which she sat behind now, regarding Bertrand as he seated himself in the smaller, rickety chair opposite.

"Let me make sure I understand, you're wondering if we can make healthier food? We don't make healthy food now?"

He raised his right arm half way, rocking his hand back and forth. "Not... quite right. I'm working out the meaning of this one myself."

"This *what* one?"

"What?"

"Go on."

"I'm not saying... I didn't say *healthier* foods. Just better *tasting* healthy food."

"You don't like the taste of… what, the green beans? The carrots?"

He was about to answer, then paused. Was *that* what he'd meant? "Not the taste so much," he muttered before he could stop himself from speaking. But it wasn't. An image of a random art class from a couple of years back. Not so much colors, as hue. Mrs. Aracknisty explained once, in her classroom that always smelled like crayons gone feral, that hue *could* mean color, but it was more subtle. It meant shade. The shade of the color.

Miriam Nourse watched him. The curious gleam in her eye had begun to dim. He was losing her.

The hue of the food.

"What does that mean?" she asked.

"Did I say that out loud?"

She sighed and leaned back, closed a folder that had been open on her desk but which he did not think had anything to do with their conversation. She simply wanted to make a gesture that meant *we're done.*

"Yes," he said, quickly. "The hue. Like a painting. You have an amazing selection for the students here. Seriously. My buddy Munch is a vegetarian and never has a problem finding something."

"Is that why he's called Munch?"

"No. But the food's … kind of plain tasting."

She opened her perfect mouth a little, uttering a silent, "Ahhh," then seemed to relax. "We do not salt our food or, if we do, it's very slight."

"Why? Or why not?"

"Too much salt is unhealthy."

Bertrand couldn't care less about the food, truly, because *he* liked it, once he added salt. But he was on this ride so might as well let it run the track.

"Salt is unhealthy for the students?"

"For anyone."

"Too much of anything is unhealthy. Even happiness."

"I - what?"

He shifted forward in his chair a little bit. "Listen, what about salting just a wee bit more? It's not like there are many, or *any* students with high blood pressure or salt allergies, right?"

She didn't respond.

"If we salted the food just a little more, could we also offer other options?" This idea just popped in his head and it made sense, at least to him.

"Such as?"

"Soy sauce! And Sriracha, too."

"We generally don't add ingredients on any *extreme* level, sweet or spicy."

"Well, you should, but that's just a matter of taste and I agree, people should have options. You've got the condom station over there, right?" He vaguely gestured to his left indicating the cafeteria beyond.

She rolled her eyes. "It's a condiment station, and yes we do." When he started to respond she lifted a finger. He stayed quiet.

Miriam Nourse swiveled in her chair, flipped her manicured fingers over the tops of a set of manila folders standing upright in slots, then procured one in particular. She slowly rotated to face him as she read whatever was on the topmost sheet.

"That's actually quite a good idea, Mister… what's your name again?"

"Bertrand. Bertrand Irizarry."

"Irizarry," she said. Then smiled. "That's right. You gave that funny campaign speech for class president the other day."

He tried to smile back. "Yes, ma'am."

She got all serious. "Didn't hear it, but people were talking about it. They seemed entertained."

He shrugged. "It was kind of funny."

She hesitated midway to putting the folder back. "Was this one of your campaign promises?"

He nodded.

"Do you know how many times making the food better has been used as a campaign promise?"

"Every year?"

"Every year." The folder went back into its place with a tad too much force. She said nothing else.

Bertrand said, "I like the food here. I really do. You've got good variety."

"Thanks. Just not enough... hue, I guess."

"That's OK. Everybody needs hue now and then, right?"

"Meaning?"

Uh, oh. Where was he going with this? He'd won! She was going to do his suggestion. "Not sure, it just kind of came out. But we all need a little bit of salt added in our lives."

"Or Sriracha?"

He laughed. This was getting weird. "Exactly. Sometimes we need to add something to the mundane parts of life to make them interesting."

She leaned back in her chair. "I have plenty of hot sauce in my life, but thank you for your concern." Her brows lowered. Was that look, he wondered, what people called smoldering?

He suddenly felt like he should invite her to church, something less spicy, or just run off and leave his multicolored coat behind. In any case this conversation was becoming a bad metaphor for something he couldn't quite get his brain around. Bertrand stood up and said, "So, did we agree on anything about the salt? Or adding the other stuff to the condiments?" He was *so* glad he said that right this time.

She looked down at her desk, considering, then stood up herself, offering a coiffed hand to him. He shook it gently, hoping she didn't expect him to kiss it. "We did. I'll add hot sauce and soy sauce, maybe some other spices if there's no obvious allergy issues. And I'll at least *consider* bumping the initial salt levels," she held two fingers close together with her free hand, "just a little."

He let her go, suddenly wanting out of there. "Excellent. Thanks!"

"Thank you, Mister Irizarry. I enjoyed our conversation."

He navigated his way around the shining silver countertops and into the school-proper. No reason to think anything but a purely civil conversation occurred, even if it got weird at the end.

Too much talk of spices and heat for one day.

XI

"How'd it go with Miss Nourse?"

"Nothing happened!"

"What?"

He and Tina were walking down the wide, central corridor, alone for the first time. Monday with his awkward glances and guilty looks still went to practice after school every day when there wasn't a game.

He did not like this jealous side of himself, nor the vulnerable side of being smitten with someone.

They were walking along the pathway leading to the parking lot. "No, I mean it went well. She agreed to look into pre-salting the food more, and they're going to be adding more items to the condiments station like sauces and stuff."

"Well done, Mister President," she said with a sudden burst of what sounded like genuine excitement. She even hip-checked him as they neared the small concrete stairs leading to the parking lot. He focused very hard on not falling.

"Thank you. I aim to please."

She was smiling at him, then suddenly looped her left arm around his right. They continued walking. He had no idea what to say. Wisely, he said nothing. She was going to be the over-ramped extrovert in this relationship, anyway.

"Next plan?" she asked.

"I have a meeting with Sal Lund about the award and the senior project. He was out today, some sort of principal convention in Boston."

"Sounds exciting. Can I come with?" They were at her car.

"Will I be able to stop you?"

"Probably not. After that?"

"Right now, homework."

"You have a plan for that one already?"

He blinked, then smiled. "No, I mean I have to get my homework done, then practice America The Beautiful."

"Star Spangled Banner."

"...yea, because it's, like, tomorrow."

Tina said nothing at first, and didn't look too hurt. Bertrand had a feeling he'd just blown her off. Can't do that if they were dating, could he?

A stern look eventually came across her face and she crossed her arms. "Well?"

Oh boy. They haven't even had a proper date yet and she wanted a goodbye kiss or something? "Well... what?" Should he lean in and kiss her? Should he even be *thinking* about kissing her -

"Bert?"

That brought him back.

"Bertrand."

The smile relaxed him a little. "I know. You went away for a bit. Anyway, I was *very* unsuccessfully trying to get you to invite me to do homework and watch you practice singing."

His face turned red. "Oh, no. No audience. I practice with

my door closed, alone."

She shook her head. "Tomorrow night, you adorable idiot, you're going to be singing in front of hundreds and hundreds," she lowered her voice to mock-menacing levels as she leaned in, "just itching to watch you make a mongoose of yourself." Instead of leaning back, she stepped closer. *Very* closer. "You need to practice in front of an audience who will laugh if you make a mistake."

He reached out, put his hands on her shoulders, and smiled, feeling suddenly more comfortable in this semi-intimate pose than he'd ever been with anyone, even Monday. Not that he'd been in many semi-intimate poses with Monday. "Fine. Come to my house so you can insult me."

She laughed, then *he* leaned forward, a little, and kissed her. Just a small one, but the requisite fireworks were sailing overhead for most of the ride to his house. She drove unsteadily behind him in her own car.

XII

"…and I almost peed myself from laughing so I had to make him stop." She said this, and everything that came before the ellipse, without the slightest concern that Bertrand's feelings would be hurt. Yes, she'd held her amusement during his first attempt at the *Star Spangled Banner*, at least through the first half of the second stanza. As soon as he'd reached some broken crescendo with, *And the rockets' red glare*, there was no helping it, even with her hand over her mouth. The wet gales of laughter came spitting out the sides and she rolled backwards on the floor where she'd been sitting.

He was staring at her now across the dining table with a mix of rage and, possibly, some affection. She focused solely on the affection, remembering for the millionth time the brief kiss in the parking lot and how she almost passed out. An exaggeration, a little, but it had been one of those stars-falling-from-the-sky kind of moments.

The bedroom door had been left open while they had distractedly finished their homework and he'd announced his intention to sing. Just to get it over with. The rest of the evening would hopefully be a fond memory between them for years to come, unless he took her affectionate description of how miserably he sang the wrong way.

"Do you like the fish?" Mitchum asked.

Mitchum was Bertrand's father and, yes, they both had old-fashioned names. She'd asked the origin of *his* name, as her mother had long instilled in her that asking this would be a compliment, never an insult. Unless you used the word *stupid* in the sentence somewhere. He'd proudly explained that he was named after an old movie actor whom his mother adored. As she had with Bertrand, she asked if he liked it. He smiled with an expression she eventually learned was *not* an indicator that the man was about to burst into tears and said, ironically, "No, I despise it, but I hate the name Mitch worse so...." He shrugged.

She liked him instantly. He seemed like an older, more nervous version of Bertrand.

"I love the fish," she said in answer to his question. "Did you make it?"

"He did," Mrs. Irizarry said, because Tina hadn't learned her name yet. "Chummy keeps us well fed." She laughed. Her husband leaned over his plate and said, "Only she calls me that." As an afterthought, added with that sideways smile of his, "Yes, I do like that one."

"You were supposed to be encouraging *me*," Bertrand said with a pout.

"No," she said through a piece of fish that tasted like it had been rolled in quite a lot of dried parsley then left to cook in the sun. She would throw up at home, if she didn't die of food poisoning first. "I was supposed to make you face your fears and see that the worst anyone could do to you is laugh."

He raised an eyebrow.

She continued, "Just make sure you play it straight, so Monday doesn't get into trouble, but in your beautiful mind -"

"Love that movie," Mrs said absently.

"- you are deliberately being funny. As long as *you* think that way," she pointed first to him with her fork, then to the window, "*they* will, too, and you'll smash it."

He took a bite, winced then wiped his mouth with a napkin. He eventually looked up and smiled at her. "You really think so?"

She laughed. "No, you're going to look like an idiot and I'm going to have an accident in the stands for real and it'll be a glorious, unforgettable evening that will be spoken of at Hillcrest High School for years!"

Mitchum raised both of his hands in a silent "yay" then continued eating the semi-edible meal he'd prepared for them all.

XIII

"So, let me get this straight," the principal began, all wide-jowled seriousness emanating from the other side of the table. Sal Lund looked like someone who had been muscular and intimidating in his youth, but softened enough over the years to become wider and fatter, but still intimidating. The fact that he began with those specific words warned Bertrand that this might not be as straight forward as he'd hoped. Which was odd because these should have been the two easiest promises to keep.

"You want to establish a service award for the staff. Someone the senior class would choose each year? And yes, of course, we need to discuss the senior community project, as well."

They were in a large conference room adjacent to the principal's office. Tina would later theorize it had grown over the years, slowly taking space from every other office and cubicle around it. "Like a succubus," she'd add, and Bertrand wouldn't ask her to explain further.

He and she were on one side of the long table. Opposite, hunkered the principal, vice principal Samaira Patil, a tall thin woman of Indian descent whose cold, crystalline approach to leading children involved mostly suspending them or calling the police. It was a long, complicated story which only grew into legend the longer she somehow kept her position. She watched the two of them like a cat to goldfish. Bertrand tried to pretend she wasn't there. He'd seen the third person occasionally in passing, but wasn't sure of her role. She was a younger woman with brown hair, hands folded in infinite patience on the table. She looked alternately at the two students, smiling. Bertrand felt both queasy and comforted under that gaze.

He made it a point not to shuffle in his chair as he replied to the principal. "Correct. The senior project is, of course, something that's been done forever." Ms. Patil looked about to say something in reply, but held her words in check. He continued, "The staff service award is new, so might take the most discussion."

Sal Lund nodded and leaned back. The nod was encouraging, and set the man's large cheeks to jiggling. "I checked," he said. "We've given out recognition plaques in the past." He gestured vaguely to the wall behind them. "They're in the hallway."

"By the trophy case, yes. But the last one issued was a few years back and if I'm not mistaken had been chosen by you and Ms. Patil." She would be "Ms. Patil" for the duration of his time at school unless otherwise ordered. Less chance of setting her off and losing a limb.

Lund said, leaning a little more in his quietly protesting chair, "Or whoever was principal and VP at the time."

"Right. *This* award would be picked by the student class."

"Oh, I don't know if we'd be able to hold another vote. I remember the chaos when you got elected, Bert. Every year this sort of thing disrupts the normal flow of the day and…" he raised his left hand slightly from his belly where it had been resting, "…buzzes up the energy level a little too much."

The smiling woman at the other end of the table offered, "But that's part of the fun of kicking off senior year, yes?"

Sal begrudgingly nodded, and offered a noncommittal sound. Samairi (he would think of her on a *first* name basis in his head, Bertrand decided) seemed not to hear. Maybe she was replaying the last terrible punishment she'd inflicted on a student.

Tina had been uncharacteristically silent to this point. She now put her left hand gently on Bertrand's arm. "Actually," she said, "since the student body elected Bertrand as their voice and representative with the administration, it might simplify things if each year the class president chose to whom the award should be given."

He was suddenly very grateful Tina had come along. The mention of an election had thrown him off, never intending the award to be democratic.

The vice principal looked directly at her, moving only her head like a robot slowly coming to life. "You are the one who calls herself TinTin?"

Sal chuckled. "Like the dog?"

Tina smiled, unabashed. Bertrand's heart expanded. "No, sir, you're thinking of Rin Tin Tin." Back towards Samaira, "I believe my name was derived - quite unconsciously I assure you - from the classic adventure and mystery character TinTin, from the comics."

"Was he a dog?"

Quick glance back to the principal, smile unwavering. "No, but he had one with him."

The third woman said, "Why would you name yourself after a boy?"

Tina laughed. "I might be suppressing displeasure, Doctor Jordan, at how society has treated my sex for so long, and felt the inner need to express myself outside of its normal gender stereotypes. That," and here she raised a finger, "and the confusion brought about by the onset of adolescence in middle school and society's recent and almost pathological need to deny the obvious differences between genders, all serving to make me desperately grab onto a name which both parries anyone's expectation on first meeting me, and keeps a wall up because of its nonconformity."

Doctor Jordan (based on Tina's reply just now, Bertrand decided she might be the school psychologist, though why they'd brought her in was beyond guessing) stopped smiling, tried to start again, managed a little. Before she could reply Tina added, with a small laugh that seemed to release some of the pressure her rant had built in the room, "Or I simply wanted a new, anonymous identity when I moved here. Since my name is Kristina I decided to pick a nickname that would sound ironic, in a cultural way."

"Linda," Sal said with a sigh, "I have another meeting in fifteen minutes so let's go with TinTin's second explanation and move on."

Linda Jordan's expression had slowly fallen from quiet amusement to a sad, hurt puppy look. Tina seemed ready to go on another tirade, probably explaining something about her reply not being an insult, something about her upbringing making her insecure when faced with questions on her motivations, so Bertrand said, "Doctor Jordan, Tina didn't mean anything against you in her reply, she's simply fascinated by your profession and gets verbal diarrhea whenever she's around someone she thinks is smarter than her. It's an adorable trait and maybe you two could talk more about what you do later. Right now," he looked at Sal, "my suggestion for the first award, perhaps given out at the Homecoming Rally next month by the Senior class, is Manny Lindberg."

Linda, who's expression had transformed into blushing pride for all of her life choices to this moment, said, "Oh, I like Manny. He is such a kind and simple man."

The robot turned her laser gaze his way. "Why him, if I might ask?"

When Bertrand explained his reasoning about Manny's quiet protection of the bullied, something changed in the vice principal's expression. Samaira Patil's stone face softened, just a bit, and her eyes melted into a deeper blue. She said quietly, "Bullying has always been an issue in schools. I hadn't realized the dependency you've all felt on that man's presence."

It was a bit more dramatic than Bertrand would have put it, but she'd gotten his point. He only nodded.

Sal muttered, but not in an angry way, "There's only a couple of cylinder's firing in that guy's brain, but he's nice enough." He hesitated, glanced quickly to his compatriots then away, maybe realizing he sounded like a jerk. "I have no objection to this whole thing. Homecoming, you said?"

Samaira and Linda were both smiling at him now, but their approval paled in comparison to Tina's hand returning to his arm and the gentle squeeze she offered.

"OK," the principle said, "let's get this done sooner then, maybe tonight at the game. I'll talk to Missy to see if she can get something put together in time for it." He glanced at his bare wrist, then added, "Sorry, force of habit. Decided last month I don't need a watch anymore because of my phone. I miss it though." He shrugged. "What's your plan for the senior project, quickly?"

What *was* his plan? He had no idea.

Tina replied as if her speaking on this topic had been the plan all along, "Well it needs to benefit all of humanity, according to my boyfriend's promises during his campaign."

It was spoken so casually, he blurted, "Boyfriend?"

She looked at him, eyes wavering between amused calmness and utter heartbreak. "Aren't we official yet?"

"Well," he said, wanting nothing else *but* be her boyfriend but … he finished aloud, "just using it the first time in here kind of threw me, is all." He shrugged, feeling like a dolt.

Her eyes began a slide towards the utter heartbreak side. He had to decide something that, twenty-eight years later he would remember in a strange, unconnected moment as he was checking their bank balance before buying his wife - OK, yes, it was her, this all ends wonderfully, though with a lot of screaming and destruction in between but I'm getting ahead of myself - as being one of the top five choices in his life to that moment. He smiled at her falling expression, made sure they were both looking into each other's eyes, and said with the same calm as he felt, "I want nothing else in this world than to be your boyfriend."

"Awwwwwwwwwwaa!" That was Linda Jordan. The psychologist had, by the way, been called in to this meeting because Sal had been warned by Vice Principal Patil that both students were considered a little slippery in the gears. At the moment, however, the stern woman was trying her best not to laugh out loud at the idiots across the table from her. Why, she thought, did kids this age think everything was a TV Hallmark movie? Hallmark or Cinemax late night. These two seemed more like Hallmark, though. And, yes, I switched to omniscient narrator for this scene.

Bertrand put a hand gently to Tina's glowing face, where all trace of heartbreak had fled, and whispered, "I don't suppose you remember what you were about to say to Mister

Lund about the project?"

"Oh, right." She turned and blushed before giving her attention fully to the situation. "We would like the senior project to sponsor, until he or she is eighteen years old, whichever child is listed on Compassion International's 'longest waiting child' list. At the moment that's," and here she opened her phone and swiped twice, "Oumaima, a six-year-old girl from Burkina Faso." She began typing furiously with her thumbs. Everyone assumed it wasn't yet time to speak. "That's in Africa." She looked up. "We'll collect the money by spreading the word, maybe have special secure collection zones, details like that can be worked out another time, because I know you have to go, but the main point is this: we raise enough to cover the..." she glanced down at her phone, "fifty-five hundred dollars it would take to sponsor her until she turns eighteen, all under the name of the class."

Bertrand's head was spinning. She looked up at him and smiled. "Woke up around two-thirty last night with the idea. Assume He gave it to me." *How could this beautiful human being,* he thought, *have run under everyone's radar for so long? Especially in* this *school?*

Sal cleared his throat and said, "Well, that sounds lovely. Magnanimous, even, but it hardly changes the world. It benefits only one child."

Tina glanced at the principal, then to Bertrand. "Bertrand, honey pumpkin, you can explain."

He laughed. "Only if you never call me that again."

The vice principal visibly rolled her eyes.

Bertrand said, "If we don't sponsor this child, someone else will, yes, and someone will sponsor the next. At some point, someone will not. If we take care of the education and raising, with love, of one child, we're doing what we've all been commissioned by God to do, and that's love everyone around us. Doesn't matter who it is, *that* child will live, be cared for, and change one small corner of their world."

"The rest," Tina added, "will ripple out from there."

The psychologist blew her nose and wiped her eyes. She got up from her seat. "I have another meeting." She looked at the two students and Bertrand wondered if he'd ever seen such a perfect mix of joy and sorrow on one face at the same moment. "Thank you both," she said, and left.

The vice principal said, "We don't do religious projects."

"Most charities," he said, "are based on some religious leaning, or support. To not do anything, not *support* anything simply because it reflects another's faith is, itself, a religion in the purest sense."

Sal Lund muttered, "You just make that up?"

Bertrand nodded but did not break eye contact with Ms Patil. "Yes, sir."

"I have a good BS meter, that's all."

"And a good heart," Tina said.

"Now you're just - "

Bertrand looked at the man, tired of the dance. And he had to go to the bathroom really badly. "Can we do it? It's an extremely awesome idea and will make a great story for the school when word gets out."

"Yes of course. It's actually pretty brilliant."

His vice principal looked about to argue until Lund raised his hand. "Not now, Samaira. I've got to get to my next meeting. Are we good, you two?"

They both nodded and *yes, sir*'d him, then left the room.

XIV

The crowd rumbled like a burgeoning mob as Bertrand fidgeted at the bottom of the steps. The portable staging had been erected along the midfield sidelines (the Hillcrest Hawks home team had to split into two factions to make room, though the podium would be collapsed and rolled away after these pre-game ceremonies). Bertrand stared across the manicured playing field, towards the visiting team mingling on their own side. Better not to look at his audience until he had to. The sunglasses in his shirt pocket (long-sleeved white shirt and black denim pants, his concession to Mom and Dad who were somewhere up there behind him, eagerly waiting) would help hide most of the faces.

At the moment Sal Lund was awarding Manny Lindberg the new Senior Class Award for Outstanding Service. Not a bad title. It was printed hastily this afternoon and signed by the staff. Manny, a massive, lumbering man with a slight limp, grinned and held the paper up to the crowd who cheered and stomped their feet. Manny did the same, then gratefully stepped down the opposite stairs.

Sal had already informed the audience about the fundraiser to sponsor the child in Africa for the next twelve years. All of this had gotten everyone in a roaringly exuberant mood.

Of course, if the principal announced Lucky Charms breakfast cereal was now made with actual puppies the crowd would still have cheered. Because no one was really paying attention. Half were there to watch football, the other half for the flaming car crash that would soon be Bertrand Irizarry and his massacre of their country's sacred, and terrible, national anthem.

He closed his eyes, took in a breath, and prayed. "Lord, don't let me make a complete fool of myself. But if I do, let it be for Your glory."

"That was awesome," Monday said beside him. Bertrand flinched, not realizing his friend had arrived. The guy smiled, in full uniform with helmet in hand.

Bertrand said, "Not now, buddy."

"Oh, stop worrying. Have fun."

"Have to play it straight, remember?"

"Well, yea, sing it. But good or bad, seriously, dude, I'm proud of you. For all of this craziness."

"Yea? Not too much craziness I hope."

Monday laughed and patted him on the back. No, he wasn't patting, he was pushing Bertrand towards the steps because somewhere far away, Sal Lund was saying his name. "Always too much," Monday said. "That's why I love you. Go do it."

Just take your medicine, Danny, the crazed writer said in that horror movie. Bertrand accepted the microphone from the exuberant principal, removed the sunglasses from his shirt pocket and donned them. The crowd faded into shadows, but did not disappear completely. He saw Tina a few rows back, sitting with her mother on one side (he assumed it was her mother, they looked alike), his own parents on the other and tried not to think of all that implied.

He closed his eyes and imagined Tina staring with loving support down at him. Imagined her nodding her head in a silent, *Go on, my Prince,* and whispered a curse just before he began to sing. The curse, and the *Star Spangled Banner* were broadcast throughout the small stadium, but it was too late to worry about it. He sang to her, seeing in his mind her encouraging stare of pure unadulterated love. Every line was perfect, no words forgotten. He wasn't hitting the notes exactly but wasn't destroying them either. After keeping to a low octave for the crazed *rockets red glare* crescendo, he finally finished with, "…and the home, of the, brave!"

He opened his eyes and slowly removed his sunglasses. The entire crowd was laughing and clapping and shouting with such utter joy he was forced to smile back. Tina had fallen backwards off the bench. He could see part of her legs. Her mother was smiling and handing the girl a large towel. He would need to ask her about that later.

Bertrand waved his hand and the volume rose one last time

before he gave the mic to the principal. As he stepped off the stage, the referee's whistle announced the opening kickoff.

XV

"You know, buddy, if you ever decide to take that one for granted, let me know."

"Stop being in love with my new girlfriend."

Monday laughed and leaned back against the porch railing. He was still in uniform and certain his body odor exuded far beyond where he sat. Not that he'd played much this game. "Dude, now that she's coming out of whatever bizarre shell she'd been cowering in, the whole world is going to be in love with your new girlfriend."

"A shell made of TinTin," Bertrand muttered distractedly. Monday laughed. They were sitting outside on Tina's front porch, one similar to Bertrand's only wider with wooden rails instead of iron, waiting for her to re-emerge with clean clothes. She had to wrap herself in a towel because, as promised, she'd laughed so hard she peed. Stayed for the game, though, gross as that seemed to both of them.

The front door opened and Marilyn Gambrelli stepped out. She was comfortably pretty like her daughter, but in an older way. She sat between them without preamble and said, "I made her shower and now she's getting dressed. She'll be out in a moment. Where are you all going?"

Both made motion to answer, then realized the same thing. Monday admitted, "We actually have no idea, ma'am. After walking her home, she said she'd be right back out so we just sat to wait. Not sure if there is a plan. I mean, it's a school night."

Bertrand added, "She has that effect on people."

Marilyn laughed. "Yes, she does. Nice job tonight on the singing, by the way. Not sure if I said that yet."

"Was I any good?"

She patted his knee. "Nice job on just getting up there."

Monday snorted but said nothing. He liked this family. The woman got to her feet and, as she stepped inside, added, "Sometimes the best evenings are spent hanging on a front porch and talking about life." Then she was gone.

The two men looked at each other. Monday offered, "You want me to get going?"

Bertrand reached out and punched him gently on the arm. "No way. Deep conversations require as many deep minds as possible." The front door opened again and out stepped such a radiant vision in jeans and white blouse that Monday knew his friend regretted telling him to stay. Still, no take-backs.

Like her mother, she sat between them, a little closer to Bertrand but not before smiling warmly at Monday. "Mom says she put a post hypnotic suggestion into your heads not to take me out anywhere because it's a school night."

Both nodded.

"You were awesome," she said.

Bertrand smiled. "Thanks. I did my best!"

"Oh, and you sang pretty good, too, sweet 'ums."

"Funny."

Monday sighed. "I didn't play once tonight."

"You hardly *ever* get put in," she said. "But you show up every game and every practice."

"Dad thinks it's good to stay connected to the sport. Thinks colleges will like seeing it on applications."

"Why, because they stereotype?"

He shrugged. "Maybe, but mostly because I haven't done much of anything else in four years."

"You've been Bertrand's best friend. What's more important than that?"

He shrugged. "More volunteer hours?"

Bertrand said, "You hang out at the church food drive

every month. That's two hours right there. Make sure that goes on the list."

Silence, but a comfortable one. Tina finally turned back to Monday and asked, "So what's the story around your name?"

"Edwards isn't an uncommon name."

"Except it's a last name that's a first name, but you know that's not what I'm asking."

A nod, thinking. "Edward Monday would make a good stage name."

She waited. Monday got a little uncomfortable. "Only seventeen people know the reason for my first name."

"You made that number up."

"Yea. But not many know."

She looked to Bertrand. "Do *you* know?"

"Of course. It was the first thing I asked him."

Back to Monday. "Tell me, quick, before you lose your nerve."

"It's a very stupid reason."

No response. Monday sighed, then said, "I was conceived on a Monday."

"Really?"

He felt himself flush. "Yep. They thought they were being clever or hippie-ish or some such thing."

She didn't immediately respond, only looked out to the street, deep in thought. Finally, "You need a new origin story. I mean, how many times has Marvel changed Spider-Man's."

"Never."

She gave him a look, then, "I saw all the movies."

"Hollywood productions don't count."

"Let's see," she said, hands flat on her knees and looking up and slightly to the right. Then to him, "Both parents alive?"

"Yep. You?"

Slight lowering of her shoulders. "No, Daddy died when I was five."

"That stinks."

All this time Bertrand wasn't speaking, content being their audience.

"Yea, but for you…." Another stare out to the sky. She was so pretty in the glow of the street light. Maybe Bertrand would be willing to fight him for her affection. *Stop it,* he thought. *And yes, I'm talking to you.*

Fine. So much for added drama.

"When your parents were first married, they both worked at a restaurant in New Orleans, deciding to pursue their dreams of acting - well, your father wanted to act, Mom was going to be a singer. With those dreams carrying them like clouds of hope into the future, there would be no room for children. Not until their own selfish goals had come true.

"Then one day, as she was taking the order of the oldest man she'd ever met sitting at a corner table… wait, what's your mother's name?"

"Sky."

That threw her. "Really?"

"Yep."

"And Dad?"

"Parlance."

She laughed and said, "It is not," looking to Bertrand who only nodded.

"Sky and Parlance are your parent's first names?"

"Yep."

She giggled again then leaned into Bertrand as she looked out to the street. "Never mind. Anyone asks, you just say, 'My parents are named Sky and Parlance, so they were mentally unable to name me Bryce or David.'"

Another comfortable moment of silence. A car approached, hissed by, and finally Tina said, "And why Bertrand? Have I asked that yet?"

"Not the why part, no. My father, when he was sixteen but

pretending to be older so he could enlist, killed a man in the war. It shook him to the core. The enemy soldier, lying dead on the ground in front of him, had the name 'Bertrand' stenciled on his helmet. Dad swore if he lived through all of that chaos and death, and had a boy someday, he'd atone for what he'd done. Hence, my name."

"Wow. You should be a writer."

"You realize," Monday said, "we're down to the last three promises." A sudden, wide yawn overtook him. When he was done and could open his eyes again, he looked at the others, who were also yawning. "Sorry about that."

Bertrand rubbed his hands down his face and said, "Yea, it's getting late, and school's still on for tomorrow."

Tina said, "I have an AP English test on Hemingway."

Monday shook his head. "Why does everyone in AP classes always have to add the 'AP' to the name? Isn't that bragging?"

"Only if you say, 'I have an AP English test on Hemingway and I'm getting an A because I am so much better than you and always will be."

"It's still bragging. Just say English class."

"Guys," Bertrand interrupted, "I want to go home and sleep. Anything from the hippie parent front, out of curiosity?"

"Well, Mumsie thinks…"

"Mumsie?"

"I don't actually call her that. Mumsie believes we need to look at the whole communism angle differently. With this list, everything is a matter of scale."

No reply, only nods. No one knew what he was talking about. Monday wondered suddenly if he'd finished his map of Ancient Rome's territory for World History. His mother had come in with her idea last night after he'd put the bug in their ear about the Big Three items on Bertrand's list. After putting aside the homework … he was losing the thread. He hated not knowing, needed to get back home and double check. The map was due tomorrow.

Finally, "Just realized I've got homework I need to finish before I go to bed, but in short, she had a bizarre idea that's *kind* of cheating but easier than flying over to Russia or China and having it out with them."

Bertrand raised an eyebrow. "And...?"

"Beat someone at chess. If they lose, they agree not to spread communism, and as such trigger the inevitable slide into a totalitarian, murderous government throughout the world."

After a pause, "But if they win...?"

"Well, they'll most likely still not do all that, but you would have to promise not to do it, either."

Tina looked at Bertrand with a strange, unreadable expression.

He said, "What?"

She focused on him. "Nothing, just thinking. It might work, in a mocking, sarcastic way." She sat straighter. "But you have to put a serious effort into it, for it to count."

"I can't play chess."

Monday was smiling, looking between them.

Bertrand saw the look, then pointed to Tina. "You mean, I have to beat TinTin at chess?"

Monday laughed and got to his feet. "Yep. And when you do, she'll have to promise never to spread communism around the world."

"That could take years! I haven't played one game, ever."

"And I'm really good at it," she said, also standing and suddenly far more animated.

"And again, every time you lose *you* need promise not to spread communism," Monday walked the flagstone path to the street, "and subsequently the inevitable slide into a totalitarian, murderous government throughout the world."

Tina was literally bouncing on the pads of her bare feet now. "We promise!"

Bertrand raised his hand. "Wait, wait. Again, guys, this could take years!"

"I know!" she said and wrapped him in their first, major hug.

XVI

He had no doubt this was all temporary but on Friday, Bertrand Irizarry was the most popular person in the school. Not only with everyone who'd been at the game, but those who'd merely heard about the performance, or discovered that Manny Lindberg's award had been his idea. "You'll always be our president!" shouted Amy Benson and Melissa Forbe (pronounced Four-Bay because she liked to pretend she was French, though in truth the clerk at Ellis Island mis-wrote her grandfather's last name, leaving off the 's' and no one over the next three generations ever corrected it) as they passed him in the hallway. Thankfully, Tina wasn't with him. He offered them a flourishing bow.

It was, as far as he could remember, the most fun he'd had at school since kindergarten when they made their own Playdough.

At lunch with the usual gang, opinion was split on the viability of chess substituting for the promise of defeating communism.

"I just don't see the connection, even as a metaphor," complained Munch as he sorted through his fruit cup with a fork, looking for cherries.

Monday finished chewing his pizza (which always tasted better on Fridays) and pointed. "Who are the biggest chess players in the game?"

"The queen!" That was Jowell, looking smug with his intellect. "Everyone knows that."

Monday offered a scornful glare, then, "Anyone else?"

"Bobby Fisher," offered Tina.

"Well, yea, but aside from him."

Looking around the room, Munch said, "Why don't you tell us?"

"I'm telling you, guys, it's the queen."

Monday shrugged. "I actually don't know, but they're all Russian. Or mostly."

From the table behind him, a tall Junior with crazed red hair shouted, "Spassky, Karpov, Botvinnik…" He let his voice trail off.

Tina nodded in agreement, though she would admit, if pressed, that Spassky had been the only name remotely familiar to her, from various conversations during chess club. The Junior who'd spoken was called Murph, current club president, and she would defer to his expertise.

"Well at this point the week's almost over," Bertrand said beside her. "Best we work out how I do the last two over the weekend."

Emil asked, "What are they again?"

"Solve world hunger and defeat global warming."

"Almost feels," Monday said, "that we already solved the hunger thing with the class sponsorship of that kid in Africa."

"When did that happen?" asked Munch.

Bertrand hesitated, then, "Yesterday, I think."

Monday laughed. "That was just yesterday? Been a busy twenty-four hours, buddy."

"No kidding."

Twirling her straw between her fingers, Tina considered. Something felt wrong. "'Solve world hunger' sounds like it's on a slightly larger scale."

"How much bigger does it need to be?" Munch asked, the frustration they were all beginning to feel etched in his voice. "You can't expect him to start a foundation or something." He looked around the table, raised one eyebrow. "Can you?"

"No," Bertrand admitted. "At least, I don't think so." He looked at Tina. She leaned into him a moment then straightened, not wanting too public a display of affection in front of everyone.

"You've gone way over and above what I'd expected, and I expected a lot."

"Still," he said. "The chess thing feels like a clever workaround, and one 'clever' is enough for this business. We should do something concrete."

Yowell said, "Just sponsor a child *yourself.*"

He nodded, but his heart wasn't with the idea. Monday said what most of them were thinking. "Eh, doing the same thing feels like a cop-out. There should be *something* different we can do."

Tina noticed the that the Junior, Murph (aka Dallas Murphy, chess whiz and Supreme Introvert) was hunching his shoulders more than usual at his table, occasionally stealing furtive glances their way. She'd played enough chess with the boy to learn two important things. First, he had a major crush on her but was so horrified at saying anything that she felt safe around him, as long as she avoided too much eye contact. Second, and more important to the issue at hand, hunching his shoulders was a "tell" that he'd come to some kind of revelation, usually around his last few moves. Maybe that was all she was seeing, him figuring out chess strategy for the October tournament. She leaned to her left and whispered something in Bertrand's ear.

He looked back. "Seriously?"

She didn't reply, only gestured for him to *go on.*

He said, "Hey Murph, you have any ideas?"

The boy straightened, obviously surprised. The others around him at his table hadn't heard Bertrand's question, so looked at their friend's sudden change in posture with quiet curiosity. That group didn't handle change well.

Everyone at Tina's table were just as surprised. Monday turned around, always reliable to run with whatever ball was handed him. That was, if the coach ever put him in. "Yea, Murph. What's your idea?"

Dallas Murphy's face was an astonished combination of shock and pride. He turned around himself and said, "My brother used to bring cans into school on Fridays."

After a few seconds with no further details, people looked at each other for some indication what the statement might mean. Bertrand said, "You mean here? When?"

Murph shrugged. "He's a lot older than me, six years. As long as I can remember, though, Mom would pack him a can of something, like soup or beans, every Friday in his lunch. I assumed, at first, they had can openers at the cafeteria until she explained." His voice was always wet-sounding, pushing the listener to swallow more often to make up for his abundance of saliva.

Emil had his hand curled around a spoon he never used, but pressed it against his growing smirk. Thankfully he kept his comments to himself. Tina didn't think she should talk, either. Murph tended to get wiggly in the brain if she paid him too much attention. Thankfully, Bertrand was the perfect human specimen, and had already figured out how to navigate the waters with the guy.

"So, there was a food drive going on here?"

"I guess so." Murph looked like he was ready to turn around, not liking being the center of attention. "He said everyone brought in cans and stuff once a week. Became a contest between classrooms, who had the most food for the charity, that kind of thing. Probably gave it to the Wachusett Food Pantry but I can't say for sure."

Having turned sideways to listen, Monday was now leaning slightly to the side, either to allow a direct line of sight between

Murph and Bertrand, or avoid being spat on. He said, "Food pantry. There you go."

The red-headed boy nodded. "And it's local. Always a good thing. Anyway," he said, voice falling to a mumble, "that was it."

He turned away with a calmer, more assured posture about him. Tina smiled. He was a good guy. This was a major moment, speaking like that. Perhaps for no other reason than that, she said, "That's it. They stopped doing it, I assume, but you can resurrect the practice."

"Food on Fridays."

"Catchy."

"There you go."

"What about can openers?"

"What?"

"What thing ab… OK, no, never mind."

The conversation bounced about the table in that manner until a plan to approach the office, yet again, with another way to better the world was worked out.

With just a couple of minutes before the bell rang for afternoon classes, Bertrand, looking at his phone, said, "Defeat Global Warming."

In that moment Monday found himself alone in an empty room - or an empty universe. Floating in a white nothingness that felt … *eternal*. He screamed in surprise, but after a while decided that maybe he'd simply passed out. This was only a dream. It felt so real, though. He said, tentatively, afraid of getting an answer, "What's going on? Hello?"

We need to talk.

XVII

"We need to what?" Monday flailed about, but if the action

caused any change in his surroundings, it was impossible to tell. It only served to make him look foolish, waggling his arms around.

"Oh, no!" he said. "Don't play all high and mighty with me. I was doing fine a second ago. What is this? You've got no right to … What is this?"

Like I said, we have to talk.

"About what?" He tried to minimize the movement of his arms, but whenever he wasn't doing something with them, the sensation of falling was too overpowering. Monday settled on slowly moving them and his legs as if treading water.

I have a couple of ideas on the last item, defeating Global Warming.

Monday stared into the nothingness, face serious. "I'm not sure I like how you capitalized global warming like that."

There's a reason, yes. Here's my plan.

Monday listened as the plan was explained, eyes growing wider the longer it went on.

Finally, explanation done, his expression settled into an odd, defeated calm. Almost serene.

"No, not serene, and definitely not calm! Not about that plan. It's way too over the top. Borderline ridiculous. What's your other idea?"

Seriously? It'll be funny! No one will expect -

"Look," Monday (rudely) interrupted. "This crazy idea is only *you* trying to be clever. It's not any of *us* - especially Bertrand - being so. Plus, a lot of people are going to be hurt or die if we go with it. No. Plan A, we'll call it. Plan A bad. Next."

Sigh.

Reluctantly, Plan B was laid out for him in vague detail. Nevertheless, his face practically glowed like the imaginative best friend character he was.

"Again, dude, not fair. But seriously, Plan B is perfect. And no one gets blown up, burned or crushed. Definitely, without question. We go with B."

But if we just do plan B then it all ends without any big flourish.

"Bring us back some other time if you want flourish." Saying that gave Monday a jolt. What was he saying? Where was he going to go? He seriously needed counseling.

One last time, just to make sure you're not busting on me. You really like Plan B better?

"Yes. Plan A is the plot twist of a psychotic madman. And I don't think that's you." He looked around at the nothingness entombing him. "I don't think…."

But it would be funny.

"No, it wouldn't. Not at all."

Fine, Plan B then.

"Yes, Plan B. Get me out of here now, please?"

Fine, fine.

"Plan B, right?"

Yes, yes. Plan B.

Monday gasped for air and leaned back in his chair, almost hitting Murph behind him. Emil shouted, "Dude, you OK?" and reached out a steadying arm. Monday blinked, looked around warily.

"Yea." He dragged the word out.

XVIII

Naw. Plan B's boring.
Plan A it is. He'll thank me later.

XVIX

For thirty-seven years Fenton Schwartz had been one of those brilliant kinds of scientist the military invariably kept away from the public eye. In fact, they kept him away from everyone via subtle maneuverings of his life on the base. His superiors had eventually assigned him to *9-Corridor* which dead-ended at the door to his office. No reason for anyone to pass that way unless Fenton was the intended destination. There were days, entire weeks, when no one stopped by. Fenton Schwartz rarely noticed. Case 4716-222-21-0994 was his baby, his assignment, the only company he needed.

It was also, he was certain, the country's biggest joke. Case 4716-222-21-0994 was someone's brainchild longer than Fenton Schwartz had been alive, a desperate dart-throw conceived during World War II when the Powers worried Hitler and his minions would, indeed, take over the world. Not only with sheer numbers and deranged leadership, but brilliantly-twisted, scientific breakthroughs. During this time the world advanced technologically, for no other reason than to survive.

It never happened, of course. Spread too thin on multiple fronts, Nazi Germany could not defeat the Allied forces. Even its ace in the hole, Japan, fell under the horrific glare of the first nuclear attack.

Projects were canceled, then forgotten. Not all of them at once, however. Like Case 4716-222-21-0994. It had been forgotten by most in the military's upper echelon during the chaos of ending wartime emergency status, then attrition and politics then, finally, budget cuts.

All of it worked to give a handful of mid-level managers a dozen projects to keep open and fund through bullet-points in their own budgets. These endeavors survived, hidden under blankets of red tape, because if they ever were solved, the world would truly be a better place. The United States in particular would emerge on sturdier footing as a world power. Some projects, like Case 4716-222-21-0994, were too ridiculous to ever consider possible, given the natural laws of the universe. Their primary purpose was placating certain scientific individuals - and there were always these people in the business - by giving them assignments such as these for busy work, keeping them hidden in plain site from everyone else. These were scientists who scared other scientists. Their potential for destructive, horrific inventiveness gave those they worked with too many nightmares. And they smelled.

Fenton Schwartz was one such evil genius. Case 4716-222-21-0994 pulled him into the depths of *9 Corridor, Location 511, Sublevel 3*, for thirty-seven years. There were times his tinkering and designing had impressive side effects, inventions which did not directly affect the final outcome of Case 4716-222-21-0994 but often made his direct reports famous within their own spheres for such amazing advancements in robotics.

Buried three stories underground in a secret base two miles from the center of a little town called Hillcrest, Massachusetts, Fenton was a money tree for his superiors.

Today, finally, it was done. His excitement grew over the past few weeks as it became clear everything was going to work. No half-percentage point variances. On target, as planned. Lately, Fenton barely slept, rarely ate.

Balance. Renewable power source. Self-correcting targeting. And rage. So much rage. All the hurt Fenton took into himself as a child, then a teenager; everything tossed at him as if he were a leper, metaphorically left beaten on the side of the road and occasionally kicked, even by passing Samaritans. All of it borne from jealousy and spite. He was smarter than everyone. *Everyone*. They hated him for it, enough that they locked him in this room for most of his adult life to feel better about themselves.

Soon, because of this, they would know true fear.

He tapped the keys and watched the simulation. Beyond the plasticine window, a series of robotic arms were stress-testing bolts one last time, measuring and monitoring and assuring that all was ready to emerge into life outside of its private universe.

Global Warming was built entirely by these arms and robotic manipulators and, of course, Fenton Schwartz. He was the god to the machines' DNA. The wind to its sails. The fist in the palm of technological advancement. Global Warming would soon become a giant, raging robot of death to the world. A harbinger of extinction, bringer of the apocalypse to mankind. If that included Fenton himself, he accepted it. Dying by his life's work was a good way to go out.

He called his machine Global Warming as a way to stick it to both political parties ruining the country above him. One side didn't want to believe in science because it was scary. The other screamed about nothing but that, and pronouns.

Fenton laughed and pressed the final icon on the screen to fully activate his creation. It was propped up by supports in the cavernous warehouse beyond his window. The world would indeed fall under the onslaught of Global Warming now.

He laughed again, harder and harder, the act making him seem trapped in an epileptic seizure, so alien this was to his body. He laughed-spasmed as Global Warming's eyes illuminated everything, locked on the control room populated by its father, the lone madman scientist. The eyes brightened, then brightened further until a blinding flash tore like lightening from its metal skull. Fenton Schwartz's remains would never be found, nor any record of how he did what he did. Everything, *everything*, was stored locally to prevent his superiors from ever knowing his progress towards this moment. All was now burned or melted, including Fenton himself.

Then, his thirty-seven-foot newborn child of Death began clawing its way up through three stories of concrete and steel, towards its destiny.

XX

The bell to end lunch intoned through the school. Everyone was gathered around Monday in the cafeteria, including Dallas Murphy. The kid had apparently decided he was one of the cool (or cooler) kids now.

Bertrand kept a hand on Monday's arm. "You sure you're OK?"

"Yea, yea, need to get to class."

That was when the earthquake reached them. The survivors would eventually understand it had been caused by a giant robot tearing through what had, in the public's awareness, simply been a strip mall along Sterling Street on the other side of town.

Tina grabbed hold of the edge of the table when the ground began to shake but the moment was short-lived. The cafeteria fell into a shocked silence, then excited voices rose up around them.

"What was that?" she said. It wasn't just rhetorical. Since moving to New England she'd not felt a single tremor - a welcome change from the first fourteen years of her life which had been rattled often by mild earthquakes. Every time, the suppressed rage of the planet beneath her feet spread fear along her spine. This wasn't supposed to happen here, however.

The only person whose expression matched her own, because everyone else looked like the circus and local ice cream truck had pulled up outside the windows, was Monday. He looked terrified.

In answer to her question, he said only, "Plan A," then ran through the exit doors. After a confused pause, Bertrand and Tina followed him outside. The rest of the table fell in behind, then everyone else in the cafeteria, assuming they'd missed some catastrophic announcement. While the crowd ran for the doors, the teachers demanded the students get to classes right now, or file outside in an orderly manner.

Bertrand huffed, "Do you think he's having a brain aneurysm or something?"

Apparently, she was in no better shape, because her answer was just as strained. "Do you even know what an aneurysm is?"

"A brain thing."

As they rounded the corner of the school, they slowed but didn't stop. Monday stood at the edge of the front circular drive, used for drop off and pick up of students. The school was on a rise with the parking lot down a series of small steps. Beyond that, an expanse of trees glowed with change, from green to warmer, autumnal colors.

Catching up to him, Bertrand reached out and put a hand on his friend's shoulder. Tina moved to the other side. Everyone else, including most of the students and faculty who'd run from the cafeteria behind them, caught up to them as well, then looked to the distance. The school wasn't so high they could see far beyond the immediate tree line, but enough to notice a line of smoke rising in the northeast.

"Something's on fire."

It was more than that, she realized. Sounds. Like a massive construction project, screeching of metal, rusting machines coming to life in the distance.

Monday whispered, "It's screaming."

Tina's stomach tightened.

Bertrand said, "What is?"

"Global Warming."

Monday finally turned around, glanced her way first then focusing on the crowd behind them. He never raised his voice, probably afraid of anyone else hearing. "This is going to sound insane but…" He looked down, collecting thoughts, or maybe this was it, his brain was crashing. Tina grabbed his arm, but when he looked up again Monday was calm, clear-eyed. "The narrator's gone mad, I think."

I have not.

"He, or she, I've never really been able to…"

"Dude, " Bertrand shouted, "focus. What are you talking about?"

The screeching, screaming metal sound was louder, Monday's expression a little less calm. "OK. I'm just going to say it and you have to promise to believe every word."

"That depends."

He gripped both of Bertrand's shoulders. "No. Dude, I love you, and I'm not going crazy and I need you right now, no matter what, to believe me and work with me on this because I don't think we have much time." He never lightened his grip. Bertrand reached out, patted his friend's arm both with affection and submission.

"OK. Speak."

"That sound we're all hearing is a massive robot which has just crawled up from some secret base across town…"

A few steps away Emil snorted but thankfully said nothing. Again.

"…and is going to destroy the world, or something - that part was a little fuzzy." Another scream of metal. At this point, loud as it was, the concept of it being some monstrous voice began to seep into others' thoughts. The sound was followed by softer crashing and crunching.

Trees falling.

Monday's gaze never left Bertrand's.

"We need to find a way of beating it because I'm pretty sure it's coming this way. Maybe not looking for us specifically, but it's going to come through here, destroy the school then continue on to destroy everything else."

Most of the students had begun slowly backing away, heading for the front doors. The few still in earshot, however, began to laugh. Monday, all three of them in fact, had that reputation.

"Wait," Munch said, leaning in and looking scared. "Did you just call it 'Global Warming' earlier?"

Monday nodded and let go of Bertrand's shoulders. "Yea, the crazy super scientist who created him named him that. Not sure why. Probably some hipster irony or such."

"It's a hipster scientist?"

He raised his hand. "Focus, please. We've got to stop the robot when it gets here. One shot, and as ridiculous as I know this sounds," at that moment the screaming/screeching began tearing through trees not far beyond the parking lot. Everyone who'd stayed outside, aside from their small group, shouted in surprise and ran for the school. Monday finished with, "we've got to stop it."

Munch tapped excitedly on the top of Bertrand's head. He swatted him away in annoyance. He was struggling to believe Monday's story. So was Tina, but she was coming pretty close to doing so simply by listening to the angry sounds drawing close. Unphased by Bertrand's reaction, Munch shouted, "Defeat Global Warming!" He laughed. "This is your chance!"

That was when things clicked in Bertrand's mind. He looked up, mouth opening. Monday's face was serious, a dark stone of exhausted frustration and determination. He only nodded. Tina wasn't a hundred percent sure what was communicated between them, but the dynamic changed.

"What do we do?"

Monday glanced at Tina, winked, then cringed as Bertrand

punched him in the chest. "Don't wink at my girlfriend."

Hearing him say that word sent a shiver of joy through her.

"OK, OK. Well, right - big robot. Walking this way and… it's going to go right through the school, I'm guessing."

Tina gasped at the implications. Everyone, except for their table and Murph, had run back inside, many staring at them through the large windows of the main lobby. "Everyone's in there. They'll be killed."

The approaching sounds were now accompanied by others: human screams. The monster was probably destroying homes and neighborhoods.

"Listen," Monday said, walking now, but having no real destination, "you need to come up with the solution. It has to be you. Something. Quick!"

Bertrand looked down, back up. "It's stupid and I don't even know where to get enough."

"Enough what?"

"You boys! And girl, ma'am," a rough, thick voice said behind them, "need to get inside!"

They turned in unison to see the hulking form of Manny Lindberg hurrying towards them with his off-balance gate. "Mister Lund sent me out here…"

"Manny, we need your help!" Bertrand said.

"Anything for you, Berty. I heard what you did." He blinked. "But you gotta come back."

Bertrand took hold of the large man's arms. "Manny, it's Bertrand not Berty and you need to listen to me. No time for questions. We need rope. A lot of it right now! Can you find us some strong rope, enough to string between some trees and trip a robot without asking why?"

"Why?"

"Without asking why, I just said."

Monday half-smiled. "The Hoth Maneuver, love it!"

The janitor must have decided Bertrand held more sway in

this moment than his bosses because he said, "Nothing much rope-wise in the school, but I have a boatload in my truck."

Jowell looked at him and said, "Why do you have a boatload of rope in your truck?"

Manny looked like he'd just been asked why there was air. "For my boat. I just said."

"OK, Manny, great. Lead the way. Now!"

The world screeched and crashed. Manny whispered, "What is that?" He was looking up in fear. Tina stepped in, took his hand. He looked down and smiled.

"It's a killer robot and we're going to stop it. Don't ask, just do," and she pulled his hand towards the stairs leading to the parking area. He said, "OK, fine. Not like they can fire me the day after giving me an award, right?"

"Right," Bertrand said from his other side. Then the man was off, running faster than even Monday could manage, though the young linebacker tried. "Everyone else wait here," he said at the edge of the lot. They tracked Manny's progress towards his car, waited as he lugged, with Monday's help, a large roll of double-braided nylon rope.

That was when the thing everyone was waiting for rose up at the far end of the parking lot. It was big and square and would have been comical if it hadn't screamed in rage, a section of the head lowering with the sound, like a jaw.

"It's an actual giant robot," someone said, without humor.

Mostly silver in color, both legs stomped in an awkward rhythm, moving the rest of it forward. They *were* actual legs, the entire structure designed like a tin robot from the 1950's, only more ergonomically designed, with smaller counterbalancing appendages emerging then retracting as it walked.

Scorch marks rose half way to hinge-like knees. After working itself free of final fallen trees it moved with force over the parked cars. They crumbled and twisted beneath its weight. Occasionally a piece of metal would spark and ignite gas fumes, engulfing everything in flame.

Someone grabbed Tina's hand and pulled her away. She spun around. It was Bertrand. "Sorry," he said. "Time to save the world!"

The other two had returned to the edge of the lot with the rope. Bertrand shouted to Manny and the others, glancing back towards the monstrosity behind Tina. Monday and the janitor wrapped one end around a large tree trunk. Emil, Jowell and Munch carried the other end across what Bertrand decided was the robot's path and wrapped it around a yellow-painted pole filled with concrete. There was a loose chain hanging from it, probably for blocking access to the parking lot once upon a time.

Murph was at the top of the small rise leading back to the school. "You think it'll trip and not just step over it?"

Bertrand shrugged helplessly. "No time for anything else. Pull that tight!" That last command was shouted to the three at the pole. Emil pulled, wrapped it around twice more. They began to argue over how to tie it off but it was too late. The robot was ten feet away and ignoring them all, glowing eyes fixed on the school. At least they seemed to be, hard to tell with illuminated eye sockets. Tina ran to Bertrand's side then they, Monday and Manny took a few steps backwards. The other three, opposite, stayed their ground and held the rope, crouching as if that would prevent them from being seen. Murph looked alternately at everyone, paralyzed with indecision.

Between the two groups stretched a braided, nylon rope a few feet above the ground.

The robot stopped. Something whirred inside it.

The entire structure bent over at the midsection, as if looking down. Murph screamed and ran back to the school. Everyone else took a few more steps back. The thing lowered its jaw and another inhuman scream emerged. This close, the sound vibrated through their chests and teeth. One arm reached out, the end splitting into an equivalence of fingers that grabbed the middle of the rope. The robot straightened, pulled. Beside Tina, the tree groaned at its base, bending impossibly sideways until the rope snapped. The massive oak straightened and groaned as if in pain. Everybody ran.

"To the school," Bertrand shouted. "We have to get them out before it reaches the top of the hill."

Halfway up, the machine's voice returned, this time it had a human quality. If they'd ever heard Fenton Schwartz speak, and most in the human race hadn't, they would have recognized it in this twisted, vibrato rendition, volume turned to eleven.

"Nothing can stop Global Warming! Nothing will survive!"

A flash of light, too bright to look at directly, flashed beside them and tore apart the hillside, sending dirt and grass and shards of stone falling over them. Monday stumbled then shouted, "The things got a heat-beam! This is nuts!" In the chaos Tina lost sight of everyone. Wait ... there! Manny Lindberg was far ahead, closest to the school entrance and shouting to the faces staring through the glass.

Where was Bertrand? There, on her left.

No, no. He was getting to his feet unsteadily. He was hurt. Beyond, thrown off course as well, Monday was as far from his friend as she. The Robot stepped up the hill, burning gaze focused on Bertrand alone.

"You dare to stop me! Nothing ..." the eyes grew brighter, "...can stop ..." Tina and Monday ran as fast as possible, converging on Bertrand as the robot shouted, "me!" and blasted them all with -

XXI

Monday floated again in the white, eternal nothingness, rolling over and over in surprise, though he did not yet realize this because he was screaming.

OK, OK, OK, OK, OK. Bad idea. You were right.

The high school senior finally stopped screaming and looked around.

"What? I was… what…?"

You were right. Plan A was *so, so* wrong. It got *way* of hand *way* too quickly.

His shocked expression tightened, pulled into a mask of rage. "Out of hand?!? Out of HAND? You s-"

Plan B then!

XXII

Monday gasped for air and leaned back in his chair, almost hitting Murph behind him. Emil shouted, "Dude, you OK?" and reached out a steadying arm. Monday blinked, looked around.

He looked really, really mad. He tried to catch himself, took in a breath, let it out slowly. Repeated the process.

Finally, "Yea. Yea, I'm fine."

The bell to end lunch intoned throughout the school. Everyone at the table had already stood and gathered around him, including Dallas Murphy. The kid had apparently decided he was one of the cool (or cooler) kids now.

Bertrand put a hand on his shoulder, "You sure you're all right, buddy?"

Monday looked at him, then at each of his friends, including Tina "TinTin" Gambrelli. He smiled. "Never been better."

They walked together out of the cafeteria, working on a

plan to defeat global warming which didn't involve anyone getting hurt by giant robots, all the while laughing and growing closer in their friendship. After Jowell and Emil turned down the science hallway for their class, Monday suddenly broke off from the group.

"Wait, wait," he shouted to no one in particular. "You're not going to explain what Plan B is to anyone else?"

"Dude," muttered the red-headed junior who'd continued to insinuate himself into their group, "what?"

It would be anticlimactic. This is a good place to end it.

They all gathered around their friend and laughed -

"No, no! Bertrand here made a promise!"

And he kept them all. The Week of Bertrand Irizarry became legend in a school buzzing and murmuring with a thousand lives moving through its halls, like life-giving blood in the veins of Education. Distantly, from deep within its thick walls, one young man shouted, "Come back here with your terrible metaphors and finish..." but the voice blended into a chorus of life singing its melody throughout Hillcrest High School.

The school itself was much the same as the week before, but small moments, small acts of grace had strengthened it, and opened it a little more to the light which God insisted all of us share with the world. In many ways it was a flower, opening its petals more to the light.

"...stop it....!"

THE END

Afterword

I tried to work out if there was a common theme with these stories, and one I can see pretty obviously is that a person's faith might start out private, even secret, but if nurtured it will have to grow and expand, becoming a very public thing.

There are many ways to look at the life we're given from birth to death, but pulling back to a high-level view, there's light and dark. Life is good, with constant promise of surprise and joy, but it can be dark, pressing down on us as a reminder that pain and hurt are also promises. Trying to find a place in the middle of all this, bearing through the dark times and relishing the light, is hard enough. Taking an extra step or two farther into the light takes more energy and determination than we're used to exerting sometimes, but can be the difference between a life well-lived and one squandered. Coins invested or buried in the yard.

Jesus has promised to be there with us, helping us take those extra steps, seeing other people with new eyes, opportunities to grow instead of fail. This Yin and Yang of being a Christian makes for a pretty interesting life. Trust Him, and you'll find out for yourself. Always remember: you're immortal. There's so much more and better waiting beyond the veil. So enjoy this little experiment we're given, this gift called life while you have the opportunity to be here.

While here, do your best to help others see the light.

As far this this humble little experiment of a book, well, Psalm 15 took on a life of its own and got away from me, but hopefully in a fun way. Honestly, there has been little I've written as an author that I've enjoyed as much as this collection of devotional stories. I did so without knowing if there is anyone would might want to read them.

More than writing, I also felt more connected than ever with the Spirit as we built something new together. That sounds a little pompous, sorry, but it was meant in humility and gratitude. I hope there is something here worth passing on to you, my wonderful reader. I also pray, since you've made it this far, that you got some pleasure, and blessing, from this book.

What's next? Well, I get back into the writer's chair, pick up where we left off with Psalm 16 and beyond for Volumes 2 and 3 and... until I'm done. I'll probably type Psalm 150's story sitting in a rocking chair in a retirement home, but that's OK. Every good recipe takes its own time to cook properly.

Special thanks to my amazing wife Linda for her support of this obsession of mine (one of many), and her early feedback.

Paul Keohane and Marty Holman, for their proofreading prowess and constant encouragements.

Ramon "Tony" Matias, and his *madre* Magda Perez, for their priceless help translating (and improving) the Spanish dialogue.

Holly Wang and her family for their wonderful and detailed Mandarin translation work.

Andrew, Amanda, Audrey, Elias and so many kids and adults who've passed through our lives and who have put up with someone like me, a flawed and broken man who loves you more than I could ever say.

Debra Butterfield for your insights and suggestions.

Fran Bellerive, for whom I will always be grateful, for her unabashed purple markups of my early work. They made me a better writer.

Mom and Dad for putting up with their twitchy child long

enough for me to figure out how to walk in this world my own way, with an unconditional love I've always tried (but don't always succeed) to mirror with my own family.

For everyone reading and supporting my work through the years. You are the lifeblood of every writer and I am so grateful you have enjoyed walking with me.

Of course, I'm forever grateful to God for this amazing life He's given me, a life full of good and bad but everywhere: His presence beside me. Jesus never promised us perfection in this world. He leaves those promises for the televangelists. But He did promise a life walking alongside Him. If you say Yes to that, that's a surrendered life worth living. The adventure and the journey is a giving one, growing us beyond what we ever imagined possible.

Thanks for reading. With much love,
Dan Keohane

About the Author

Daniel G. Keohane, is the Stoker-nominated author of *Margaret's Ark, Plague of Locusts, Solomon's Grave* and *Plague of Darkness*; the young adult novel *The Photograph* (with David Hilman), contemporary horror novels *Destroyer of Worlds* and *Nightmare in Greasepaint* (with L.L. Soares) and the collection *Christmas Trees & Monkeys*. His short fiction has appeared in *On Spec, Cemetery Dance Magazine, Apex Digest, Borderlands 6, Fantastic Stories of the Imagination*, and dozens more. A founding member of the New England Horror Writers, he previously co-edited their "Wicked" series of anthologies, and is an occasional film reviewer. Dan is an active member of the SFWA, foster parent, and member of the leadership team at his church. More information on his work, and life in general, can be found at dankeohane.com. To purchase signed copies of his work, visit otherroadpress.com.

Afterword

Made in the USA
Middletown, DE
12 November 2023

42255236R00182